ISBN: 979-8-9990858-0-1
Printed in the United States of America

https://www.manishaholmauthor.com

SPRING MAIDEN

Contents

IV ~

Spring Maiden

MANISHA HOLM

Chapter 1

The Summit

It seems our luck is shifting.
    Yes.
The horse and rider picked their way through the boulders of the pass, pausing at a small patch of grasses that waved gently between tumbled stones. Miichal slid from the horse's back and wandered along the twisting trail, while Tronder pulled at fresh grass, breathing its rich scents.

There's water here.

I can smell it. I'll come in a moment. Tronder continued to pull at the grass.

Miichal shrugged off his heavy cloak and knelt down at the trickle. He knew Tronder was giving him time to drink first, before his wide hooves muddied the pure water. He drank, then sat back, enjoying the sun on his face, letting his body adjust to the wonder of running water to fill his belly.

An hour earlier they had battled, heads down, through bitter winter. His fists clenched at the remembrance. On this summit, he heard birds calling. He did not recognize their voices, but knew the complex trills to be mating songs. A sign of spring. Sudden spring. Early spring?

He sat in silence for several minutes, bent and drank again. Retrieving his cloak, he walked farther along the trail, breathing the thin air, musky with the scent of watery herbs.

The warmth of the sun soaked through his shirt; even the rocks were warm. Winter held no sway here, lurking in crevices to overwhelm a tenuous spring. No. Winter was long forgotten on this summit. Miichal turned and waited, watched Tronder move through the boulders, making his way toward him.

There is makta growing there, behind those rocks strewn below that ridge.

Tronder's thorough awareness of his surroundings always surprised Miichal.

Makta?

Makta.

Miichal paused at this enormity. *Have you ever seen it?*

Tronder blew his breath in a great huff. *No one has seen it. For generations.*

Miichal's heart thudded in his chest. *How do you know it's makta?*

It tells me its name.

Miichal stared at the ridge, lost in the wonder of it. Makta, growing here, in the isolation of this summit. And it *spoke* to Tronder. And Tronder heard.

Makta.

Yes. Blankets of makta.

Excitement warmed Miichal's belly. He shaded his eyes, squinting up the steep hillside. Were the stories true? Did makta carry magic? *Shall I bring you some?*

Tronder tossed his head and pawed away several rocks to find surer footing. *I do not relish the thought of climbing that slope.* Tronder had borne the brunt of the winter's ferocity. Miichal recognized exhaustion in his whisper. The stories claimed that makta had the power to revive. If the stories were true. If it did carry magic.

Will you wait or go ahead?

Tronder gazed around them, breathing deeply. *I will wait.*

A question burned Miichal's mind. *Is there danger?*

Tronder shifted and turned his head to gaze east to the valley they had struggled to leave behind. He rested the tip of a hoof on the ground. *A mile back along this trail we were in deep winter. Now we are in spring. Why?*

You're testing me. Makta, early spring; these are signs of Spring Maiden.

Yes.

Miichal looked at his hands, fighting to calm his excitement. There was dread there, too. *If we do find a Spring Maiden, will there be danger? To us? To others?*

Many Spring Maidens have come. Most have not survived the double moons.

Some have.

Yes.

The tales of evil...

That is what we are meant to prevent.

Miichal unclenched his fists. *The risk is great.*

The blessings are enormous.

How can we know what to do? When it happens?

Read the signs. Pay attention. Listen within.

This I know.

Yes. This you know. Tronder huffed. *Trust yourself.*

Will you be there?

I am here now.

Miichal shook his head and came back to the warmth on his shoulder. He spread his damp cloak on a rock slab that slanted itself toward the morning sun, a grey face drinking in the season's first warmth, and scrambled up the rocky slope. As he moved, he emptied his mind, clearing the way for thoughts to come unbidden. He quieted his heart, wiped damp palms on wool trousers. Trousers meant for winter, not balmy spring.

As he walked, he took in his surroundings, noticed the rocks of whites and grays, their silvery sparkles. They were above tree line, so his view stretched unhindered as he clambered along the ridge.

He reached the rocks Tronder had indicated and climbed onto the relatively level plateau beyond. Thoughts rose in his mind like balloons floating through the air. He noted them and let them pass, waited for the next thought to touch his mind, float, disengaging the thought as soon as he recognized it, keeping his mind clear and still.

He found it easily. The makta had found rich soil on the plateau that tapered and melted into the steep slope at its furthest end, a plateau carpeted in makta. Miichal crouched and ran a fingertip along a leaf's edge. The scent was intoxicating. He sniffed his fingers and found that the scent lingered, even with that single, delicate touch.

He drew a knife from his vest pocket and opened the honed blade. He bent to his task, cutting outer leaves, leaving the tender inner leaves to grow and flourish. He brought a leaf to his nose and breathed in the full awareness of makta. He closed his eyes against a subtle dizziness that twirled his head. He recognized power.

He ran his fingertips across the crisp leaves, relished the life held within the fronds, all the while opening and clearing his mind, moving more deeply inward. He gathered the stack of cut leaves, relishing their pungent scent as he settled them next to a boulder where no breeze could ruffle them away. He bent to cut more.

When he felt satisfied with his forage, Miichal wrapped the makta in a loosely woven cloth and tied them onto the strap at his waist. He rose and looked toward the winter they had escaped. The sky was gray and thick, and slanted lines of rain fell beneath their clouds. Snow gathered in the deeper valleys where no birds sang of love and nesting.

Miichal made his way around the curve of the hillside, taking care not to dislodge rocks that crowned amidst the burgeoning makta. A breeze quickened as he came from the leeward shelter of the hillside, and he looked into a long valley, toward distant mountains that formed the western horizon.

Sunlight blazed on the green patchwork of the valley, dotted with thin stands of white-barked trees and larger stretches of evergreens surrounding the myriad greens of tended fields. In the near distance, an orchard clouded with blossoms surrounded white buildings of a village that crowded the banks of a river that wandered the length of the valley.

The breeze refreshed Miichal as he sat on a large boulder whose warmth seeped into his thighs, spread up his travel-weary spine. Miichal closed his eyes and rested, stilled his breath and observed thoughts that bumped along the edges of his mind.

Would they know what to do if they found a Spring Maiden? Would they find one? Why had Tronder chosen *him* for this pilgrimage? Even after all this time, he felt the need for more time to learn, gain wisdom. He hated the uncertainty. He wasn't prepared. What would they face? How would they know?

The barrage of questions chased Miichal from stillness. He gazed at his surroundings with half-slit eyes, the boulders cleansed from a recent rain.

A lizard sunning itself nearby shifted away from an encroaching shadow. Its tail wound long and thin across the face of the rock. A pair of white butterflies flickered at the edge of a grassy verge, danced over a cluster of clover blossoms that sweetened the air. Miichal could hear the gurgle of water here, too, a trickle hidden by boulders. The breeze caught the leaves of the blanketed makta, lifted their edges in the warm sunlight.

Miichal's gaze returned to the frozen valley behind them that contrasted dramatically with the inexplicable clover flowering at his feet, nudged by fat black bees that buzzed clumsily amongst the sweet blossoms.

Early spring. Makta. He quenched the excitement in his belly that lay waiting to engulf him. The weeks and months of training threatened to desert him. Would they know what to do?

He rose and waited for blood to flow into cramped legs, tingling along thigh and calf. He retraced his steps down the hillside to find Tronder waiting silently, his hoof tipped up, perched on hard ground, resting his leg. The two friends studied each other as Miichal closed the distance between them. He lifted his palm to smooth the soft hair along Tronder's cheek, reached higher to stroke upward between gentle brown eyes. Tronder lowered his head, and, foreheads touching, they stood, leaning into each other, Miichal's hands smoothing, smoothing the long curve of Tronder's neck, eyes closed, with Tronder's ears laid easily against his head.

As Miichal shifted his weight, Tronder blew out his breath and tossed his head. Miichal retrieved his dried cloak and rolled it into a tight bundle. Sitting against a boulder, he unwrapped the crisp makta leaves and together they ate several nourishing leaves. The stories held true. Miichal felt replenished. He cut two slivers of cheese, rolled them in the last of the leaves he had set aside for their meal, and held one out to Tronder. As Tronder's soft lips took the food, Miichal chewed his own piece, then stood, wiping his knife and hands on his pantleg. He tucked the cloth encasing the remaining makta into his shirt front. He stooped for his rolled cloak, and after stowing it safely in the pack strapped across Tronder's withers, he swung onto Tronder's back, and they continued picking their way along the narrow track that readied itself to plunge into the rich valley.

Chapter 2

The Valley

Bolin stepped from the shade of thick forest and squinted against the brilliant sun of early morning. His hand automatically felt for the empty bag swinging from his belt. Its emptiness brought satisfaction that glimmered anew, evidence that the seedlings now nestled in new homes, tucked into the rich soil that covered his forest's floor.

Bolin dug his pipe from his shirt pocket, struck a match, and lit the tamped leaves. The scent of burning herbs swirled around his head along with hearty puffs of white smoke as Bolin encouraged the flame to catch and settle in for his morning's smoke. Satisfaction filled Bolin's belly.

The seedlings came from a forest that sprawled two valleys away. Bolin had long admired that forest, an abundance of trees not found in his valley. A fortnight had passed since Bolin had made the trek to the neighboring valley, its forest mysteriously deep in the sleep of winter, the night dark with the absence of moons. The contrast between the two valleys baffled Bolin. How could his valley be in the full blossom of spring, while winter raged in a neighboring valley only two ridges away?

Thankfully, snow had been light under that winter canopy and reflected the light of his upheld glorb. The seedlings had been easy to find, his soft murmur rousing them from their frozen slumber, encouraging their roots to release their hold of dormant soil. The care of the lifting, the trekking, and now the replanting under the streaming light of Ero, this first night of the moon's fullness. The rightness of Ero's light softened Bolin's worry of whether the seedlings would succeed in their new life here in their new forest. His forest.

Bolin's heart swelled anew with hope as his thoughts returned to the night of planting. He had been quick and thorough under the powerful rays of Ero. The spirits would do their part as well to help the seedlings find purchase. In sixteen hours Era would rise, her own fullness flooding the world with her rare glow to join Ero, double moons swollen in their double ecstasy.

The forest whispered around him. He tasted the anticipation that seeped up from ferns that brushed his knees, from moss underfoot, drifting down from fresh leaves of the canopy overhead. The forest bustled with life, a rowdiness that Bolin had anticipated during the long winter, but had never witnessed this early in the new year. He shared the forest's anticipation for what the season would bring them.

Bolin snuffed his pipe and lifted a flask to his lips, drawing clear water into his tired body. Replenished, he stoppered the flask, wiped his sleeve across his forehead, and swept his gaze across the valley floor.

Flowers danced and insects swirled above swaying grasses. Even though the early spring defied the stars' seasonal placement, Bolin believed the evidence before his eyes, that this early spring was firmly entrenched. It would not be swept away by a killing frost or freezing torrents pelting from the sky. His seedlings were safe, despite the stars' insistence of weeks of winter still to come, with its icy storms and howling winds.

He wiped his forehead again, secured his empty pipe in his pocket, his flask to his back strap, pulled his cap lower over his eyes, and set off across the fields.

Lambs frolicked in a far pasture, too many to count. Bolin had never seen so many. He wondered anew at how the ewes knew their own lambs from the rest, especially now, when each ewe must have at least three apiece. Perhaps it didn't matter. Perhaps with this many lambs, every ewe cared for whichever one was nearest and all were fed. He had not the gift of husbandry and could only speculate, but it was easy to recognize the abundant herds that cropped their pastures, a boon for their village. Bolin hummed a merry tune, his rich tenor vibrating his chest. Many new cloaks would be woven this season, with the promise of new wool to come for many seasons ahead.

Bolin crossed the main road and saw that the masons had smoothed away the winter ruts, murmured them into a gentle dome along the road's center with solid ditches at either verge to carry away spring's runoff. Wagons and carts would find easy travel on this fine road. Bolin felt pride in his village, at the craftsmanship held in high esteem, practiced and admired by all. His eyes followed the road as it wound its way toward its climb to High Pass, the summit that separated their valley from Broad Valley beyond.

High Pass kept their village serene, for few wanted to trek that summit, and most outsiders wanted easy access to Broad Valley, whether for distraction or livelihood. He sent a blessing to High Pass, the natural barrier that kept his world separate from the busy world beyond.

His sharp eyes caught motion, far up the sloped road. He turned to gaze fully, hoping to recapture that glimpse, turn it into certainty. Two figures, one tall, one drooped, trudged along the groomed road, obviously weary, probably hoping for lodging in the village that lay behind Bolin. He would tell Gosikk, and see if he could help with preparations for receiving early guests.

He crossed an empty field and ducked into the flower-laden orchard that bordered the village. The orchard was heavy with scent, and insects hummed around his ears as he passed below limbs, taking care not to disturb the insects' flirtation with their beloved flowers. The abundance promised by this orchard was not lost on Bolin, as he strode along his shortcut. Fruit and drink and sweet leather would enrich their stores this season. The stars had not foretold this abundance either, and yet here the early blossoms spread farther than his sight could reach; wealth beyond measure.

Bolin glanced along the well-kept road and admired the garden colors that tumbled from neighbors' yards. The mixture of scents intoxicated the very air, and Bolin could hear the hum of busy insects. Turquoise birds darted from bush to tree, flitting across the road to knit together the stretch of blossoms that waved from every garden.

Bolin tore his gaze from the splendor, lifted the latch to the inn's side door, and slipped inside. A carpenter murmured in the rafters, persuading a wooden plank to lengthen and curve, blending it into its new home, melding with its newly murmured sister to frame a high opening where a broad dormer would grow, a new room for guests who would soon descend on their quiet village. Their village, which was readying itself, with carpenters and masons and thatchers busily murmuring and coaxing, shaping into form, into function, into beauty.

Bolin watched Stevven's sure hands as he bent and murmured. The work advanced quickly, displaying the carpenter's skill. The new rooms would be ready in a matter of a day or two.

Bolin tore his eyes from the craftsman and strode across the common room, eyes scanning for Gosikk. He nodded to Yonce where he stood drying cutlery, practicing the murmuring of an exploratory trade, murmurs of cleanliness, readiness, purpose. Bolin bent to scratch Pharlan's ears, who looked up with red, rheumy eyes, panting her rancid thanks and thwacking her matted tail against the floorboards. Bolin palmed Mackey's back where he sat hunched over his watered ale, startling him out of a morning doze to gaze at Bolin with red, rheumy eyes before nodding mournfully over his tankard.

The inn smelled of cinnamon and cider, baking bread and dried herbs. The inn welcomed Bolin with its charm and promised delights.

Bolin found Gosikk in the storeroom, moving boxes and barrels from that morning's shipment into their places on the broad shelving that climbed from floor to ceiling. Lighted glorbs lined the high ceiling, their soft glow enabling the storage and fetching of all the needs of Gosikk's fine kitchen.

Stevven had been busy here as well, with new shelves hugging the tall walls, boxes and barrels waiting for their fill of roots and grains. The sight of those high shelves, the waiting boxes and barrels, brought home to Bolin as nothing else, the reality of the invasion about to descend on their village, upending their quiet lives. High Pass might protect them from the busy-ness and hustle of Broad Valley, but nothing would prevent the approaching hordes from sweeping into their streets from neighboring farms and villages, filling every available bed and sleeping cloth. Nothing could stop them.

For Rosa, darling Rosa, was to be wedlocked.

Chapter 3

Darling Rosa

Rosa glared at the frock that would not stay still on her mother's pressing board. She had not the gift of homemaking that blessed her mother and older brother. This frock needed pressing, and Rosa's murmurs had no influence on its unruliness. The source of its unruliness most likely stemmed from its habitual residency on the floor at the back of Rosa's cupboard. Rosa's murmurs offered no remorse for the frock's abandonment, her carelessness, and so could offer no coaxing into a pressed presentability.

Rosa startled at a gentle touch on her shoulder and the sweetness of a kiss planted on the top of her head.

"Let me help," whispered Romane, as he slipped the frock from beneath Rosa's irritated palm. He held up the crumpled material, gave it a practiced shake, and settled it back onto the pressing board. He spread his fingers wide, softened his eyes, and murmured lovingly over his work. Rosa watched the sullen fabric stretch itself like a purring cat, spreading beneath the gifted caress of her older brother. Romane could gentle any household task into cooperation.

Relief flooded Rosa, and she breathed gratitude, to the frock as well as Romane. The frock huffed its shoulder at her, and Romane whispered, "Leave this to me, Rosa. I will finish it for you. No one need know."

Rosa reached on tiptoes to kiss Romane's temple, breathed her gratitude again, and gently touched the relaxing frock. "That's better," Romane smiled, as the fabric accepted Rosa's touch.

"I have to wear it tonight, so I need to be its friend."

"Yes," nodded Romane. "Off with you now."

Rosa slipped out the back door and trotted to Gosikk's inn. She had promised to come early to hear her duties, and she was adept at keeping promises.

Rosa heard Stevven's murmurs and stopped on the street below to watch the enthralled artisan murmur the enthralled wood of Gosikk's new roof. When Stevven stooped to begin a new murmur, Rosa climbed the steps of the inn, pushed open the double doors, and began her search for Gosikk.

She found him in the storeroom, listening to a capped man who stood with his back to her.

"There are two men walking down from High Pass. They look weary."

"Two men?" Gosikk asked.

Realization flashed through Rosa. The man standing between her and Gosikk was Bolin. Heat flushed Rosa's neck and face, and she was grateful for the dim light that cloaked her blush that betrayed her schoolgirl crush.

Bolin bent his head and rested his hand on the shelf beside him. Rosa knew he had closed his eyes in concentration.

"One man," Bolin corrected himself. "One man and one horse. Walking together. They look weary," he repeated, an important part of his message.

Gosikk rubbed a hand over his face. "The horse is no problem. We've room in the stables. In a week, a guest would be no problem as well. But now..." he gestured in the direction of the carpenter with his murmuring and sighed. "We'll have to pull something together to welcome him."

"I can help," Rosa said from the doorway where she had lingered. Both men startled at her nearness, appearing seemingly out of nowhere. She grinned an apology. "I can help," she repeated.

"Right." Gosikk straightened. "Let's clear out the corner room and move all of the extra furniture in here. We'll sort all of this," his arm swept to take in the new shelving, "once the new rooms are finished, and we're able to move the furniture to where it belongs." He frowned. "It will make sense of itself soon enough. We need Katernn's gift of organizing to do it justice." He nodded at Bolin and Rosa. "Yonce can help with the room."

Rosa skipped behind the men and followed them to the corner room, where they made quick work of readying it into a welcoming snug, with bright splashes of color on pillow and rug, white curtains drifting with the breeze finding its way through the window, its shutters thrown wide. Rosa relished the busyness of the inn, her newfound freedom in helping Gosikk, releasing her from her mother's habitual frown and constant irritation.

Once the room gleamed, Gosikk turned his full attention to Rosa. "Now, girl. Let's get you settled so you'll be of some use once the bustle is on." Rosa nodded and followed him into the passageway toward the main stairwell that emptied into the common room below. She glanced back and met Bolin's eyes. She smiled an unknowing dazzle that smattered across Bolin's cheek, but turned to fly down the stairwell without seeing the smile's effect on the discomfited woodsman.

The inn was as familiar to Rosa as her own home down the road, but she had never entered as hired help. She followed Gosikk closely as he pointed out cleaning cloths and extra tankards, opened cupboards that released their aroma of vinegar and lemon oil, and drawers that revealed the inner workings of the village's public parlor that doubled as welcoming respite for travel-weary wanderers making their way from here to there.

Rosa's excitement bubbled into a giddy grin and bouncy steps. The thought that she might finally discover her true gift ignited a dizzying frenzy inside her head. She forced herself to concentrate on Gosikk's every word. He was like a second father to her, and she longed to please him. His hearty laugh and hand on her shoulder made her feel welcome and essential. His instructions and demonstrations were clear and simple. Rosa grew more confident that she could succeed. A future as barmaid thrilled her, worlds more than her past as daily hang-about.

All too soon, Gosikk stood with Rosa in the center of the common room, her gaze sweeping across benches and tables, along the pleasing lines of trim and beams, the warm glow of scattered glorbs, soft textures of rugs and cushions. He nodded at her. "Let's bless."

Rosa followed as Gosikk roamed the edges of the large room, listened to his murmured gratitude and welcome, watched his floating arms and half-closed eyes. She added her own fledgling murmurs of welcome and readiness, leaning into the aura that wafted behind Gosikk, feeling his love of his life's purpose, his gift of hosting. She melted into the ritual, floated after him, and learned more about the world of wanderers and innkeepers than she had in her young lifetime of merrying within these cozy walls.

Finally, Gosikk turned to her with a question in his eyes. "What else?"

"I'm ready."

He glanced at her stained overalls and raised an eyebrow.

A blush warmed her cheeks, and she reassured him. "All I need to do is ready *myself*." He nodded, and she dashed through the nearest door to head home, to bathe and don the pressed frock that she knew awaited her.

Chapter 4

Wanderers

Bolin watched the girl dart across the wide porch of the inn, trotting toward home. He puffed his pipe and pondered the fate of a young woman fated to a wedlock that would take her away from the village of her youth, away from all who knew her, all who loved her. Would her promised mate please her? Would her fated life fulfill her, help her blossom into her potential? He puffed his pipe solemnly, worriedly.

His own fate had blossomed into a love of forest, with its trees and ferns, its scattered meadows and busy streams. He looked up to the blossomed limbs that hung above him and murmured admiration for the cultivated and domesticated. But his true love lay with the wild, the unstructured reaches, the dips and curves, the ravines and hillocks. He cherished the wild.

Perhaps that was why he was drawn to Rosa. He sensed her wildness, a wildness that her mother could not quite domesticate, could not quite tame. Would her fate tame her? Would her wild dampen and flicker out? A tremor of sorrow darkened his heart.

Bolin considered the repairs to the inn, the expanded loft with its extra rooms. The work had started early, timed with the early spring, and the roof lay open and vulnerable below the dazzling sun. Bolin felt no concern for unexpected weather blasting through the open roof, drenching the new rooms below. The early start in this early spring felt right and fitting.

Bolin sat cocooned in wafting fragrances of burning herbs from his pipe and bountiful blossoms that jostled above his head, heard the buzzing busy-ness of a myriad insects, felt the warmth of the scattered sunlight that drifted through the bedazzled orchard. It was time to meet the wanderers, these early guests who trod the well-groomed road that plunged from High Pass, the road that led wanderers to the welcoming glow of Gosikk's fine inn.

Bolin tapped his pipe to empty its spent leaves against the boulder atop which he sat and tucked the warm pipe into his pocket, checked for his swinging bag, bereft of seedlings, yet redolent with their memory and promise of an enriched forest. His forest. His wild, cherished forest.

He clambered to his feet, glanced in the direction of Rosa's flight, the road now empty and waiting for the next passerby to tread its domed perfection. He turned and stepped onto that perfection and walked away from the village and its wild girl whose fate remained obscured. His eyes swept the road before him, squinted against the noonday glare, and he walked toward the wanderers, the horse and its man, who, in their turn, walked in weariness toward Bolin, the village, and the inn that waited, glowing with expectation and welcome.

They first came into view as a shimmering in the distance, the warmth of the sun radiating up from the road and its gentle curves. As Bolin walked, his awareness reached to the forest that crowded its way up the hillsides along the far edges of the groomed fields, even as his eyes held the road before him, his heart beating in unison with the doubled steps of double wanderers. His ears drank the birds' song as they flitted above swaying grasses and the tumble of the river that swept along its ancient path at the far reaches of tidy pastures.

The shimmering silhouettes gained substance against the brightness of the sloped road. Bolin sensed their peace and tranquility along with an expectation and curiosity of what awaited them. His greeting would be their first welcome to his village, and Bolin felt the rightness in that beginning.

Bolin halted a hundred yards from the newcomers, his arms relaxed at his sides. They walked toward him, a fine stallion and a lithe man, walking side by side, shoulder to shoulder, their paces perfectly timed, one to the other, their eyes observing Bolin. They halted ten paces away. The horse tossed his head and touched the tip of one hoof to the perfection of the domed road. The man nodded and placed his palm against the horse's neck. The three paused their breaths, waited, each assessing the other.

Bolin nodded and addressed the man. "Gosikk has a room ready for you and a clean stable for your horse. His food is good, and the inn is clean." He gave a slight grimace. "Except for some repairs that will not inconvenience you, given their distance from your room. Welcome."

The horse nodded and stepped forward. The man followed. He spoke. "Your welcome is gratifying. We come in peace, hoping for rest and quiet. We have journeyed far."

Bolin turned as the duo reached him and matched the wanderers' pace, side by side, shoulder to shoulder. "You crossed High Pass. How was the crossing?"

"The summit was clear and warm. Beyond the summit, we left deep winter and a furious storm of ice and wind. Yet as we made the summit, the clouds opened, the sun turned brilliant, and spring ushered us into a remarkable contrast."

The horse lifted its forefeet high and stomped for several steps. The man nodded and glanced at Bolin. "We are curious about all of this...bounty..." he gestured at green pastures and sparkling sunshine "...despite our gratitude for its presence."

Bolin breathed air deep into his lungs. "It is an early spring, to be sure."

"It is not always so?"

Bolin guffawed. "Nay. This is rare, this beauty, this abundance, this early in the year. Exceedingly rare."

The horse's steps slowed, stopped. The man turned to watch the stallion, lifting his hands to plant them on his hips. Man and horse looked around them, silent. After a few moments, the horse tossed his head and stepped forward. The man turned and once again matched the horse's stride, side by side, shoulder to shoulder. Bolin joined them.

The man spoke. "Have you lived here long? In this valley?"

"Since my birth," Bolin replied, "and all the days since."

"And you've not seen this before? This...early spring?"

"Not in my remembrance. It is a blessing to our village."

"Yes," said the stranger. "Let's hope for that."

The threesome walked in silence, feeling the day, wondering, one about the others. Bolin, unused to words, walked comfortably in their silence. The horse and the man, unused to spoken thoughts, walked purposefully in their outer silence, watchful. They walked past frolicking lambs and grazing ewes, past orchard trees bursting with color and fragrance and the hum of busy pollinators. Bolin led them to Gosikk's inn and past, around the corner, and through a wide gate opening onto a cobbled courtyard where Yonce waited, a silent welcome for horse and rider.

With no lead, harness, or saddle, Yonce paused, unsure of how to attend to the horse. With a toss of his head, the horse stepped forward as the man said, "He will follow you." And he did. Through a high door and into the fragrance of fresh straw that crackled beneath weary hooves, and rich hay piled high, a bucket of grain, another of clear water. Bolin followed the man into the stable, waited while he looked at the sturdy walls and generously strewn straw. The horse stood in his stall, turned, tossed his head at the man, and nickered softly. He lowered his nose to the bucketed water and drank deeply, eyes closed, radiating peace.

Yonce lifted a brush from its nearby basket, stepped into the stall, and began the end-of-day ritual of currying away the day's travel.

Bolin led the wanderer from the courtyard and through the inn's nearest door. The man's glance roamed the common room, brushed across Mackey who sat nodding at the far end of a trestle table, Pharlan peering from beneath, and turned as Gosikk strode from the kitchen, wiping his hands on his lifted apron, who reached past Bolin to the wanderer standing just behind. Bolin sensed that the wanderer still listened back to the stable, to the stall, where his horse sighed into the stiff brush traveling across his withers and back, lifted one hoof to rest its tip atop the crackling straw. Bolin saw the wanderer regain himself, stretch his hand out to meet Gosikk's welcome, waited through the customary exchange of host and guest.

Gosikk gestured to the gaping hole at the far end of the room. "We are preparing more space for additional guests arriving in a few days' time. We are celebrating the wedlocking of a neighbor's favored daughter. You will find the village abuzz with preparation. I trust the work will not disturb your rest, for the length of your stay in our village."

"A wedlocking," breathed the man, eyebrows raised. "We had not expected that."

"Yes. It is a rare occasion, but a blessed one." Gosikk sent a quick glance toward Bolin, returned his attention to the man. "Would you care for a meal? Or is rest your immediate need?"

"A short rest, perhaps. Then I will see to Tronder, to make sure all is well. Your evening meal will suffice, I am sure."

"Tronder is your horse? My apprentice, Yonce, is seeing to him. You may rest easy. Yonce has the gift of husbandry. A strong gift, it is."

The man smiled. "Yes. Tronder says he is well cared for and is resting easy. I only want to settle with him before evening falls." He bowed slightly. "I am remiss. Miichal, kind sir. I am Miichal, and exceedingly grateful for your warm welcome and kind hospitality."

Gosikk laughed heartily, his round belly shaking up and down. "We are happy to have you with us, Miichal. And Tronder as well." He rubbed his palms together and turned to Bolin. "Will you show Miichal to his room? The kitchen beckons..."

Bolin nodded and gestured toward the stairwell. "Your room is just here, Miichal, away from the bustle of the inn's evening. And it will bustle tonight, of a certainty. We have several guests and many neighbors. After a long day of crafting and preparation, an evening of camaraderie always beckons."

Bolin led the way up the stairs and along the low passageway, ducking under a beam. He swept open the door of the corner room, bright and cheery after its morning transformation. The scented breeze ruffled the curtains edging the open window, and the trill of birdsong floated from the orchard beyond.

Miichal stepped into the room, glimpsed the bathing tub through an arched doorway at the far end, and breathed in a deep contentment. "This is the perfect ending to a long day. Thank you, Bolin. We will both rest well in this serene inn."

Bolin gestured to the open window. "You will want to shutter your window at dusk." He pointed to the clasps that held the shutters against the walls, shielded by the fluttering curtain. "Ero and Era are both at their fullest tonight, and their brightness might challenge your sleep. Be forewarned."

Miichal swiveled toward the window, and stood as if listening. After a quiet moment, he said, "We have been in deep winter, without stars or moons. We had lost track of the moons and their cycles." He looked fully at Bolin. His face seemed drained of color, but perhaps that was only the light streaming through the window. "Double moons, at their fullest." A shadow crept up from beneath his collar. "Thank you for the reminder, Bolin."

Bolin nodded, touched his forefinger to the brim of his cap, and backed out of the room. A momentary worry tickled the edges of his thoughts as he made his way along the passageway and down the stairwell. Why had the man's face darkened? And Bolin couldn't remember telling the wanderer his name.

Chapter 5

Upending

Mandra hefted another basket onto the table and turned to the wall shelf, lifting down a stack of earthen plates. Each plate went into the sturdy basket, wedged between layers of straw. She leaned against the full basket and reached across to swing open the large window, taking a moment to marvel at bright jonquils nodding in the breeze. She took in a deep breath. She had to admit that the fair weather would make an easier time of it, living under cloth until the house was finished.

What a time to be upending households. But Marlow would insist, so upend they would. Mandra huffed at the added inconvenience of Gosikk's sudden need of Rosa's help. Rosa might not have the gift of householding, but she could lift and carry with the best of them. Now, Mandra and Romane would work alone, packing and sorting as well as lifting and carrying.

She bent with a grunt, reaching to the back of the low cupboard to bring out empty wine bottles. They would not be needed during the family's brief stay under cloth, but she would not leave their delicacy in the path of careless carpenters and thoughtless masons. Artisans lost themselves in their murmurings, and she did not trust them. She refused to add replacement of broken bottles to the chaos of wedlocking and housebuilding.

She frowned anew at Marlow's extravagance. Why, now that their family was diminishing by one, why was he determined that artisans murmur a newer, larger house for them? The house was fine as it was. Why disrupt everything, upend their lives? She huffed in disgust.

Mandra could not begin to understand the workings of her husband's mind. As often happened, he felt as a stranger to her. A stranger at home in this village that remained foreign to her, even after these many years.

Mandra had never fit in since arriving to this new life as a young bride. Her father had been sure that she would adjust, given her youth. He had brushed aside her misgivings. But she had already been set in her ways, even at that young age, and adjustment wasn't in her nature. Mandra frowned. *Marlow* should have been the one to adjust. *She* was the household-maker. He was out and about, from dawn to dusk. Why should she adjust, when the household was her domain, not his? It rankled, his authority over her and their household. This foreign village was not her own. Why should it be? She was not born to it.

And why this elaborate display over Rosa's wedlocking? Mandra huffed again. A simple ceremony would have sufficed. Mandra could not understand Marlow's insistence on pomp and splendor. She was skeptical that Rosa was as beloved as he claimed. Why should the neighbors have any say in their daughter's wedlocking? Absurd.

Romane came through the doorway from the garden and paused, hands on hips. He nodded approval at empty shelves and packed boxes. "The other rooms are cleared, except for beds and linens in the sleeping room. I was thinking we could stay under this roof for a few more nights."

Mandra straightened from rummaging in the low cupboard, hands pressing into her back to ease the ache that clamored there. "Why would we stay? The artisans begin tomorrow. It is high time for us to leave so we can move past this nuisance."

Romane shook his head. "I've spoken to them. They will begin their work at this end of the house. Our sleeping room will be undisturbed for several days."

"You expect us to sleep in an upended household?" Mandra stared at her son. Had he gone mad, along with her husband and the rest of the village?

"It will be more comfortable. And..." he paused, reluctant to speak of superstitions. "The moons will both be in the sky tonight. They'll be full."

"Stuff and nonsense," scoffed Mandra. "Children's tales and midnight whisperings. I will not listen to your tales of mystery and fear."

Romane, ever the diplomat, moved across the pavers that lined the kitchen floor and wrapped his arms around his irritated mother. "It's only for sleeping. We will live under cloth during the day. All will be well. It will be quiet and calm in our familiar beds, our familiar room. We will sleep soundly. Much better than trying to sleep under flapping cloth and the patter of rain."

Mandra's irritation ebbed at Romane's soothing voice and comfortable embrace. He could always calm her. She sighed, resigned. "Yes. You're right. We would sleep better here than under cloth." She pulled back to study his face. "Will the artisans be able to finish on schedule? The wedlocking is fast approaching."

He nodded. "The timing works well. We'll be fine. We'll be right here, both of us. We'll finish everything with time to spare."

She nodded against his chest and moved out of his embrace. She patted his chest where her head had rested and turned away, looking for her next task. Romane lifted the basket of plates to carry them to their temporary tent.

"I'll set these up in the tent's kitchen to be ready for tomor-row's meal."

She nodded absently as he disappeared into the garden. Such a fuss, over extravagant wedlocking and childhood tales of bright moons and mysterious magic. She huffed and opened the next cupboard door.

Chapter 6

Draymon

Draymon whistled his way back to Gosikk's inn as the sun passed its zenith and began its descent toward western ridges. Today's circuit through the countryside had been happily successful, and Draymon chortled to his mule with boisterous cheer. The approaching wedlocking had reminded these simple folk of the countless odds and numerous ends that they surely needed to prepare for the upcoming festivities. Draymon's money belt hung heavy at his side, reminding him anew of his happy success.

He remained undaunted by his dwindling supplies and empty barrels, knowing that his partner, his Greggor, would arrive any hour now, his wagon piled high with bright cloths and baskets of trinkets, with hats and scarves and all manner of sparkling and tinkling loveliness to tempt wedlock guests into adding one more flourish to their celebratory costumes.

Draymon had noted the simple houses and unlavished rooms, so the bulk of Greggor's wagon would be filled with pillow covers and blankets, footstools and side tables, candlesticks and vases, glass and crockery, lace and ribbons, all manner of brightness to fill these simple houses with color and cheer. Their trade would continue long past the wedlocking, when villagers and country folk alike returned to the plainness of their lives and dreamed of more.

One customer had even asked him to open his box of medicinal herbs, feeling certain of the need for extra boluses and poul-
tices to treat heavy heads and thickened brains on the morning
following the splendor of this extravagant wedlocking. He sent a
whistle of gratitude to his foresightful Greggor, who had insisted
that the bulky box was a necessary addition to his inventory.

Draymon turned his mule into the cobbled courtyard behind
the inn, and handed the reins down to Yonce, the innkeeper's
capable apprentice, who had a gift of husbandry, as it happened.
He climbed from the high wagon, straightened himself to his
full height, and shook his trousers into their rightful crispness
of line and fashion. He strolled across the cobblestones, his eyes
following the flight of a flock of turquoise birds that swept over
the towering trees that waved their crowns above the high roof
of the inn.

He held his hat secure upon his head, braced against a sudden gust and wondered if a storm might be brewing. He scanned
the cloudless sky, shrugged his silk-clad shoulders, and entered
the inn through the nearest doorway, his mule and wagon put
out of mind.

As his eyes adjusted to the dim interior, he noted the drunkard with his dog at their usual place next to the far window. His
nose wrinkled in distaste. The strapping Bolin was disappearing up the stairwell, followed by a newcomer wearing the dust
of long travel on his boots and shoulders, the dust thickly evi-
dent as the tall man passed below the cavernous hole in the roof
through which the midday sun glared.

Draymon cleared his throat noisily. "Ahem!"

Gosikk appeared through the kitchen door, paused upon seeing Draymon, and strode toward him, preceded by his usual
friendly greeting.

"Mr. Draymon, sir! Welcome, welcome. How was your trade
this fine day?"

"Very favorable, Mr. Gosikk. Your countrymen are exceedingly generous with their wants and needs. I was able to fulfill many a wish." He rolled up onto his toes and smiled his happy smile as his heels regained their firm place on the worn floor. It was hard to stand in one spot, with all this cheer bubbling through his veins. He could dance a jig. "Has Mr. Greggor arrived?"

"Not as yet, though we expect him shortly. You mentioned that he will be heavy-laden, perhaps moving slower than anticipated."

"Just so. Just so." Draymon smoothed his waistcoat and looked around the common room. "Might I trouble you for a draught, while I await his imminent arrival?"

"To be sure. Young Yonce is most likely settling your mule, so allow me to pour you our best vintage."

Draymon's smile widened. "Yes! Of course! Your very best, if you will. Today is a day for happiness and cheer." Draymon wandered to his favorite table, happily situated at the opposite end of the room from the wretched drunkard and his pathetic dog, the drunkard who smelled faintly of ammonia and moldy apples.

Gosikk carried a tray filled with a shallow bowl of roasted nuts, a plate of melting cheese that dripped tantalizingly over crisp crackers that were themselves covered with roasted seeds, and a brimming glass of Gosikk's best cider, the thick glass frosted so that it glistened in the sunlight as the tray passed below the roof's gaping hole. Draymon breathed in the blended aroma of cold cider, toasted nuts, and melted cheese and hummed approvingly.

"Thank you, Mr. Gosikk, thank you!" He beamed. "Just the ticket."

Gosikk straightened and beamed in his own right. He bent forward slightly, conspiratorially. "I'm afraid that I must return to

the kitchen. Until young Yonce returns from our happily popu-
lated stable, you have only to call out, and I will attend to you
at once." He bowed to the full extent allowed by his round belly.
"Enjoy your respite."

"Thank you, Mr. Gosikk, thank you!" Draymon repeated, eyes
twinkling. "I may now await Mr. Greggor happily and splendidly."

Gosikk bowed a final bow and turned lightly on his heel for
such an ample figure, intent on the demands of partially as-
sembled bean stew, a pile of cabbage in need of chopping, and
spongy oblongs of bread dough, ready for the hot oven.

Greggor would arrive, his wagon heavily ladened, but not until Yonce had brought a second glass of their best cider, along
with a single, thick cigar, whose smoke Draymon drew in, slowly
and lovingly, as he watched the carpenter busily humming and
murmuring wooden planks into their assigned destinations.

Draymon hummed cheerfully as he leaned back, exhaled the
cigar's fragrance up to the high ceiling where the carpenter murmured his captivating artistry.

Chapter 7

Treasure

Stevven did not notice the raven that glided through the opening in the roof he was murmuring into shape. Stevven did not know that the raven's name was Cam, and that Cam had been waiting for Stevven to turn his back, offering the chance to peak into that opening with its fascinating aromas drifting up, the hole that yawned below Cam's tree. He did not see it alight on a wide beam, hop to the edge to peer down at the tantalizing glimmer of a frosty glass and aromatic nuts passing below.

But when Stevven *did* turn his back to reach for his water flask, Cam fell forward into a silent glide and swept into the darkened common room. Cam blinked, and was only *just* able to land on a wide beam, along which he did hop, over which he did peer.

The glass might no longer glimmer under the light of the gaping roof, but the nuts were certainly the source of the enticing aroma that drifted on the air. Cam ruffled his feathers and shifted his weight from one foot to the other and back again. Cam would not risk discovery by giving in to his yearning for those glorious nuts, but he would keep his eye on them, lurking in the deep shadow of the high beam, awaiting his chance.

A second glass arrived, briefly glimmering as it passed underneath Stevven's gaping hole, then immediately dimmed into mediocrity. The glass held no attraction for Cam. But the nuts. Oh, the nuts!

At long last, the tall man stood with purpose and excitement. He strode to a door leading to the courtyard beyond, waving and calling exuberantly. Cam seized the moment for which he had waited so patiently. He swooped down to the low table, picked one, two, three nuts into his long beak and flapped back to his perch on the high beam. He excitedly discharged his treasure, taking care that none rolled away, a carefulness that had taught him much over the span of his young life. Riches!

He peered again over the edge of his beam, down to the table, to the waiting aroma of additional treasure. The coast was clear. He swooped, scooped one, two, three, and flapped once again to his high perch. He remained undetected, a silent wraith, with treasure beyond his wildest dreams wobbling at his feet.

Just in time. The tall man returned, pounding the back of a shorter man who grinned up into the excitement of the tall man. They crossed the room to the table still rich with treasure. The tall man raised his arm, held up two fingers, and nodded happily to the round man at the far end of the room. The tall man and the shorter man sat at their table, laughing and using their words in a flurry of noise, slapping each other's backs, arching in laughter, unceremoniously ignoring the treasure spread before them.

Cam looked down at his own collection of nuts and bent to the nearest one. He cocked his head. He had enough. He could leave the tabled treasure for a later time. He watched the round man bring two more glasses with their brief glimmering, and turned his full attention to his treasure. He picked up the nut that wobbled nearest his foot, and lifting his head to the ceiling, he swallowed it down, just in time to see the opening in the roof blink out and disappear.

***

Stevven rolled the thick tarp over a length of slim wood and laid it in place next to the unfinished base of the new dormer. Gosikk had insisted that the hole be covered completely by the tarp, all edges securely fastened, ensuring that no wind or rain might enter the common room until work could be resumed tomorrow. Stevven would have to use nails instead of murmuring his gift of carpentry, since wood did not touch wood on this impromptu covering. He tacked down the first edge, tap, tap, tap, and stretched the canvas tarp, covering the hole entirely. He wound the second edge of the tarp around a second length of wood and nailed that edge securely as well.

He hated piercing these wooden lengths, and especially hated piercing the wooden roof with iron nails. He murmured condolences, apologies, and the wood softened a pinpoint of its depth in order to accept the nails, one by one, in deference to the artisan who murmured the secret language of wood. Once the third and fourth edges were nailed in place, the tarp was thoroughly secure. Stevven gathered his few tools and scattered supplies and moved with sure feet to a lower roof, then another, making his way back to his ladder that led to the cobblestoned courtyard.

He edged into the kitchen where Gosikk shaped loaves of dough into bread pans, ready for their final proofing. Stevven raised his voice. "I've finished for the day, Gosikk. The roof is secure for the night. I'll start again tomorrow at first light."

Gosikk wiped his hands on a nearby cloth and motioned Stevven to follow him into the common room, where they craned their necks to look into the rafters. Not the faintest sliver of light, proving a secure fit. Gosikk nodded his approval and wiped his floured hand once more before offering it to Stevven.

"Thank you, sir. Your murmurs took you far today. The dormer will be finished in no time and we can easily add new walls and flooring. It'll be grand, having that extra room."

Stevven stood, hands on hips, peering into the dark reaches of the partial roof above them. "Yes. It'll be fine for the night, and will have its final covering tomorrow. This wood is young and compliant; easy to shape. The work is going well. I'm pleased."

"As am I," replied Gosikk. "Have a restful evening." His eyes glinted. "Katernn and Jullia will be here soon, and dinner will come soon after."

Stevven brightened. "Jullia is here tonight?"

"Yes!" Gosikk grinned. "*And* Katernn, don't forget. They'll both be sure to bring you ample food and drink." Gosikk turned, chuckling. He turned back, abruptly. "And Rosa joins us tonight. She is helping out, in exchange for her wedlock feast. We have many guests arriving over the next days, and the more she learns now, among friends, the better she'll be able to help when the bustle grows larger and less familiar."

"She'll serve at her own wedlock feast?"

"Nay, nay. Only up until then. She'll cease when it's time for her to cease." Gosikk rubbed his chin. "She's not really needed," he said in a lowered voice, "but it seemed best to remove her from her mother's scolding; give her time to relax before her wedlocking."

The men fell silent. Gosikk motioned his thumb over his shoulder, gesturing toward the kitchen. "I've been abandoning guests all day long. I do need to finish the meal." He pointed at the dark roof. "Thank you for covering it. It's probably nothing, but I'm uneasy about the wind that's been building all afternoon." He paused. "Plus, the moons will be full. They'll both be up there, and one...one just never knows," he finished awkwardly.

Stevven gave a short laugh. "Our aunties did a thorough job of bewitching us, with those old stories of the danger of our moons. But it's rare to have both of them overhead during their fullest light. I expect many people will be somewhat nervous, remembering those stories." He looked up again. "One never knows." He stepped toward the stairwell. "I will clean up, get out of your way so you can finish the meal. I'm certainly ready for your fine cooking."

Stevven continued upstairs, and Gosikk returned to his kitchen were the proofing loaves rested and the stew simmered.

* * *

Cam had followed their movements, watched as they parted and left the room. He looked down at the two men who remained at their table, nonchalantly picking up treasure and popping it into their mouths, speaking their words and laughing their laughter.

Cam looked down at his own trove, gauging again that he had enough. He peered to the far end of the room, where a dog sat under his man's bench. The man dozed, but the dog's eyes stared back at Cam with an intensity that gave his heart a rush. He puffed his feathers, settled them back into place along his wings, down his back. He reached his neck to toss a nut down his throat, relishing its saltiness. He kept one eye on the dog and waited to know his next move.

He had already waited throughout the day for the chance to dart into this room, to see inside. He had been rewarded with hoped-for treasure, most of which still lay scattered at his feet. But his exit through the roof was gone. Only black stillness hung above him. He had lost the sky.

He cocked his head, looking again toward the window at the end of the room. That window stood open, a freshening breeze ruffling the sleeping man's hair. But the dog. The dog watched him intently.

Cam glanced at the other windows. He knew they were closed. No air moved there to ruffle the light they admitted; no sound or scent came through. Only light bouncing from the road beyond. A world beyond his reach. His heart beat faster at his entrapment. The certainty clutched at his breath; no escape offered itself anywhere but the single, open window. But the dog. The dog made that escape unattainable.

Cam hopped along his beam, leaving the remaining treasure behind. He would wait. He had waited all morning to get into this room. He would wait the rest of the day for his chance to escape it.

He watched the dog.

The dog watched him.

Chapter 8

Love

Jullia hefted straps of the heavy sack more securely onto her shoulder. Gosikk would love this new batch of fermented vegetables; quite an array. They would be a tantalizing side addition to his soups and stews.

She stopped at Katernn's house, as was her habit, so they could walk together to the inn, as was their habit. They greeted each other happily, linked elbows, and set off along a meandering village path.

"I need to stop at Elss and Laurr's," Jullia said. "Elss has new crockery for me, and wants to know the style that would work best for pickling."

As they rounded a curve in the path, Katernn gasped. "Look at Laurr's garden. I've not seen those colors anywhere before. How does she do it?"

Jullia's hand flew to her mouth. Accustomed as she was to the village's extraordinary gardens, the vibrancy of Laurr's garden stood out from all the rest. "Her gift has outshone itself this spring. These blossoms are glorious!"

"And the scent! It's heavenly."

Insects crawled busily amongst the flowers, pollen thick on their backs. Birds trilled overhead, chortling in the midday sunshine. The women stood in awe, taking in the glorious garden tucked along this back lane.

Katernn pointed. "Are those the jugs? The new ones? They certainly look sturdy enough."

Jullia hefted a crockery jug and nodded happily. She loved the feel of the solid shape; it was easy to lift; roomy enough for a grand batch of pickles. "I can bury these and fill them with long-haul pickles. I don't like giving up pantry space for long-hauls, but these will work perfectly in that shady area behind the house." Jullia lifted the heavy cover and peered inside. "Elss can make anything out of clay." Her words echoed inside the jug. "How she keeps them from cracking is a mystery."

"I love long-haul pickles. Especially in the winter. Will they be crunchy? Those are the best."

Jullia nodded. "Those are my favorites, too. Yes; I'm planning on quite a variety of winter crunch." She stood and swung her sack back onto her shoulder. "Maybe Elss will be at the inn tonight. I can tell her she got them just right."

Katernn stooped to closely examine the remaining crockery. "How does she get those colors in her glazes? They're beautiful!"

Jullia pulled on Katernn's arm. "We should go. Let's stop for Rosa, make sure she's ready."

Katernn followed Jullia's pull. "We need to see about her shoes. She's not used to standing for hours on end."

They gained the main road and slipped through the gate into Mandra's garden, slowed to gawk at the tent that stretched next to the house. Jullia whispered, "They'll be cramped in that wee thing."

Katernn nodded and copied Jullia's whisper. "It won't be for long, though."

Jullia whispered even more softly, tenderness filling her heart. "May be that Rosa can come to the inn during the day, too, instead of only at night."

"What could she do?" Katernn asked dismissively.

Jullia knew that Rosa, sweet as she was, held no special place in Katernn's esteem. Rosa's gifts remained obscure, hidden from discovery, if she even had any. What use was a gift-less girl? Still, Mandra's nagging of Rosa was widely acknowledged in the village, so Jullia thought that perhaps her gifts were simply smothered. To be honest, could anyone blossom in that angry house?

Also widely acknowledged was the consistent absence of Marlow, Mandra's soft-hearted husband. Daily, he stopped at the inn for a clandestine breakfast, before climbing onto his mule's back, a midday meal wrapped in cloth tucked safely in his pocket.

Jullia shrugged, grasping for ways that Rosa might be kept occupied. "There's dusting and straightening and sweeping."

"She hasn't the gift." Katernn scoffed.

Jullia shrugged again. "She won't need a gift for the lightness of tasks that the inn demands." She abandoned her attempt to change Katernn's mind and silently bemoaned the weight of her sack of ferments. She switched the sack from one shoulder to the other and looked toward Mandra's door, hoping they wouldn't have to wait long for Rosa. As an afterthought, she said, "Not for these few days, at least. 'Twill give her some experience of managing a household, without constant disparaging from her mother."

Katernn shook her head. "For *that*, she *will* need a gift." She stepped away from their conspiratorial whispering and called, "Rosa! Rosa, are you ready? We can walk together to Gosikk's."

Mandra's shrill voice blared from an open window. "Rosa! Rosa! Move, girl! You're keeping your new *colleagues* waiting." Mandra's voice sneered the word, colleagues. She leaned out the window and glared at Jullia and Katernn. "And I'll thank you not to stand in my garden, bellowing for my daughter." The scowling face disappeared, and the window slammed shut, muffling another shrill "Rosa!"

The women's backs stiffened and their eyes slid a sidewise look at each other at the unexpected onslaught from their least-liked neighbor. But they stood their ground. They continued to wait for Rosa, Jullia thinking that Rosa might need some soothing on the short walk to Gosikk's.

Sure enough, Rosa stumbled from a doorway in a flurry, face flaming, cheeks wet with tears. She kept her eyes on her feet as she walked to where the women waited. Jullia reached an arm to encircle the tearful girl, and the threesome turned to the garden gate just as Romane hurried after them.

"Rosa!" he called softly. She looked back obediently, and a sob shuddered her belly.

"Hey, hey. There, there. Look. I've brought you a ribbon for your glorious hair. It will keep it out of your way as you tend to all the guests at Gosikk's." He turned her shoulders to face away from him and gently gathered her unruly curls, running his fingertips softly across her temples and up her neck. Rosa closed her eyes and let flow the last of her tears at his tenderness.

Jullia felt her face blush at Romane's words. His kindness to his sister swept her with admiration. Romane was the kindest man in all the village. Jullia sighed. Katernn rolled her eyes.

Romane tied a wide ribbon securely at Rosa's nape and embellished it by fashioning a tidy bow. The emerald of the ribbon set off the dusky red of her bountiful curls. He turned her again to face him and wiped her cheeks dry, kissing each one and smiling into her eyes.

"You have fun tonight, okay? Remember; you're only learning for now. Tonight and tomorrow and as many nights as you need, in order to help Gosikk..." He glanced at Jullia and Katernn, "...and these fine ladies." He kissed Rosa's forehead. "They are lucky to have you, and they'll fall in love with you all over again, just as they do every time you visit the inn."

Jullia, meanwhile, reached out and palmed Rosa's shoulder. "We *will* have fun tonight. You'll see. Katernn and I are thrilled to spend the evening with you, showing you all of our secrets."

Rosa looked up at Romane and nodded a shaky smile. "I know." She glanced at Katernn and Jullia. "I've been looking forward to it all day. Truly."

Mandra's voice blasted through the open doorway. "Rosa! Get on with you! You're already late, and on your first day! What will Gosikk think of you? You'll have no one to blame but yourself, if he sends you home in disgrace. Get a move on, girl!"

Jullia grimaced at the venom in Mandra's voice. Even Katernn flinched. Romane tweaked Rosa's nose, a favored gesture often employed, and whispered, "Off you go. Have a grand time."

Jullia and Katernn stepped to either side of the girl and linked arms with her. "Thank you," Rosa called over her shoulder to Romane, as they pushed open the gate and walked briskly to the road, side by side, shoulder to shoulder.

Jullia leaned into Rosa. "We're actually early, you know. You're already off to a brilliant start, with your early arrival, your wide smile and sophisticated ribbon." She squeezed Rosa's arm. "Everyone will be ever so glad to see you, wearing a long apron and with a towel draped over your arm." She mimed the length of the apron and the drape of the towel. "Quite professional and ready to help. We *will* have fun."

"We'll have you trained and ready in no time," quipped Katernn. "Just you wait and see if we don't." Jullia's heart lightened at being gone from that unfriendly garden, pleased at Katernn's kindness to the beleaguered girl.

Rosa's step took on a determination and her chin lifted in a tilt of bravado. Her sweetness peeked from behind its protective shell and took a tentative step toward bubbling forth, as was her usual deportment.

The trio clumped up the inn's steps, across the wide porch, and through the doubled entry whose doors stood open, beckoning to sunlight, fresh breeze, and passersby alike.

Jullia called out, "Gosikk! Your prize has arrived, ready for whatever the evening may hold for her. And, I've brought you more ferments!"

They heard Gosikk's voice drifting from the kitchen. "Good! Good! Get her settled and aproned. Bring your jars in here, will you Jullia? Yonce!"

"Yes?" Yonce answered from the courtyard.

"Come have your dinner, before the guests arrive with thirsty gullets and empty bellies to demand the full of your attention! Be sure to try Jullia's latest ferments. They'll be gone before we know it."

Jullia disappeared into the kitchen with her heavy sack, greeted with delight by Gosikk's exclamations, while Katernn took Rosa by the hand and set about tying a crisp apron just so over her bright frock. Jullia rejoined them and led Rosa on a tour of the room, pointing here and there, murmuring instructions, demonstrating techniques.

The low sun slanted through the front windows, catching dust motes in their slow-motion dance. The quiet hour would pass quickly to usher in the busy-ness of the village's nightly gatherings.

***

Rosa followed along, nodding and touching, lifting and touching, seeing the logic and efficiency of the inn's hosting prowess. Jullia's instructions sang clearly across her quick mind, and she felt eager to learn as much as she could. A light flickered in Rosa's belly. Had she a gift after all? Had it lain hidden and dormant, waiting for this night to blossom into certainty?

Two men descended the staircase, one tall, the other shorter, intent on their conversation, with eyes only for each other. They strolled to a table and sat, with nary a pause in their exchange. Rosa followed Jullia, who strolled to the men's table, swapped pleasantries. The flickering light grew into a warm glow in Rosa's belly.

When Stevven appeared, Rosa turned, oblivious to his lingering gaze aimed at Jullia, and darted to his side, led him to an empty table. She dutifully heard his story about his day and brought him brimming bowl and chilled tankard, a basket of crusty bread with steam drifting from the thick slices. Her delight was complete, her laughter restored, springing from that glowing warmth in her belly.

Neighbors arrived and conversation ebbed and flowed around the room. The three women drifted amongst tables and benches, offered tankards and pitchers, bowls and platters, wiped away crumbs and spills with quick efficiency.

Jullia smiled and winked at Rosa again and again. At one point she pulled Rosa in for a hug and a whispered "Wonderful!" Rosa glowed, happier than she could ever remember. Evenings at Gosikk's were always grand, but this...this helping and toting and serving...This was beyond anything Rosa had imagined.

The glow in her belly spread to fill her eyes and spill from her lips. She seemingly floated on air, amidst neighbors long-known and friends newly met. The scent of roses filled the inn.

She did not notice the wanderer who descended the stairs, who froze at the sight of her, who stared at her red hair as he moved to a dim corner and sat watching her fiercely, sipping sparingly from a single tankard as the evening lengthened and the room gradually emptied. Yonce barred the double doors against the blustering wind that swept from High Pass to plunge across the darkened valley, sweeping along the scurrying wisps of clouds to reveal a single moon rising, full and regal, above the eastern ridge.

Chapter 9

Peace

Miichal's eyes scanned the busy room, noting every person there, counting their number yet again. Mostly he watched the young woman with the red hair, hair that tightened the expectation in his belly. With a bracing sip from his tankard, he rose, slipped out the back door, and crossed the courtyard, holding his shirt front tight against the gusts of wind that threatened to steal what warmth the shirt afforded.

He found Tronder easily, from the colors that glowed in the air above his stall, the rumble that greeted him as he entered the stable, the familiar whisper that drifted into his heart.

The moons will rise soon.

Yes. Ero is clearing the eastern ridge even now. Miichal paused. *I've just counted. There are too many souls.*

Tronder lifted a hoof, scraped it through straw to touch bare earth.

Perhaps we are in the wrong place, Miichal worried.

We were led surely.

Yes...Era has not yet appeared. There is time. Miichal hushed his worried mind. *There's a young woman here, with hair the color of Spring Maiden.* He paused. *Another sign.*

Yes. Are you ready? Can you call up the words?

Yes. They are well engrained.

Miichal wiped his palms down his thighs and once more sought to still his heart. He moved into the stall to touch his forehead against the one that Tronder lowered to greet him. The two stood silently. Miichal's heart pounded.

Miichal smoothed his palms along the silky hair of his friend's neck, relishing the familiar strength that lay beneath his touch. He moved along the length of the stallion, smoothing and caressing. The long tail twitched.

I would stay. I should have brought my cloak.

If you were meant to stay, you would have remembered to bring your cloak.

Miichal nodded. *Truly spoken.*

Truly heard. They breathed together for several breaths. *Do not hesitate, now that the time is upon us.*

Miichal yearned to linger, to avoid this challenge for which he felt sorely unprepared. Tronder had worked with him incessantly, but still. But still. He knew in his core that he had duties to attend, a birthing to usher forth. He drew in a shaky breath. All the signs were there. The early spring. The abundance of lambs and blossoms. The promise of the stars. The makta.

This village.

This inn.

The red hair.

The double moons, steadily approaching their rendezvous.

Miichal's hands jittered, his entire body electric despite the peace of the stable. He sought nonchalant words.

The moonrays will not find you here, in this sturdy stall, under this thick roof. All will be well.

All is always well.

Truly spoken.

Miichal encircled Tronder's neck with his arms, stood pressing his face onto Tronder's cheek.

You are frightened.

Miichal nodded, wiped his palms along the familiar neck. His heart pounded against his ribs.

All is always well.

As Miichal took in deep breaths, calming himself, he felt Tronder's peace fill his heart, helping him soothe himself. At last, he could acknowledge that all *was* well, just as it *should* be. Anything was possible, when preluded by this deep peace.

All is always well.

Miichal smoothed his palms on Tronder's neck one last time, then turned, latched the stall door behind him, and left his friend to his solitude. As he crossed the courtyard, he glanced at the scuttling clouds that raced above the valley, driven by the gathering wind. Ero had risen fully, shrouded by clouds for now, and begun his sedate journey across the night sky. Era's light was brightening the eastern horizon. Her erratic path would carry her close to Ero, close enough to roar across his face. The double moons were fast approaching, would quickly disperse, but Miichal felt before him an eternity; an eternity through which he must wait, in as much peace as he could garner.

Chapter 10

Sound

Cam had waited throughout the day. Once, when the wide doors had been flung open, he gathered himself and swooped out and away. He rose on the wind and banked happily in the freedom of sky.

But then he remembered his treasure. How had he forgotten his treasure? They were his. They were enough, it was true; he had not needed more. But the nuts remained on the high beam, forgotten by Cam, pinned as he had been by the stare of the dog.

So Cam decided to return. He waited in a flowering tree and assessed the inn's door. It stood wide and beckoned to him. He knew the room beyond. He knew the placement of the high beam and the treasure that awaited him there. He plucked up his courage and launched, flapped high, and without hesitation, swooped through the double doorway, up to his beam, and hopped to where his treasure lay, awaiting him.

He swallowed one nut. A second. He peered over the beam to where the dog lay under her man's table. The dog's eyes stared at him, followed him as Cam hopped back to his treasure and scooped up another nut. He would not leave them behind this time.

Suddenly, three women burst through the brilliance of the opened double door. Loud voices careened around the room, blasting Cam's sensitive ears. He squatted low, eyes mere slits, waiting for the cacophony to end.

The voices did soften, calling one to another in friendly tones, but the room was horrifyingly busy. The women moved everywhere and were soon joined by others, who also moved and called to each other. Why were their voices everywhere? So incessant? Why did their voices go on and on, bouncing off walls, one over the others then back again, others over the one.

The voices paralyzed Cam. The quiet room of the afternoon had vanished. Chaos threw itself everywhere. Cam peered toward the dog, who also cringed and retreated against the wall, only her belly and the tail curved against it visible. The dog could no longer see Cam, no longer send her stare along Cam's spine. But a larger threat pinned Cam to his beam. The cacophony and chaos of men and women enjoying each other's company spun around the room, obliterating thought, obliterating action. Cam could only cower. And wait.

The final nut lay forgotten on the wide beam. Un-treasured.

At long last, the din of voices slackened. Only a few people remained, content with the tankards before them, the conversations shared across tables. Sound softened and once again became bearable.

Cam felt his calmness return. He rose from his crouch and looked around the room. It was mostly empty. His thoughts returned. His mind settled. And yet he could not fly. The doubled doors stood barred. He had once again lost the sky.

Cam hopped along his beam, rustled his feathers, spread and tucked his wings, and as his heart beat and pounded, he gave voice to his plight, voiced his frustration and fear, called out his despair. He filled the room with his sound, hushing the people below, people who stood bewildered, staring up at him, startled into silence, mouths agape.

Chapter 11

Light

The sudden wind tore the inn's back door from Miichal's grasp. He could not find its handle and groped unsuccessfully for several moments. It was then that he heard the raven's call...and knew the time had come more quickly than he had realized. He had no more time for fear, no more time to long for someone to rescue him from his ordained duties. He turned hastily and strode into the common room, automatically counting the people who stood gaping into the shadows above them.

Gosikk hurried from the kitchen, wiping his hands, pink from washing up, on a towel that he unseeingly set on a nearby tabletop. Draymon and Greggor stared from their table. Katernn and Jullia stood frozen in mid-step. Stevven rose from his bench, hand atop tankard. Even Mackey stared, roused from his drunkenness. Young Yonce leaned across his countertop, wondering how a bird could have appeared above them. Bolin sat across from Yonce, breaking his revery of Rosa to stare up to the rafters, searching for the raven whose call he knew as well as any other.

Only Rosa moved. She stepped slowly, quietly, to stand in the center of the room. She looked up to the beam, where the dark eyes glinted down to her, and held up her hand in an attempt to soothe the frightened raven, who called and called.

"Hush, little one. You are safe. Quiet your fear. You are safe."

Several things happened suddenly, in quick succession.

A ferocious wind burst through the double doors at the front of the inn, rattling free the bar that had held them fast. The same wind circled the outer walls of the inn, caught the back door whose handle had eluded Miichal's groping, and slammed it shut. The trapped wind inside the inn swirled through the room, whipping cloths and forelocks as it passed, and swept upward to knock Cam from his high beam, slamming him, flailing, to the wall beyond, and burst through the gaping roof, tearing asunder the straining canvas, which had done its best the entire evening to withstand the mounting gale, but which now tore from its paltry, unmurmured moorings, and sailed daintily across the road to wrap itself amongst the torn flowers of the orchard's splayed branches.

And Rosa, with outstretched hand and upturned face, stood full in the searing light of the double moons.

Chapter 12

Calmness

And suddenly the guilty wind was gone. Nothing moved, not even Rosa, who stood enthralled, reaching toward those treacherous moons, who bathed her with their mysterious glare. Era moved quickly, as was her wont, and the doubled rays shifted and waned, leaving only Ero's light to bathe Rosa's upturned face.

Rosa crumpled into a heap.

Her eyes stared; her breath stirred a red strand that had escaped its emerald bondage. Her pulse beat against pale temples, while her arms and legs lay sprawled, incapable of function.

Ero drifted unconcernedly, his duty realized, washing Rosa with a lingering incandescence, awaiting the twelve.

Miichal scanned the room quickly, counting faces. Only ten, including him. Not enough, then. Not enough.

An unfamiliar whisper echoed across his heart.

Look above and below.

Miichal stepped softly to the center of the room, pointed an arm toward Rosa while his eyes scanned, scanned. "Do not touch her," he said. "We cannot touch her yet."

The calmness of his voice, his movements, calmed the others' hearts. They remained where they stood, where they sat, glancing at Rosa, but watching him.

"We do not yet know, and until we *know*, we must wait to act."

Look above and below.

He turned where he stood, wondering.

A flicker of motion caught his eye, and he saw the raven hop from the high ledge where he had been thrown, watched him float down to a tabletop to stand, looking up at Miichal in calm expectation.

Eleven?

Look below.

Miichal's sharp eyes pierced the corners of the room, beneath tables and benches, and there he found bright eyes gazing back at him.

The dog rose from under Mackey's table and padded forward to stand, sit, in full view of all. Pharlan's calm gaze trapped Miichal as he turned to face her. Miichal looked to Mackey, whose jaw stood open and unbelieving, and back to Pharlan, sitting alertly.

Twelve.

Yes.

Pharlan's coat shone in the flickering light of glorbs that burned merrily from walls and rafters. She held herself strong and magnificent, her eyes bright and attentive, waiting for Miichal to speak.

Miichal felt a terrifying emptiness yawn in his heart.

You must speak your words.

It was not Tronder's voice that filled his heart. It was another's. Miichal was dizzy with confusion and wonder. He could not find words.

You must speak.

I have no words.

You must find them.

Miichal tore his eyes away from the magnificent dog. He took in a deep breath and turned to take in all the eyes that watched him; eyes that glanced at Rosa, but watched him.

He drew himself to his full height.

"Rosa is Spring Maiden." He waited for their words, but none came. They had all been raised on the murky fable of the Spring Maiden, as many variations of the story as there were aunties in the world. As adults, few found credence in the stories. Most scoffed. But in this room, with this girl crumpled on the floor, bathed in magical light, Miichal could see the lifting of skepticism, the dawning of awe, could feel the certainty of their witnessing grow, a blossoming calmness brightening their eyes...and knew that they knew.

Rosa was Spring Maiden.

Chapter 13

Wisdom

Miichal stepped across the room to stand near Rosa's shoulder, just outside the moonlight pouring through the roof. Rosa's unseeing eyes unsettled him, but he saw her chest rise and fall. He glanced around the room, reconfirmed his count of twelve, and spoke his words.

"Rosa is Spring Maiden. We must help her awaken."

He gestured to the others to move forward. "We must encircle her, taking care to avoid any touch, either with the Maiden, the moonlight, or with each other."

Rosa's champions broke their frozen poses and quietly moved across the room. All, except Jullia; Jullia who backed away from the fallen girl, who shook her head in denial and dread.

"She cannot be Spring Maiden. Rosa is kind and joyful. There is no treachery in her heart; no cruelty. No evil."

Miichal's eyes pierced Jullia's heart. "That is what we are meant to prevent. Without us, there will be only treachery and cruelty. Only evil."

Jullia backed further, head shaking denial.

Miichal's voice was gentle and clear. "We must act swiftly, Jullia. We have not the time to ponder."

"How do you know my name? Who are you? Why should we listen to you?"

Miichal glanced at the dog and knew her name. "Pharlan told me your name. She has known you all of her life." He paused. "She urges you to trust me. Trust Pharlan if you cannot trust me."

"Trust the dog? This is insanity. All of this." Jullia gestured to Rosa, crumpled and staring, Ero's light pinning her to the floor.

"Jullia." Bolin moved toward her.

"Do not enter the moon's light!" cautioned Miichal.

Bolin hesitated and made his way carefully to grip Jullia's arms, to turn her to face him. "Search your heart, Jullia."

She frowned at him, squinted her wariness. Bolin rubbed his palms up and down her arms, imploring her with his touch. Her breath caught, and she gulped back a sob.

"Spring Maidens destroy," she whispered. "Rosa could never destroy."

Bolin spoke from a wisdom outside himself, a wisdom that whispered across his heart. "That is why we have to help her. It's up to us to keep her safe and reasoned. So she can stay her cheerful self."

Miichal clenched his fists. This couldn't be happening. Tronder had never spoken of this possibility, that one of the twelve would refuse. His mind frantically searched for Tronder's whisper, his guidance. He could not think what to do.

"Jullia." Katernn moved to take Jullia's hand. "Put aside the aunties' tales and feel for yourself." Jullia's crazed eyes moved from Bolin to Katernn. Katernn nodded at her. "Feel for yourself."

Miichal willed himself to stay still, to allow Katernn and Bolin the time to coax Jullia into her right mind.

Bolin lifted Jullia's hand and squeezed her fingers. "You can do this. Feel for yourself."

The world stood still while Jullia stood and breathed, her stare flicking between the two who held her. Just as Miichal readied himself to step forward, Jullia closed her eyes and breathed deeply into her belly. She stood for several moments, transfixed.

At long last she nodded and stepped forward. Bolin dropped her hand, and Katernn patted her shoulder. They looked to Miichal and took their places at the edge of Ero's light that flooded still through the gaping roof.

Miichal let out a breath that he did not remember holding. The others moved across the room to stand around Rosa, 'til they were ten. Miichal felt Cam's soundless flight, the rightness of his alighting on Bolin's shoulder. Of course the animal would touch its human companion, sealing their bond.

Eleven.

Pharlan padded forward and stood panting just beyond the circled humans. Her gaze held Miichal's eyes. Miichal stared back.

Twelve.

Pharlan continued to hold Miichal's eyes. She panted patiently. Miichal cocked his head, wondering. All eyes turned to the dog. Shifting her gaze to Rosa, Pharlan padded around the circled humans, slipped her head beneath Miichal's hand, and sat.

Astonishment flooded through Miichal. How could Pharlan bond with *him*? He was already bonded to Tronder. A cold dread trickled down his spine. What had happened?

You must speak your words.

Miichal's thoughts spun.

You must speak your words.

Miichal fought past the confusion of the unfamiliar whisper. He had duties to attend, a birthing to usher forth, a birthing Tronder had trained him to bring forth. He drew himself to his full height and turned his attention to the gathered champions.

They were twelve.

Twelve collections of wonder and awe, curiosity and trepidation, courage and faltering hearts. Together, they must unite. Together, they must birth this fellowship. Together, they must awaken Rosa and pledge their protection, guidance, and loyalty.

"You will have questions," Miichal spoke at last. All heads swiveled toward him; some nodded. "We will talk later. For now, we must waken the Maiden, before Ero leaves the sky."

Miichal looked around the circle. "Please join hands."

Yonce, standing next to Miichal with Pharlan between, placed his hand atop Miichal's where it rested on Pharlan's head. Cam fluttered from Bolin's shoulder to perch atop the clasped hands of Bolin and Katernn. Miichal felt a current run through him, around the completed circle, connecting them all. He closed his eyes and spoke his words.

"By the majesty of Ero, the sacredness of Era, through the mysteries of their crossed paths, and the wisdom of the ages, we twelve enter into covenant, one with the others, together to protect and defend, to serve and guide, through all our days."

Without prompting, knowing in their wisdom what was to be done, the others repeated each phrase after him. Miichal heard Pharlan's vow whisper across his heart and knew that Cam's vow whispered across Bolin's.

It was done. They stood together, linked, their fellowship newly birthed, strong and ancient.

Chapter 14

Power

"We must kneel. Kneel in Ero's light. We must not loosen our hands. We must not touch the Maiden."

With unpracticed grace, they knelt, one knee, two. As their heads entered Ero's light, the air tingled against their skin. The wind died, clouds stalled, curtains settled, trees paused their dance. A power entered them, transmitted through Ero's light. The power whirled and built. Clothing fluttered. Strands of hair lifted. Feathers and whiskers tingled.

"We must place our clasped hands on the Maiden. Without loosening our hold of each other." They did as Miichal described, clasped hands, a paw, a wing. Sparks of light flashed where hands met the Maiden, under a paw, around a wing. The flashes increased in brilliance and rapidity. Clothing flapped. Hair flew.

They knelt in Ero's power and knew they were transformed.

Sudden silence.

The world blinked and remembered itself.

Clouds resumed their silent drifting, and Ero hid his brilliance. The sky above them darkened.

Rosa closed her eyes, rolled onto her side, cheek resting on forearm, and slept.

The fellowship lifted their hands at her first movement, held them ready to assist. Rosa sighed. The fellowship sat back on their heels, hands folded in laps. Cam climbed Bolin's arm to perch again on his shoulder. Pharlan sat and set her tongue to panting.

All eyes turned to Miichal.

"All is well. The Maiden is awoken." Miichal breathed air deep into his lungs and closed his eyes.

Chapter 15

Joy

Miichal spoke softly into the quiet room. "This is my calling. Since boyhood, I have been a truthseeker, searching for answers to a thousand questions, questions that, I discovered, no one could answer. It was a struggle, not fitting in; constantly staying in the background, living on the edges. It was lonely. And empty.

"But my questions drove me, and when I was old enough, yet still a lad, I took to the road. Ever searching. Ever questioning.

"At long last I found Tronder. Perhaps he found me. We found each other, and loneliness vanished. He was living in an open pasture of an abandoned farm, no one to care for him, no one to miss him when he came with me. He was old and greying, his back swayed, his hooves brittle, his coat caked with mud and worse.

"I walked into that pasture. He lifted his head and walked toward me. And as he walked, his back straightened and his eyes brightened. His ears came forward and he tossed his head. I knew he had been waiting for me. Not for just anyone to come by and care for him. He waited for *me*.

"We have been bonded since that day. Companions. He fills my thoughts and answers my questions, even questions I didn't know to ask, drawing wisdom from the stars, the trees, the ground beneath our feet, and whispering it into my heart. Our meeting was foretold by the stars and celebrated by the trees and rocks.

"We swam the river and I rubbed neglect from his coat; the river carried it away. When we found our footing and came ashore, I used grasses to dry his coat. He shone in the sunlight, glistened. I had never seen such beauty. Such elegance.

"We traveled far, watched the people we met and listened to their stories. When I tired on the long road, Tronder carried me, but mostly we walked.

"I had never known such joy.

"'Twas Tronder who told me the story of Spring Maiden, you see; the true story. 'Twas Tronder who taught me to search, to see the signs, to know their meaning. Everywhere we went, we looked for signs of Spring Maiden. We spoke of it constantly. It was our calling.

Only yesterday we bent our heads and fought through deepest winter. And then, miraculously, at High Pass we stepped into spring. We found makta growing, and we ate it. Truly makta. We rested and let warmth seep into our bones.

"We walked a well-tended road and descended into a verdant valley. Prosperity surrounded us. We met friendly people, kind people." Miichal gestured around the table. "There was room at the inn, for me, for Tronder. And we were reminded," he nodded at Bolin, "that the night of double moons was upon us. Certainty blossomed. The signs whispered to us, and the certainty grew.

"When I saw Rosa's hair, the glorious color, I knew that she would be Maiden. I could not contain the certainty that exploded within me, and I went to see Tronder, to calm myself.

"Then I heard the raven call, and saw her caught in the rays of the double moons. Dismay filled me when I counted only ten souls. How could we be wrong? How could we find so many signs and have it be wrong?

"You see, Tronder had not mentioned the possibility of you," he gestured to Cam, "and you." His gaze lingered on Pharlan. "So there were twelve after all, and I felt the rightness of it all. I used the words that Tronder taught me, whispering them to me each night as I fell into sleep."

Miichal was overcome with emotion and could not speak. The watchful eyes of his audience blinked and roused themselves. They waited respectfully for him to regain his composure.

To ease the moment, Bolin spoke, releasing Miichal from the spotlight. "This morning...yesterday morning, I thought that I had started my life's work. I planted seedlings in our forest, seedlings I brought from another valley, to enrich our forest." He paused. "I planted those seedlings and felt that I had reached my zenith, that nothing could be better than planting *those* seedlings on *that* morning, the morning before the double moons. I could not imagine a sweeter victory."

He looked at the raven perched on his knee. "Now, it feels as though it was nothing, those seedlings going into the ground on that morning; nothing compared with the joy of Rosa being Spring Maiden. Of me, meeting my companion." His finger smoothed Cam's head and stroked his neck. Cam leaned into the caress, closed his eyes in pleasure. Bolin continued, gestured around the circle, "Of us, creating a fellowship for Rosa, Spring Maiden."

They sat around a trestle table, elbows resting askew, wrists propping chins. Some sat astride their bench, some leaned stolidly forward, knees crossed, or ankle crossed over knee, relaxed and familiar. Each had positioned themself with an easy view of Rosa, who still lay curled below the gaping roof. Ero had completed his voyage across the night sky, and the slight form slept in dimness, a sleeping cloth laid gently over her. A cushion slipped under her head.

They had shuttered the windows and barred the doors. They instinctively gathered in the solitude of the quiet inn, surrounded by the sleeping village, under the blinking stars. Glorbs flickered still, soon to be indistinguishable from the dawn light that seeped through the gaping roof.

Through the quiet night, they watched her, as they spoke and compared their stories of Spring Maiden, some of which carried a slight resemblance to the miracle that had created the curled miracle laying in its impromptu nest. Most did not, and the twelve wondered at the journey those stories had traveled, from the moment of true telling, to the lips of aunties the world over.

Miichal thought fleetingly of Tronder in his stable, but was not drawn to go to him. Tronder was safe and comfortable. And the Maiden demanded watching. Miichal would go to the stable later, after the Maiden stirred.

"What happens now?" Jullia asked. "What do we tell our families? Our friends?"

"What of Rosa's wedlocking, fast approaching?" Gosikk asked. Practicalities flooded their tranquility, jarring them, as if from a dream.

Rosa cannot wedlock. The whisper streamed across Miichal's heart.

"Rosa cannot wedlock," said Bolin with the same inflection.

"What?" asked Rosa, as she sat up and rubbed a fist into one eye.

Joy erupted around the table, as Gosikk and Jullia stumbled from their benches and hurried to help Rosa rise and sit on the chair that Greggor held for her, as Yonce scrambled to bring her a tall glass of spring water.

Rosa's champions chattered and chortled as Rosa blinked and wrinkled her forehead at them. Stevven smoothed back her curls and tucked them behind her ears before planting a gentle kiss on her cheek. Bolin folded her blanket and tucked it across her lap. Pharlan padded to Miichal's side, slipping her head beneath his hand, a hand which automatically smoothed her fur and scratched her ear.

Mackey brought Rosa's shoes, which he had removed when first she curled, and slipped them onto her feet. Draymon sliced the apple left at his plate a lifetime ago, and brought it to her on a hastily emptied bread plate. Katernn knelt at her side and smoothed the sleeve of her crumpled frock.

Joy bubbled and swirled, spiraled through the air of the blessed inn to burnish the dawn sky that peeked through the gaping roof.

Rosa had awakened.

Chapter 16

Broken

A shrill wail interrupted the patting and cossetting of Rosa, who gathered her feet beneath her and stood, hand covering mouth, for she knew that voice.

The fellowship streamed into the pale morning, the twelve and their one pausing as they looked down the road in the direction of the wail. Mandra knelt in the dust, rocking over the lone figure that sprawled at the edge of the road.

Rosa cried out, hands clutching her heart, for she knew with certainty who the sprawled figure was. Her heart broke despite her clutching hands, as she stumbled forward, her mind denying the certainty that froze her blood.

Rosa blundered down the road, bordered by gardens now grey and mourning, her foot catching in the hem of her frock, the twelve following closely. She held out her arms to the two figures, her hands pleading that it not be true. She fell to her knees and lifted his lifeless hand, held it to her breast, and keened to the sky.

Mandra sat up in all her fury and grief and shoved Rosa away, retrieved the dropped hand, the lifeless hand, and bent over the fallen Romane protectively, glaring at Rosa, screeching between sobs.

Rosa could not breathe.

"Go away, you useless thing! This is your fault! Yours! If you had come home when you should, he would not have gone looking for you! Some hooligan has killed him, and it is *all your fault!*" Mandra gasped for breath. "Go! GO! Leave! You hateful, hateful girl! I will not have you touching him! You've killed him as surely as the club that struck him down! You are damned! For all eternity! Go!"

Mandra bent again, burying her sobs in Romane's breathless chest. Romane, whose eyes stared at the moonless sky, oblivious to his mother's grief and his sister's stolen breath.

Stevven drew Rosa to her feet, and the twelve enveloped her, led her away from the grief and heartbreak that sprawled and crouched at the edge of the lifeless road. She strained to look over her shoulder, but could not see him, could not believe that this could be true, that Romane lay dead, dead...that it could be because of her.

Her feet tripped on stairs, but arms caught her, steadied her, sat her in a chair. They were back inside, back in the room that moments earlier had held only joy. Gosikk brought a damp cloth to cool her face. Mackey cleaned her dusty palms. Bolin patted her hair. Jullia retied her ribbon. A dog snuffled at her elbow, coaxing her hand to rest on soft fur.

She can revive him, floated across Bolin's heart.

"She can revive him," said Miichal with the same inflection.

Before the sunlight finds him, floated across Miichal's heart.

"Before the sunlight finds him," urged Bolin with the same cadence.

Gosikk and Stevven strode out the door. Mackey lifted Rosa's hand and pressed it to his lips, lips that no longer stank of moldy apples. "Find yourself," he said. "Remember who you are."

"I am Romane's murderer," she whispered, eyes staring.

"Nay, lass," Mackey replied. "You are Rosa, Spring Maiden, and we are your champions." He grinned at her, winked a green eye.

Rosa roused herself and looked to Bolin, the raven on his shoulder. She looked at the dog and smoothed a soft ear. She looked to Katernn, and Jullia, to each who crowded around her, sending her courage.

She thought of Romane, sprawled, and a sob shook her belly. She looked at Yonce, at Greggor and Draymon. At last, she looked to Miichal, and knew his truth. She looked again to Mackey and used his shoulder as she rose shakily to her feet.

Neighbors had gathered and now stood in clusters, hands covering mouths, grasping each other's arms. Sobs shook shoulders. Disbelief froze feet.

Gosikk looked over his shoulder and saw Rosa coming, Rosa with her ten. He leant toward Stevven, who stooped over Mandra, consoling the inconsolable, murmuring to the unhearing. Stevven looked and saw Rosa, Rosa with her ten. He looked to Gosikk, and together the two men lifted Mandra, loosened her grasped hands from Romane's dewed shirt, his dusty sleeve.

Together, they turned Mandra and led her through the clustered neighbors, past the mourning gardens, supported her stumbling legs and slack arms, led her back to her own garden, where her unbelieving husband stood, eyes streaming. They gave Mandra into his arms, and he took her, bracing his round frame to support her weight, her weight that she could not carry. He led her into their empty house, to their rumpled bed, their familiar room. Together they lay, sobbing into each other's necks.

Chapter 17

Morning

Rosa led her ten, who followed her closely. Stevven and Gosikk emerged from Mandra's garden, edged past neighbors, rejoined Rosa, her twelve now complete.

Rosa stood over Romane, and a sob shook her belly. She knelt and smoothed his shirt, repositioned his arm, lifted and kissed his cold hand. She looked to Mackey, who handed her his cool cloth. She smoothed the cloth over Romane's face, his neck, and washed his cold hands.

She set aside the cloth, finding Mackey's ready hand, lowered to receive the dusted cloth. She had eyes only for Romane, her beloved, her safety, her joy. She leaned over his chest, rubbed his temples with her thumbs, stared into unseeing eyes. After a pause, she drew breath deep inside her and bent to blow the long breath between Romane's parted lips.

She sat back on her heels, one hand smoothing Romane's cheek, the other resting on his chest. She watched his eyes.

Eyes that blinked and whose corners crinkled, eyes that stared at the dawn sky, bewildered.

A sob shook Rosa's belly.

Her hands grasped his shoulders, helped him to sit, where he coughed and sputtered, unaware of the gasps around him.

As the villagers whispered and wondered, the sun cleared the eastern ridge, spilled along the fine road, and found Romane and warmed his shoulders, cleared his mind, enlivened his breath.

The village gardens raised their hopeful heads to gape at the morning miracle. Turquoise birds darted once again, and insects remembered their lists of tasks and took to the air that once again wafted intoxicating colors. The scent of roses filled the air.

Romane looked deep into Rosa's eyes and sighed, taking her into his arms. A sob shook Rosa's belly. "Hey, hey," he whispered in her ear. "You're fine. You're safe. I'm here."

Chapter 18

Afternoon

Cam did not wonder at his transformation. He had no memory of before. Something latent had opened within him, when the moonrays grasped the girl. As he regained his footing on the ledge where the swirling wind had thrown him, he knew a strong draw, a force that beckoned him to watch the light-haired man. Bolin, he now knew his name to be. When the dark man looked up at him, looked at him from where he stood near the crumpled girl pinned by moonrays...with that look, Cam had swept down to join the group, the humans, the dog, of whom he now held no fear.

When the dark man, Miichal, he now knew his name to be, when Miichal beckoned them to encircle the girl, the Maiden, he had taken his place on Bolin's shoulder, heard Bolin's amazement spread across his own mind, and knew to speak to Bolin in response.

They bonded.

Now, hours later, all Cam knew was his Bolin-bond, their Maiden-pledge, the rightness of the twelve plus one.

Cam flew through the gaping roof and regained the sky. He circled the village, with its now-empty road, the villagers having wandered their clusters on to the business of the day, and Cam felt the awe and mystery that lingered still, along the edge of the empty road.

Bolin spoke in Cam's mind, and Cam answered. They explored their call and response, testing their bond's breadth. Cam soared higher, circled wider, with no diminishing of their calls and responses. Cam banked to return to the inn, wanting only to be near Bolin and the Maiden, to feel his shoulder beneath his grip, to know her radiance and every move.

Stevven must close your roof-doorway. Will you mourn its loss?

I do not need it. The sky will always be here. You can easily provide exits wherever we are, whenever the sky calls.

Yes.

Yes.

Cam saw and felt Bolin move from the inn's deep porch and step onto the road. Cam banked and slowed, landed neatly on Bolin's powerful shoulder. They re-entered the inn.

Stevven worked on the roof, Yonce at his side. Yonce had not the gift of carpentry, but he could fetch and brace wooden pieces into position, while Stevven murmured and coaxed their shape, bonded them into place. Their work grew smoothly, and the view of the sky slowly shrank, and was gone.

Gosikk worked in his kitchen, preparing a midday meal. Mackey washed and chopped, brought fuel for the stove, feeling a glow in his belly as he scraped greens into bowls, roots into pans. He had never found his gift, with his early penchant for emptying tankards and dreaming the day away. He watched Gosikk's movements of sprinkling spices and stretching dough, patting it into accustomed shapes, and leaving it to grow and puff.

The roots were roasted, the greens dressed, the dough baked, and Mackey's belly glowed. The glow filled the place where the emptying of tankards once dwelt. And Mackey felt the rightness of the glow.

Katernn worked with Draymon to empty Greggor's wagon. They carried pillow covers and blankets, footstools and side tables, candlesticks and vases, glass and crockery, lace and ribbons, all manner of brightness to fill the inn's new rooms with color and cheer.

Meanwhile Jullia stood behind Rosa, brushing, brushing her red curls, folding them into a shining heap atop her head, a heap that Jullia fastened into place with an emerald clasp. She bent down to press her cheek against Rosa's, and they smiled at each other through the dressing table's mirror.

The dressing table held a spray of orchard blossoms that filled the room with their scent of promised fruit and autumn abundance. Jullia plucked a bedazzled twig and tucked it into Rosa's curls, the delicate petals nestled against the shine of her hair.

Rosa stood and the two women hugged. For Rosa was a girl no longer. She had stepped fully into her adulthood, ready to begin her role, learn her fate, become her all. She smoothed her frock, and they moved across the room, elbows linked, along the passageway, down the stairwell, and into the common room, filled with the busy-ness of fellowship.

Miichal stood alone in the gloom of the stable. He had slipped away once the others were absorbed in their projects and tasks, let himself out the back door and stepped quietly across the cobbles of the courtyard. As he slipped through the stable door, the emptiness that had invaded his heart during the birthing of the fellowship and the awakening of the Spring Maiden, yawned anew, an echoing emptiness that he could not fathom.

He heard the rustle of Greggor and Draymon's mules as he moved deeper into the stable. He could see no glow from Tronder's stall. Perhaps Tronder had strolled out to a pasture, seeking the freshness of green grass or running stream. Perhaps he slept still, after the ordeal of winter storms and high passes, the birthing of the Maiden.

Miichal peered over a stall door that shielded only emptiness. The same with the next. In the third, an old dray horse stood, back swayed, ears drooped, eyes empty. The last two stalls also stood empty. Miichal searched his mind, listened for Tronder's whisper, absent all these hours. Where could he have gone?

Pharlan had watched Miichal slip out the inn's door and quieted her heart. She sensed Miichal's need for solitude and refrained from intruding with her thoughts. She padded to the door, pushed it open with her nose in time to see Miichal slipping into the stable. She followed him slowly, tail drooped, and crouched soundlessly just inside the stable door. She sniffed the air, to know who stood in each stall. She shuffled forward, keeping to her belly, shuffling until she could see into the stable proper.

Miichal stood, shoulders drooped, head lowered, eyes closed. She knew his mind searched, searched for a bond that was no more. She huffed a quiet huff, deep in her throat, a huff that Miichal did not hear. She understood his loss, knew his fear. She reached to him.

Only one bond is allowed.

He raised his head and looked at her, crouched near the door. They stared at each other. She gathered her feet and walked to him, sat under his unresponsive hand, waiting.

Where is he?

Tronder is there. She pointed her nose to the stall where the old drayhorse stood. She waited.

Miichal walked his slow steps to the door of the stall and looked again at the swayed back and dull coat. He shook his head. *This is not Tronder.*

Pharlan said nothing.

And then the old horse lifted its hoof and rested its tip on the ground.

Miichal could not breathe. He stared at the swayed back and drooping ears, the half-shut eyes. Remembrance flooded him. He saw the neglected pasture at the abandoned farm, the mud-encrusted horse that stood with swayed back and dull eyes.

He opened the stall door and crept toward the horse who paid him no mind. Miichal reached a palm to smooth brittle hair, felt slack muscles, and smelled sour breath. The horse dropped its head and snuffled at the grain waiting in its bucket. Miichal wrapped his arms around its neck, pressed his face onto the horse's shoulder, smoothed the rough coat with one hand, while the other arm clung to the horse's neck.

Sobs shook him, and he sank to his knees, arms upstretched to press against his old friend's chest, his friend who was no longer there, his friend who stood broken and dull. And no longer there.

Pharlan crept her feet forward until she lay on her belly. Her head sank to her paws, her nose gusting the dust of the stable floor. She waited.

Miichal knelt in his grief far into the day. The sun traveled the sky, and still Miichal's sobs floated from the stall, muffled by sleeve, or dull coat, or covering hands. Sobs that could not stop. Sobs that could not heal the breach in his heart.

Pharlan waited.

Chapter 19

Evening

"Will anyone come?" Yonce voiced the question on every mind.

Gosikk shrugged. "That, I have never known."

Katernn wrinkled her forehead. "The inn is always full. People always come."

"Now. Yes." Gosikk stood at Yonce's counter, elbows propped. "But not at first. It took many months for people to feel accustomed, to accept gathering of an evening, or even eating together. This thing that happened this morning, last night, this thing has rattled the village. I do not know that they will come."

Rosa sat quietly, Jullia at her side. Jullia, who reached for her hand and held it. Rosa's hand, which squeezed Jullia's, and then withdrew to its place in Rosa's lap.

Miichal came from the courtyard, Pharlan padding behind him. He looked at the faces that turned to him, in expectation, with curiosity. These faces that he barely knew, yet whom he loved well. With his empty heart, he knew not what to do.

He looked to Rosa, knelt on one knee before her, searched her eyes. "I wish to be released from fellowship. I ask that you release me."

He heard the gasps from all sides, felt their shock and dismay.

Bolin spoke. "'Through all of our days' is not the equal of a single day."

Yonce said, "It's even less than a day."

Greggor asked, "What has happened, Miichal? What has crushed you?"

Miichal's shoulders drooped. He hung his head. "Tronder is gone. I am nothing without Tronder."

The room stared.

Stevven asked, "Who has taken him? Where have they taken him?"

Miichal looked to Pharlan. "The dog has taken him."

He couldn't quite bring a sneer into his words, but Pharlan felt it just the same. She sat. She waited, her calm eyes watching the broken human. She held her thoughts, to keep them from straying into his heart.

Miichal looked again to Rosa. "There can be only one bonding. My bond with Tronder was torn when Pharlan became one of the twelve and stole Tronder's place in my heart." He shook his head. "I can do nothing without Tronder."

Rosa's eyes flashed. She understood why he spoke to her and not the others. He believed that being witness to her Spring Maiden, by the need to form the fellowship for her sake, he had been broken.

She spoke calmly and clearly. "All my life I have been told of my faults, of the harm and wrong I have done. All my life I believed those accusations, despite Romane's efforts to shield me from them. I tell you now that my time of guilt has ended. With the double moons, that time ended."

She held Miichal's gaze. "I tell you this, Miichal. You may not lay your loss at my feet. It is not mine to own. I will not be victim to your grief." Her eyes softened. She lifted her chin. "But grieve you must. It has clouded your thoughts and stolen your reason." She searched his face. "You must live through your grief, and when you are once again whole, if you seek release from me, I will grant it. I will grant it to you all.

"But now is not the time. We have much to do. I feel it in my bones. I do not know why fate has torn Tronder from you. But all is well, Miichal. All is *always* well."

Miichal blinked at the familiar phrase coming from this young girl turned Spring Maiden. Grief again threatened to pull him under.

At that moment, Marlow pushed through the double doors, and hesitant steps carried him into the frozen room. He took in the gathering, and his steps faltered. He removed his cap and turned it in nervous hands.

"Ros-sa," he stuttered. He looked around and began again. "Rosa, will you be coming home?" He paused, and then asked the true question, the question that had been assigned. "Will you wed, Rosa? Will you stand by your promise and enter your wedlock?"

Mandra's anger exploded from the road. "You gave your promise, girl. You had better keep it and be gone with you."

Marlow hung his head, hiding the tears that fell.

At her mother's shrill explosion, Rosa's resolve crumbled. She was once again a young girl, trembling before a mother's wrath. Her heart shrank, and her shoulders curved forward to protect it. She could not quite look into the waiting faces that surrounded her.

Jullia pulled Rosa into a hug, kissed her temple. Courage flowed into her anew, bolstered by the kindness of that kiss, a reminder that she was not alone, that the faces that surrounded her were her champions. She felt their protection, and for the first time in her life, she straightened her spine and brushed away her mother's scorn.

Rosa smiled at Jullia and stood. She walked to her father, picked up both his hands, held them between hers.

"Father," she whispered. His shoulders shook. "Father, dearest." He looked up to find her eyes, his cheeks trembling. Rosa paused. "Father, this is what I tell you. I gave my word to my betrothed. When he arrives, I will speak only to him, and tell only him my resolve."

A sob escaped him, and he squeezed her hands. "We are building a bigger house, Rosa, big enough for you and him to live alongside us. You will not have to leave your home. You'll see, Rosa. It will be a fine house, and he will want to stay here, with us." He drew her hands closer and whispered. "You do not have to leave. I cannot bear it if you leave." He loosened his grip on her hand to wipe his face with his sleeve. He offered his last temptation. "Don't forget Romane. His heart would break, were he to lose you."

A tear spilled down Rosa's cheek, and she leaned her forehead against his. Her voice was low, but the room could hear her every word. "I will not return to my mother's house. Not today. Never. That part of my life is complete."

Mandra burst through the double door. "You will wedlock, you selfish girl," she spat. "You WILL keep your promise to your betrothed and follow him to the home he will make for you. You will obey him in all that he wishes and keep a fine household for him. This is your purpose! Your only purpose."

Katernn blocked Mandra's path and scolded her tirade. "And that has worked so well for you, has it Mandra? All of your following and all of your obedience has brought you deep joy, has it Mandra? So much so, that you would foist the same fate onto your daughter's heart?"

Mandra retreated from Katernn, backing against the door jamb, disbelief flooding her florid face. Never had she been rebuked. Outrage throttled her words and clouded her brain.

Rosa released her father's hands and stepped to stand slightly in front of Katernn. "Mother, your rage has no place here. It has no place in your heart. Release it!" Rosa raised her arm, eyes glaring. Mandra cowered before her, raised both her arms as if to ward off a blow. Or a curse. She fumbled her way to the door and fled.

Rosa turned to the stunned room. "My wedlocking is between me and my betrothed. No one will speak again of broken pledges, until he and I have spoken together." She looked to her frozen father. "I will not be returning to my mother's house. Not tonight. Not tomorrow. Not with a husband. Not without. I will never return."

Marlow nodded, misery drooping his face, and forced his shaking legs to carry him out the double doors and into the moonless night.

Chapter 20

Practicalities

"What will we do?" Gosikk asked again. "Guests will arrive for the wedlocking, expecting a room in this inn. Whether there is a celebration or no, guests will arrive.

"Yet we have settled here and agree on the rightness of staying together, in fellowship. The inn is well suited for that, with its numerous rooms and comfortable gathering place." He gestured around the common room where they had spent the entire day, when not occupied with murmuring roofs or unpacking wagons...or grieving broken bonds and facing enraged mothers. It was clear to all that they would stay together. But what of the guests due to arrive, expecting an inn?

Draymon ventured an idea. "Five of us have rooms here already."

"Katernn and I can take rooms here," Jullia offered, "and our houses can serve as lodgings for families who would otherwise take several rooms."

"Yonce and I can stay here as well," Bolin said with a look to Yonce, who nodded, "which makes our houses available, too."

"I'll be quite comfortable in the stable," said Mackey. "I'm quite used to it." Jullia smoothed her palm down Mackey's arm, gave a small smile.

"So a room for Rosa, and four houses for guests. That makes the numbers come to the same, right Gosikk?" Yonce spoke with an enthusiasm echoed by nods and raised eyebrows from the others.

"Rosa can have my room," said Miichal, speaking for the first time. "I prefer to stay in the stable as well." No one spoke. "I'm used to sleeping in the open, so the stable is a luxury. I have no need of the bed upstairs."

"We don't know if the neighbors will gather." Greggor filled the prolonged silence. "They didn't come tonight."

Jullia spoke. "Which brings us to our main point. How do we bring the neighbors together?"

"They'll come 'round," said Katernn.

"Will they?" asked Bolin. "Fear is powerful."

"They don't need to be afraid of us," protested Jullia. "They've know us all their lives!"

"They don't fear *us*." Bolin's circling hand included all of them. "They fear *Spring Maiden*." His hand again included all. "Rumors and gossip have flown, and the aunties' tales have ignited deep fears."

Silence.

"Spring Maidens bring great prosperity," Miichal said. "The village will thrive for generations."

Bolin pointed out that the lightest of the stories, the rarest, mentioned this fact. Everyone nodded, remembering the trembling hearts with which they had listened to their aunties' persistent tales of doom and misfortune. Those tales were meant to frighten and ensnare, and they had succeeded at their job.

"And they have Romane as evidence of doom," Bolin said.

"Romane lives!" cried Rosa. "I brought him out of his stupor."

"The double moons put him into that stupor," Bolin said.

Stunned silence.

"The double moons?" Jullia's voice sounded small. "That's what happened to Romane?"

"I thought it was hooligans with clubs," Katernn said.

"There was no mark on him. The hooligans came from Mandra's imagination. Romane's stupor came from the double moons," said Bolin. "That's why Rosa was able to revive him. The moons brought him down, and he had no fellowship to restore him. He would have died if Rosa had not got to him in time, before the sun found him. It's part of the doom and gloom of the old stories."

"How do you know all this? You speak with certainty." Draymon's voice held only curiosity.

"I didn't know it. But Cam does."

Silence.

"He's teaching me. So I can teach all of you."

Silence.

"But, I revived Romane," Rosa repeated, perplexed. "Why are they still afraid?"

"*Because* you revived him, most like," Bolin said. "No one can do that. No one except a Spring Maiden. Which makes the rest of the aunties' dark tales a looming possibility. You are powerful, Rosa, and what will you do with that power? What will any of us do?"

"But everyone knows me," Rosa said. "Why would they think I would do something evil?"

"Because of fear, Rosa," Jullia said. "Fear can be strong enough to blind them and drive them into the shadows. This is our real challenge. Sorting out where to house guests is easy. This challenge will take all of our knowing and all of our courage."

Silence.

Chapter 21

Realities

"Should we stay?" Draymon kept his voice low, despite their solitude in the orchard across from the inn, the scent of blossoms drenching the air. They sat on one of the many benches scattered throughout the orchard, throughout the village, truth be told, inviting passersby to gather, to linger and enjoy.

Greggor paused his lighting-of-the-pipe ritual to watch Draymon's face. "What do you mean? What are you thinking?"

Draymon pointed his thumb over his shoulder in the direction of the inn. "We've not had a chance to talk about any of this. What do you think we've stumbled into? Should we stumble our way out of it?"

Greggor was used to taking charge and making decisions. He understood that Draymon would rather follow than lead. That was Draymon, right enough. Greggor found it endearing, since he, himself, enjoyed taking charge. He took a moment to get his pipe lit, gave himself time to think. The aroma of burning herbs swirled around his head, mingling pleasantly with the orchard blossoms' scent. Greggor considered Draymon's hesitation over this whole Spring Maiden thing.

"Well." Greggor puffed his pipe. "This certainly came out of nowhere, didn't it? Not at all what we had planned for ourselves." Puff, puff. He shook his head. "Spring Maiden?"

"I know! Isn't that just a tale? A bunch of scary stories? How can any of this be happening in real life?" Draymon looked around them. "Out here in the sunshine, last night doesn't seem real, you know?"

"And yet..." Puff, puff. "We were there. We felt it." Puff. "I felt it. Did you feel it?" Greggor's voice rose to its question mark.

Draymon looked toward the inn. "Yes. I definitely felt it, truth be told. It was incredible." He hung his head "It's just...Like I said. It's a bit hard to believe, standing out here in the sunshine."

Greggor nodded. "That's the thing, of course. It felt completely real at the time. All of it. I mean," he pointed his chin toward the inn, "we gave away half our inventory to decorate the new rooms. Without a second thought. Who would have predicted that?"

Draymon leaned back on the bench, stretched his legs out in front of him. "It was fun, though, spreading around all the pretties."

"That it was." Puff. "I don't regret it. Not for a moment."

"Nor I."

"It's just...Where did that come from?" Greggor frowned. "We've never done anything like that before, have we?"

"They're good people," Draymon said. "And Rosa's a sweetheart."

Greggor nodded, not sure what to think. They did seem like good people. But still. Half their inventory?

He thought about Draymon's earlier point. "But you're right. It feels different now, standing out here on our own, in broad daylight."

"Like it was all a dream."

The sun warmed Greggor's shoulders, chasing away the morning chill. The scent of the orchard blossoms drifted intoxicatingly. Greggor shook his head. He didn't often succumb to confusion, but his thoughts couldn't quite settle. He grabbed one, mostly to keep the conversation going.

"We don't know any of these people, really, even though they seem good. What do you make of them, really? You've had more time with them, as it were."

"Gosikk's a decent man, of course, always looking for ways to make others comfortable and taken care of. Yonce is a find lad. Bit quiet, but always ready to fetch and carry. Wonderful with the mules. The carpenter? Stevven? Another quiet one, but clearly a true artisan. I quite like him. I suspect he has a thing for the young barmaid, Jullia."

Draymon shrugged and crossed his ankles. He looked relaxed, at ease, really. Greggor squinted against his pipe's smoke, wondering what prompted this discussion. Wondered where it would lead.

Draymon continued with his role call. "And the drunkard? Mackey? He's been slumping around the inn ever since I arrived three days ago. Smelly and useless, for all I could see. And yet, now, he's all bustle and busy in the kitchen. In his element, as it were. Hasn't touched a drop, far as I can tell."

"Quite the transformation, 'twould seem."

"Yes! Completely." Draymon looked up through branches, squinting at the sky. Greggor waited for him to gather more thoughts.

"And the *dog*! Pharlan? He was mangey and groveling."

"She. As it turns out."

"Right. She. Now? She's a beauty! Alert. Following Miichal around. Quite the attentive thing."

"Another transformation, so it seems." Greggor looked toward the inn, leaned forward, elbows on knees. He struggled to make sense of his confusion. What was it, that clouded his thinking like this?

"Do you feel transformed?" Draymon asked.

"Not really. Not now, anyway. Things have been swirling all around us, of course. I can't seem to think it through, truth be told."

"I'm not thinking clear myself," Draymon admitted.

They fell silent. Greggor finished his pipe and tapped the spent herbs against his boot. They sprinkled across his toe, so he stood, shaking the herbs onto the ground.

"Should we stay?" Draymon repeated.

"I can't make sense of it." Greggor looked to the inn. "I tell you what. Let's stay until after the wedlocking. That at least fits our original plans. It'll give us more time to see what's what, with the Spring Maiden part of things and all the rest. All of them." He jutted his chin toward the inn. "We can decide after that, can't we?"

"It is a beautiful village. I've not seen one quite like it in all our travels. 'Twould be pleasant to extend our stay, truth be told, if only to enjoy the peace and welcome." He paused for a breath. "Right. Let's do." Draymon pushed himself up from the bench. He pulled Greggor into a hug and spoke into his ear. "If you can't make sense of it, no one can. We'll wait until things set themselves right again."

The hug sent a wave of relief through Greggor. He nodded against Draymon's cheek and patted his back. As they turned toward the inn, Greggor tucked his pipe into his vest pocket and put his pipe-warmed hand on Draymon's shoulder. They walked in companionable silence.

As they drew closer to the inn, Greggor found himself looking forward to seeing the others again, of all things. Especially Rosa.

The night seemed more real, now that they were climbing the stairs, walking across the inn's double threshold. Greggor's confusion cleared, and he looked around the room in cheerful expectation.

Chapter 22

Visits

They worked in pairs, those champions who had grown up in the village. It took all of two days, but the visits became easier as they went along. Word spread and doors opened.

The neighbors were especially impressed with old Mackey, who visited with young Yonce. No one had seen Mackey sober 'til now. "No, thank you kindly," he said again and again, to each offer of a frosty tankard. "I would be grateful for some water, though, and a slice of that fine cake I see sitting on your counter."

Mackey was free with his winks and nods, Yonce with his chuckles and guffaws. Katernn and Jullia held the villagers' hands and patted their arms, listened in earnest to fears and frights. Gosikk and Bolin told easy stories that brought easy bursts of laughter. At each household, in each garden or front step, kitchen or parlor, the champions listened and nodded, reassured and elaborated.

And to each neighbor, they extended the invitation. Come for a tankard. Come for some of Gosikk's renowned cooking. "Will she be there?" was the ever-asked question. "Will Rosa be there?"

"Yes!" was the cheerful response. "Yes. Rosa is always there. Come and speak to her for yourself. Or at least *see* for yourself.

Then you'll know for yourself, decide for yourself." The heads always nodded, eyes hesitant and wondering.

"Is she Spring Maiden?" The question came with squinted eyes, frowns.

"That she is. And a fine one she is at that. Not a drop of meanness. You know Rosa. The sweetest thing. You know she brought Romane back. Loves him dearly. Come and see."

And after a time, they did come, some the first night, more the second. They nudged open the double doors, clustered just inside, staring toward Rosa. Rosa who came with her calm eyes and ready smile. Who took their hands and welcomed them, led them to this table or that. She always knew just what to say, the best table for them.

She seemed innocent enough. She dusted benches with her white cloth, gestured them to sit. What could she bring them? What would they have? Sometimes she sat, seeing an open face or a curious eye. She leaned forward on elbows, or sat hands in lap, always a posture to soothe this heart or that. Some tears were shed, some voices shook. Some whispers sank into silence when Rosa drew near, for fear is a powerful thing.

Yet everyone left feeling the better for their visit, having seen, having listened. Some laughed, with nerves or with humor, as they waved a good night to Gosikk, to young Yonce. Yet their fears would meet them, as they stepped onto the road, walked to their doors. Glances were sent over shoulders, up to the moonless sky, across an empty field, elbows locked together as they walked in twos or threes, but never alone.

"It's not working," Greggor said.

"Give it time," Gosikk said.

Bolin was silent, which spoke volumes of its own.

"What more can we do?" asked Yonce.

"Make ready for wedlocking guests?" Jullia suggested.

"They are coming," Katernn nodded. "Let's do."

Chapter 23

Redoing

Romane hoisted another basket filled with kitchen crockery onto his shoulder and, huffing, carried it through the low doorway, and lowered it onto the long table. This was their second day of resetting the household into its accustomed shape, given that Marlow had abandoned his plans for an extravagant rebuild.

Romane felt invigorated, enjoying the physical work of lifting and carrying, the mental exercise of sorting and organizing, working far into the evening. Each day found him eager to rise, before dawn, it must be said. Most of the house was settled, with only this last bit in the kitchen. Then, they could collapse the tent and regain the garden, an achievement that Romane anticipated cheerfully, given his mother's love of her garden and his concern for her.

The garden had long flourished under Mandra's care, even as she flourished in the caring of it. The garden acted as refuge from the constant keeping of Marlow's household, of the neighbors' sideways glances. Would Mandra return to her garden, with muddied knees and callused hands? Romane hoped 'twould be so.

His hope was thin, given Mandra's recent retreat into shuddering silence. Her rage had left her, leaving in its wake an overriding fear, almost a terror. She crept docile and wary about the house. Her haunted eyes and trembling hands led to a useless-ness for even the simplest task. She retired early and rose late, barely touching the bowls that Romane placed before her, dis-appearing for much of the day into the sleeping room, curled under a coverlet that she clenched with white knuckles against her chest.

Marlow, too, had changed his habits, remaining home for the greater part of the day, sharing meals and wandering about somewhat aimlessly. Romane would lift a basket into Marlow's willing arms, telling him where it should be carried. Romane would find it later, its contents tumbled from a chair or random ledge.

His parents had shouted and wrung their hands the day after the double moons. They had left the house as night fell – she determined, him cowed – and returned shortly after, shaking, refusing to meet his eye or tell what had befallen them.

Rosa, he had not seen. Neighbors told of her living now at the inn, along with a curious collection of others. Over break-fast, his parents silent with lowered eyes, he had announced his intention of visiting Rosa, to learn her plans and see for himself that she was well situated.

But his mother had grasped his hands in desperation, ex-tracted from him a promise to never cross that doubled thresh-old. In confusion, he had pledged it so. He had watched the others come and go, and knew of the widespread visits. No one visited this household, though, and Romane hesitated to call out to the champions as they passed, reluctant to interrupt their intent purpose, or to bring his mother, wailing, from her bed.

So he spent his pent energy on hoisting and carrying, sorting and arranging, setting up their household as his mother would want it, but also as *he* found easier, since his hands were the only ones now, that cleaned or chopped or stirred or braised.

He wondered at the mystery of Rosa, the mystery of Mandra and Marlow, whom he now scarcely knew. He wondered at the fate of their household and the wedlocking, the wedlocking that trundled toward them with unwavering surety.

Chapter 24

Victtor

The carriage lumbered along the beautifully tended road, pulled by a team of eight horses, there more for show than for need. Four would have done the job, buy why use four, when you can afford eight? A driver in a fine uniform perched atop the forward seat, another by his side. Why shout at one, when two would go pale just as pleasingly, and offer proof for all to see, the power of the one who shouted.

The fine uniforms were heavy, now that the road led into spring, where the blue sky was bright with a determined sun, jackets too heavy for breeze to penetrate or sweat to escape. Rather, the sweat ran down arms and soaked gloves and squished inside the soles of fine boots.

Two grooms stood at the aft of the carriage, also finely arrayed, and also with soaked gloves and squishy boots. Their aching knees and bruised ankles were grateful for the well-tended road, for at long last they could relax, hands could loosen their grip, no longer at risk of being bounced from their station. One groom had lost his hat during a particularly harrowing interlude. Now he squinted against the sun and hoped the hat's absence would not be noticed, when finally they reached the inn.

A line of wagons followed the carriage, piled high with cases and trunks. Why bring only what you need, when a sudden fancy might require an elaborate change of costume, or perhaps two, come the afternoon? Each wagon rode high for all to see, over-populated with grooms and drivers and horses, for, of course, why not?

The gentleman so prone to shouting, the one propped on pillows and cushions, stared angrily out his lowered window, across field after field after field. Would they never arrive and be finished with this cursed journey? He clutched his belly. He had cast aside the many woven coverlets, much reviled under this ridiculous sun. Where had winter gone? Why was he not told? And when would this journey end?

His wife sat demur and serene, a poise that befitted her station, reflected her breeding for all the world to see and admire. For surely the world watched; how could they not? She glanced at her husband, assessing his mood, for his mood defined her world, and she took care to pamper, to please. She smiled her most beauteous when he looked her way. Despite her smile, he bellowed, "When will this journey end?"

She waved her scarf out her window, and their assistant nudged his horse close to enable his hearing, and she asked in silken tones, "Might we stop, somewhere pleasant, so the master might stretch his tired frame?"

The assistant, one Parker, tipped his hat and galloped ahead, returning in ten minutes' time. An eternity. "There is a copse, just ahead, most pleasant. I'm sure it will meet your needs."

"Send the wagons ahead, with you as well, to ready the inn for our arrival. We require a light lunch, the best on offer, and four rooms at least, for our business is pressing. We have many to receive, and receive them we must, so we require the best. At once."

Parker tipped his hat, gestured and spoke to the driver, then turned to spread the lady's instructions, ensuring not the slightest complication that might keep the party from moving smoothly, to make everything ready, for the lord would arrive in an hour, perhaps two, replete from the pause in the copse most pleasant, to ensure the lord's satisfaction, for his mood defined all of their world.

Chapter 25

Seedlings

"I want desperately to be outside in the sunshine, feel the breeze on my face, hear the birds, and breathe the beauty of the flowers." Rosa felt the press of ceilings and walls, the still air of the room. She gazed out at the dawn and felt a prickle of expectation dancing under her skin.

Bolin joined her at the window, followed her gaze. "Come with me to visit the seedlings. Let's see how they fare."

Rosa's face lit. "Your seedlings! In the forest? Yes! Let's walk in the forest. Who wants to come?"

She looked at the table where they had broken their fast, where the fellowship still sat, remnants of bread, fruit, and cheese strewn before them. Faces perked and heads nodded. They scrambled to their feet.

Pharlan stood, tail wagging and ears perched forward. She looked to Miichal who sat still, unseeing, cheek on fist. Miichal, who closed his eyes and shook his head at her silent prodding. *Not today,* he sighed.

Yonce wrapped cheese and Greggor scraped plates. Jullia fetched a damp cloth and swept crumbs and spills onto the floor. Mackey wielded the broom, and Gosikk banked the fire. The room was tidied and readied, and the fellowship sailed out into the sun and marched across a neighboring pasture.

Yonce caught Bolin's eye, a memory flickering into the foreground. "Why did you say that Rosa could not wedlock?"

"What?" asked Rosa.

"When?" asked Bolin.

"When we were waiting for Rosa to awaken. You and Miichal said that Rosa could not wedlock."

Bolin gazed unseeingly at the air before him. "Because she might disappear into wedlocking." He blinked. "Cam says she might disappear. Many do."

Rosa scoffed. "Nonsense. I won't disappear."

"Many do," repeated Bolin.

"Where is Miichal?" Rosa asked, counting noses and seeing the lack.

"He prefers to stay," said Draymon. "His spirit is low today."

"'Twould be lovely were he to come," said Rosa. "I will coax him along."

She retraced their steps, peered through the double doors, and stepped softly to Miichal, who slumped, head cradled in elbow, Pharlan morose at his feet.

"Miichal," Rosa whispered, and when he offered no response, she sat next to him on the bench, rested her hand on his knee. She patted his leg. "Miichal, why don't you come? I cannot bear your sadness on such a fine morning. The sunshine will do you a world of good. Won't you come and see Bolin's seedlings? They will enliven your heart."

She stood and repeated, "'Twould be lovely were you to come."

Miichal raised his sad face and said, "I must tend to Tronder."

"Nonsense," said Rosa. "Tronder is over-tended and will be happy for your mood to shift. 'Twould be lovely," she said for a third time as she tugged at his arm.

Miichal sighed and stood. Pharlan's ears perked but did not take her place at his side, but rather, followed, respecting his grief, patient beyond belief.

The trio joined the others who had wandered toward the forest, throwing watchful glances behind them, relieved to see Rosa walking briskly, Miichal and Pharlan in tow.

Bolin cut across fields, unerringly on track to the seedlings, to the first of the many he had planted only a few nights before, in readiness for the double moons. Birds sang from bushes and fence posts, from overhanging branches and hidden places. Bolin pointed out his favorites and whistled their song back to them. The scent of the warming pastures, with their herbs and grazed grasses, swirled around the fellowship's footsteps and intoxicated their noses.

Rosa's spirits bubbled to the surface. She hugged her arms to herself, cast a sidelong glance look at Miichal, plodding in their wake. What were they to do with him? Perhaps all wanderers were like this. Rosa knew only the village and the stories that her papa carried home with him. She was at a loss how to cheer him.

The sun cleared the eastern ridge and beamed its glory across the valley. Though the shadows it cast were long and slender still, the bright rays held the promise of another glorious day. The rays found the fellowship as they crossed one field, then another, boots and pantlegs soon drenched with dew. Pharlan trotted alongside, panting and raising her nose to take in the still air redolent with its thousand scents telling their stories, ears alert, enthusiastic. Cam flew overhead, circling and banking, chortling his joy to Bolin, the two bandying back and forth, on this, their first outing as companions. Into the wild, their beloved world.

As Rosa entered the forest, she paused for her eyes to adjust and breath to catch, taking time to admire Bolin's obvious awe and reverence. She stood in silence, breathed deep to still her thoughts, to feel what Bolin felt, to appreciate his gift of wild.

Bolin led them to the first seedling, small and frail, nestled in the rich soil, reaching as best it could to the light splattering down through the mature forest above.

"It needs more light, maybe, Bolin. What do you think?" Greggor asked.

"More light would help it greatly, but I cannot bear to cut back any of the canopy. It must try its best. Once it is larger, it will do fine. It was harvested on the new moon, and spent its first night under the double light of double moons. I can do no better for it than that."

Rosa knelt next to the seedling and ran her hand up the single branch. "It's so sweet, Bolin. And beautiful. I don't recognize it."

"I brought it from two..."

"Oh, my!" exclaimed Rosa, palms now pressed to the soil at its base. "I can feel its roots! I think they're spreading..." Rosa closed her eyes and pressed the soil, radiated her hands outward, away from the seedling. Her eyes sprang open, and she looked up at Bolin. "I can feel them growing..." She ran her hands up the single branch.

Bolin fell to his knees next to Rosa and the seedling. He watched her face, the seedling, and forgot to breathe. He placed his hands opposite Rosa's, encircling the frail seedling. His face filled with awe. He certainly felt the life bubbling below the surface of the soil.

Bolin's gift of wild joined Rosa's gift of Maidening to breathe life into the soil. Subtle vibrations pulsed beneath their hands, and the soil blossomed into liveliness. Buried biomes interwove their networks, nutrients flowed, moisture hydrated. Roots extended and thickened; their fine hairs multiplied and explored the rich world around them.

Bolin raised his head to stare at Rosa, who stared back. The power of Spring Maiden filled the pair, fed from below and blossoming into the air around them. Their skin glowed, spilling light onto the frail seedling, sent it to trembling.

Before their eyes, the seedling thickened, straightened...and grew. It sent out new branches and sprouted leaves. It reached shoulder height while Rosa's hands petted and stroked, while Bolin's hands smoothed and nurtured. Finally, Rosa sat back on her heals and looked to Bolin, where he perched on his heels, mouth agape.

"I didn't know I could do that," she said, eyes wide.

"No, I suppose you didn't." He swallowed and stared. "I've certainly not done that before. This is not a gift of wild. This is magic."

The fellowship stood silent, awestruck. Eyes blinked and heads tilted.

They erupted.

They chortled and hooted, danced a jig. Katernn stood, hands on head, laughing in wild abandon. Draymon leaned into Greggor's chest, eyes wide, hands covering his mouth.

"Let's find another!" exclaimed Mackey. The champions and their maiden looked to Bolin.

Bolin asked, "Do you think we could do another? Do you *want* to do another?"

"I would *love* to do another! Let's try!"

They trotted through the forest, Bolin pointing out each seedling. Rosa dropped to her knees, smoothed her enlivening palms, Bolin falling to his place beside her. Together they magicked the soil alive, let their light blossom and engulf the seedling. They imagined growth into being, first the root system, then robust branches.

With each caress, a stillness spread through Rosa that she sent to the young tree. Bolin closed his eyes in concentration and celebration. Again and again, they knew exactly when to break their trance, to leave each sapling to its astonished awakening, blinking its new leaves at the morning sun.

They left behind a scattered string of saplings, seemingly into their fourth or even fifth season of growth, shimmering in the quickening air.

Pharlan panted her enthusiasm and delight of the adventure, always with an eye on Miichal, a soft whine escaping from time to time. Rosa felt the dog's yearning for Miichal's attention. She petted her head, smoothed her ears, smiled into her eyes. Pharlan accepted Rosa's caress with a quick lick to the hand, then resumed her courtship of Miichal. For himself, Miichal paced himself with the others, yet kept to the side, watching with only slight interest as Rosa and Bolin transformed seedling to sapling, again and again.

Midway through the outing, Rosa locked her elbow through Michael's and matched his lackluster stride. They walked in silence, Miichal unresponsive to her concern. She thought his face brightened momentarily, if only the slightest. But even a slight brightness is brighter than no brightness at all. Pharlan licked Rosa's hand in thanks, catching her by surprise.

"Oh, hello!" Rosa said. She bent over Pharlan, releasing Miichal in the bending, to pet Pharlan's silky fur, to again scratch her soft ears. Miichal stuffed hands in pockets and watched the exchange, a frown snuffing any brightness. Rosa straightened, and the fellowship continued to the next seedling, which Rosa and Bolin coaxed from seedling to sapling, the next, and then the next.

At last the final sapling stood, strong and sure, and the fellowship threaded their way out of the forest, across fields, to gather on the roadway, under the midday sun. Rosa welcomed the sun on her shoulders after the cool of the spring forest. Bolin took Rosa's hands in his and smiled his solemn thanks.

Rosa's heart brimmed with a camaraderie richer than that which blossomed whenever she and Romane and Bolin had trekked the wild together in the days of their youth. The magic of Spring Maiden enlivened them still.

The fellowship made their way toward the inn, until, even from a distance, Rosa could see the gathered wagons piled high with cases and trunks, the fine colors of the drivers' clothing, a lone man pacing their porch.

Gosikk frowned. "Who might this be? I was not expecting any delivery. I wonder what they need..." As the fellowship walked closer, the pacing man spotted them, ceased his pacing, and strode along the road to meet them.

"At long last," the man called out. "I feared the entire village to be abandoned."

Gosikk held out a hand in greeting and they shook, palm to palm. Rosa noted the man's obvious relief. Gosikk said, "My apologies for not being here to greet you. I had no inkling of your arrival." He gestured to the fellowship who trailed him. "We run the inn." The man nodded to one and all. "How can we help?" Gosikk asked.

"Oh, thank the stars. Exactly who I need." He shook Gosikk's hand and again nodded smiles to all. "My lady requires four rooms; your finest. She and the lord arrive within the hour, and all must be ready." His eyes roamed over the collection of dirty knees and drooping socks that adorned the motley crew. "Also a robust lunch; your finest." Being a fine diplomat, his face betrayed no judgement, only a readiness to put things to right. "Parker's the name, good sir. I am much pleased to meet you."

"Yes. Parker. A pleasure to meet you as well. Gosikk's the name, and this is our fine inn. And these, these are..." and he rattled off each name. At the last, his hand touched Rosa's sleeve. "And this fine lady is Rosa, Spring Maiden newly birthed."

Since Gosikk was watching Rosa, he did not notice the startle in Parker's bearing, his quick step backward, but Rosa saw it. She took in the pallor of his face. Rosa swallowed and stepped closer to Gosikk, who tightened his hand upon her arm.

"Rosa?" Parker's voice quavered, despite his diplomacy. "Spring Maiden?" he queried, looking from Rosa to Gosikk and back again. "Oh, my."

Chapter 26

Arrival

It was at that moment that the heavy carriage chose to rumble around a curve of high hedges and sway into view. Parker's face, if possible, drained to a paler hue. "Oh, my," He repeated, but with a shading of dismay. He looked to Gosikk and pulled himself to his full height. "The rooms, sir? Will you show me the rooms?" He looked back at the approaching carriage. "Quickly, if you would be so kind. And lunch? Can a prompt lunch be arranged?"

"I offer sincere apologies, my good man," said Gosikk, "but four rooms? Four? That won't be possible." Gosikk felt irritation rise at this last minute inconveniencing of the hosting of guests.

Parker pressed his lips into a thin line, closed his eyes momentarily, and turned to skuttle to his place at the front steps to await his lord's wrath.

Young Yonce tapped Gosikk's shoulder. "Perhaps we should scrape together a lunch? I wonder for how many..."

The fellowship walked slowly the remaining steps to the inn, all eyes on the ominous carriage, swaying ever closer. Gosikk glimpsed Yonce hurry around the corner. Gosikk nodded. Good lad. He would at least bring the fire back to life.

The carriage rumbled to a halt, the driver dragging back eight bits, bringing eight horses out of their high-stepping trot. The lead horse tossed his head and struck his polished hoof on the fine road, adding the slightest mar. Several things happened in a rush.

The grooms jumped from their high perch at the back of the carriage, retrieved filigreed steps to place beneath the door at either side of the carriage. The driver seated his dancing whip, removed his wool hat, hurriedly wiped his wet forehead, and fanned his red face. His travel partner jumped to the ground and hurried to hold the lead horse's halter, precluding any forward lurch. Both carriage doors opened with perfect timing on the doubled grooms' part. Several pillows and coverlets spilled forth, which were swept up by the attentive grooms and held behind backs, the offence hidden from reprimand.

A delicate shoe peeked from the off-side door, displaying a slender ankle. The groom held out a hand, keeping the door propped on his shoulder, his other hand otherwise engaged with pillows. A pale glove clutched the offered hand, and a slender, delicate lady, stepped her delicate way down the delicate steps and onto the suddenly rough-seeming road. She retrieved her hand from the groom, ignored the clutched pillows and trailing coverlets, and swept her way forward, around the long team of eight horses, and floated to take a place next to, but slightly in front of, Parker, who stood stiffly expectant, a splotch of red blossoming on each pale cheek.

The carriage swayed a final sway as Victtor swung himself down and frowned into the sun, at Parker, at his wife, and all around. "This can't be the inn," he bellowed. "I was told it was newly built, even added to, the grandest in the town. This hovel cannot be the inn." He turned and shouted into Parker's face. "You fool! Can you do nothing right?" He turned to remount the carriage steps. "Take us to the inn, you fool! Gosikk's inn!"

Gosikk grimaced his rising irritation at the presumptuous newcomer, with his rebukes and disdain dripping from every word. Gosikk felt disinclined to be of service.

Parker's glance swept across the front of the inn and caught the lady's eye, which flashed a query to him. Parker's red splotches paled, and he bowed to his lady. "This is Gosikk's inn, m'lady." He paused. "The only inn to be had."

Victtor whirled at the words, one foot on the bottom-most carriage step. "What?" he bellowed. "That can't be true. This is not what I was told!"

Gosikk drew himself to his full height and walked into the fray. "This is the inn, kind sir, gentle lady." The irony would be lost on them, but he would speak it nonetheless. "This is Gosikk's inn, and I am Gosikk." He bowed. "How may I help?"

Victtor spluttered and fumed, unaccustomed, as he was, to being caught in the wrong. His wife stepped forward and offered her hand, over which Gosikk made a short bow, nothing more. "Yes, m'lady. How may I help?"

"We require four rooms, your finest. And an opulent lunch, for we have journeyed far. Immediately, if you will."

"For you and all your servants?" Gosikk asked, to buy himself thinking time, eyes scanning the various wagons with their various attendants.

"No. No. For my husband and myself. The others will find their own way."

Gosikk stiffened at her words, his gaze passing again over the numerous drivers and grooms and maids. She would leave all these folk to fend for themselves? He let loose her fine hand, for he needed no more thinking time. His words were ready, and he spoke them. "I fear, dear lady, that we have none. Neither rooms nor meal to share." They deserved no further explanation, and he would not offer it. He gave a second short bow and stepped back to join the fellowship, a newly united front, who had arranged themselves along the steps of the inn, Gosikk's inn. Gosikk's fine inn.

He smiled benevolently at the stunned gathering, cataloguing responses. He turned abruptly and led the fellowship through the double doors of his inn, left the doors to swing, shutting out the unwelcome intruders where they stood under the midday sun.

Chapter 27

Upending, Redux

Romane opened the window and leaned out. He had not heard the rumbling on the road, neither of wagons nor of carriage. The bellows he *did* hear. They caught his attention, not only for their volume, but also for their cadence and fury, which sounded vaguely familial, and the voice, which he abruptly knew.

Romane trotted into the road, stared at the wagons as he passed their long row, and came to the carriage with drama bellowing at its side. He peered over horses' backs and shuffled along, skirting the team of eight, sweat darkening their coats, to arrive just as Gosikk pronounced, "I fear, dear lady, that we have none. Neither rooms nor meal to share."

The disbelief, astonishment, and fury that met the pronouncement and abandonment through the double doors was something to behold. Before faces exploded, before words were found and bellowed, Romane, gentle Romane, found his voice.

"Uncle Victtor?"

The tableau at long last relocated itself to Mandra's garden, where Uncle Victtor reclined on a cushioned chair, with his wife...what was her number? Aunt...what was her name? bravely seated beside him, and Parker standing near.

Grooms and drivers and maids and...others, scuttled from house to hastily re-erected tent, carrying baskets hastily stuffed and pillows hastily fluffed, emptying the house of all that was familiar, to make room for the cases and trunks that came down from the wagons, for Marlow's house had four rooms, and though small, it was all that could be had.

A cook was hastily promoted, a driver transformed into scullery maid, for lunch must be served, and Romane had departed for the inn, dismissed by his uncle, despite tears from his mother, who had fled to cower in the back of her tent.

Uncle Victtor fanned his flushed face, glared his displeasure, frowned his unfulfilled expectations. This journey, long planned to the finest detail, lay unraveled at his feet, defying his clout, indifferent to his demands.

It was not to be borne.

His healer placed a calming infusion at Victtor's elbow and stepped back, watching intently. When Victtor remained unresponsive, stubbornly furious, the healer reclaimed the infusion and circled Victtor's chair, standing in full view of the lord's wrath.

"My lord. This infusion will help put things to right. All you have to do is drink it, and all will be well."

Victtor glared at the healer, his frown shouting his displeasure. The healer stood firm before the frown and the glare, calmly offering the calming brew.

The wife's gentle voice filled the void. "What a lovely suggestion, Healer. It sounds just the thing."

Victtor glared for two more breaths, then reached to accept the delicate cup on its fine saucer. As he sipped, the garden and household took their own deep breaths, and settled into the rhythm of creating solace for their cantankerous lord.

Chapter 28

Anticipation

Over the next two days, guests poured into the village, for a wedlocking approached, and not just any wedlocking. This was the wedlocking of Rosa, darling Rosa, whose birthing as Spring Maiden was conveniently tucked away, stowed safe and sound, hidden from outsiders' ears.

The guests poured down the road, from High Pass to the east, from far valleys to the west. Marlow had spread his invitation far, and everyone loved a wedlocking, and everyone who knew Marlow, knew of Rosa, darling Rosa, and her wedlocking they would witness.

They camped in the fields, they cooked meals along the road's generous edge. They bartered and traded and clustered and roamed, for country folk know how to find wonder in forest and stream, and curious eyes would see the village, quaint as it was.

They arrived walking solo; they arrived by the dozen. They clogged the road and invaded the walking paths, and it made no matter that the inn was full, for the pastures were wide and the forest infinite. And as country folk born and bred, they left nothing thoughtlessly behind on their wanderings, not fluttering cloth, nor crust carelessly tossed.

For the spring was abundant, and grass and herbs grew anew, edging roads and paths, pastures and fields. The sun warmed all, and the breeze refreshed in its turn. Clouds floated and lambs romped, fluffy white above and below.

Rosa remained in the inn, secluded, as befit a bride-to-be. None would lay eyes on her before her bridegroom arrived and proposed, whence she would emerge, blush and accept, and the wedlocking would commence as always they did, with celebration, rejoicing, and feast.

Vows would be spoken, pledges would be promised, applause would be clapped, and the wedlocking would be sanctified by joyful observance. Then cheers would rise, tankards would empty, and Rosa, darling Rosa would be wedlocked.

Chapter 29

Revelations

Rosa sat with her twelve, her twelve plus one, for Romane sat at her side, their hands interwoven, reunited after all these days.

Romane had come agreeably, accepting his uncle's dismissal, for though he could soothe his mother's anger, he was inept in the face of her fear. It was clearly unfounded, this terror that gripped her, or perhaps it had always lain there at the base of her rage. Romane had neither the wisdom nor experience to understand, no way to soothe.

So he had left her to her brother's care, the two who had grown up side-by-side, each bolstered by the other. Perhaps her brother could reach her. Perhaps he could soothe her. For Romane surely had no solution to give.

"How will we spend our day?" Draymon tapped his forefinger on the table, fretful.

Gosikk mused. "The feast preparations that can be finished, are, all of them, finished. The next two days promise much busy-ness, but today?" He shrugged. "Nothing."

Bolin rose from the bench and stretched his arms to the ceiling. "The forest remains out of reach. Visitors walk every path, linger along every stream." He shook his head sadly. "There's no place for us there."

Miichal was the next to rise. "I must see to Tronder."

He shuffled to the back door, despondency trailing in his wake. Pharlan padded behind him, head low, tail drooped.

"He's not getting better," Katernn said.

"No. He's broken," Jullia said.

"What broke him?" Romane asked, perplexed.

Everyone contributed to the answer, and for the most part, Romane was able to piece together the tragic story of the broken bond that had broken Miichal.

"Ma is broken, too," Romane said, a weariness burying his heart.

"Whatever do you mean?" asked Rosa.

"When she and Pa came to demand you keep your promise of wedlocking...I don't know. Something happened to her." He shook his head. "She's not the same." He looked at Rosa. "No one had ever defied her, Rosa. Something broke inside her. She hides and cowers. I've never, in all remembrance, seen her cower before anything."

He brought his cup to his lips. "I thought Uncle Victtor might help." He sipped. "Maybe he will, still."

"Why is Uncle Victtor here? I've never seen him 'til now. Why would he come for my wedlocking?" Rosa turned from the uncertainty that lapped at her heart. Had she broken her mother? Had she been the cause of Miichal's broken bond, despite her declaration otherwise? Had she a double blame to her credit?

Romane stared, incredulous. Did Rosa not know? "He came for your naming, soon after your birth. He is your guardian. Of course, he has come for your wedlocking. It's his duty."

Rosa's breath caught. "What? What are you saying? Papa is my guardian!"

Romane shook his head. "No. No, he's not, Rosa. Ma insisted that Uncle Victtor be your guardian. Did they never tell you? Ma? Pa?"

"No!" cried Rosa. "I've never heard this! Are you certain, Romane?"

"Yes. Yes. I was only a lad, but I remember it clearly. He claimed your name and claimed you." Romaine watched Rosa closely. He wished he had told her long ago, privately, in order to calm her through the revelation. It had never occurred to him that she didn't know.

"He claimed my name? He chose 'Rosa'?"

Romane shook his head. "Nay, nay, Rosa. *I* chose your name." He delighted at the memory. "You *were* a rose, so pink and fresh, with the scent of the bushes in Ma's garden floating always around you." He hurried to be clear. "But my name for you wasn't real, you see, until Victtor agreed and claimed 'Rosa' as yours."

"What else did he claim?"

Romane hesitated. He hated telling her anything more that might upset her further. "Well, he claimed your bridegroom and set the day of your wedlocking."

"How do you know this, and I do not?"

Romane wiped his sweaty palms on his trousers, wishing to be anywhere but in this room, having this conversation. "I saw his letter, where Ma left it in the kitchen. Ma doesn't know I found it, but it was there an entire afternoon, before she noticed and snatched it away." Romane felt shame blossom anew at his indiscretion.

"Why didn't you tell me?"

Romane searched for an explanation. Why didn't he tell her? "I expected Ma to tell you, or Pa. And when they *did* tell you, they left out the part about Victtor's claim." He paused; plunged forward. "It may be that Pa didn't know either. He most likely gave in to Ma's demands and agreed, if even reluctantly."

"And why didn't *you* tell me any of this, Romane, since you knew it all?"

He saw the truth then. He knew why he had said nothing. He turned to face her squarely. "Because *they* didn't tell you. I didn't know the reason, but I couldn't betray them, go behind their backs and tell you what they chose to conceal."

"And why tell her now?" Draymon asked, genuinely curious.

Romane felt his face flush. Would this enquiry never end? "Because she asked." Romane understood his own logic clearly. He straightened his spine. He was a born diplomat. Why speak of things that might cause turmoil, when the outcome could not be influenced? But nor would he lie, when asked a direct question. He drew breath to defend himself, persuade them from asking even more questions.

With a blast, the double doors slammed back on their hinges, and Victtor himself strode into the inn.

"What is this nonsense about you not obeying your husband-to-be?" His words roared through the room and spilled from doors and windows to startle a passerby.

Romane startled and spun on his bench to face the storm that invaded the inn. The blank stares and gaping mouths of the fellowship seemed to enforce Victtor's belief in his dominion, as he stood, towering, over pale Rosa.

Rosa gaped silently. She shrank against Romane, further invigorating her incensed uncle. Her guardian.

The power he held over her was unquestioned, unchallenged; every societal belief convinced the room of this truth. She cowered before him, thoroughly trained by a lifetime of cowering before her mother. Romane knew that she stood no chance in the face of her uncle's wrath.

Victor grasped her arm and tore her from her bench, which would have toppled had Romane not steadied it. Victtor dragged her and shook her, bringing his face within an inch of hers. Benches toppled as champions sprang to their feet, spacing themselves to intervene, should need arise. Separating them from action was the specter of guardianship and all the power it imbued. Victtor spat his words in a low growl.

"You will be wedlocked, you worthless girl! You will follow your husband to his home. You will obey him, in all that he orders. And you will honor his name, just as you will now honor mine! You will do as you're told, you wicked, selfish girl. Do you hear me? Do. You. Hear. Me?"

"She hears you, dear uncle. Of course she does." Romane stepped forward and steadied Rosa from behind, hands firm on her shoulders. "She will be wedlocked; she has given her promise. And Rosa always honors her promises."

Victtor stepped back from Rosa, dropped her arm. His eyes still glared, still demanded Rosa's eyes to remain locked onto his. "See that she does." Victtor's icy voice dripped his disdain. He took another step back, his glare scanning the fellowship, who inched to cluster around her. Jullia gathered Rosa into her arms.

Romane released Rosa into Jullia's embrace and stepped to shield her from her uncle's fury. He knew just where to step, not challenging his uncle, but forming a subtle shield just the same.

Victtor's glare focused on Romane and they stood, Romane graceful and respectful, Victtor all jutted jaw and clenched fists. Romane watched his uncle's rage soften, just as his mother's rage had always softened when faced with Romane's graceful respect. Romane wondered if his obeyance would heighten his uncle's attack, but for some mysterious reason, Romane's protective shield soothed the familial rage.

Victor dropped his fists and abandoned his bullying stance. He looked his nephew up and down and spoke in an almost friendly fashion. "See that she does," he repeated. He turned and strode from the inn, the double doors swishing behind him.

Romane wilted onto his bench, his heart breaking for his sobbing sister.

Chapter 30

Familial

Victtor tromped down the stairs of the inn, pushed past the guests who had clustered curiously, wondering at the bellows emanating from windows and doors. At the sight of Victtor, understanding dawned on their faces, and they turned aside, lessening their chances of being sideswiped by a familial squabble. Especially one involving the volatile Victtor.

A familial squabble! Ooooooo...Eyebrows raised and lips pursed. Heads nodded intriguingly. Could it be that Rosa was wavering over her wedlocking? Had she misgivings? Had she defied her parents? Darling Rosa, a rebel? Oooooo...

The clustered guests scuttled away, intent on gossip and the spread of speculations. Excitement to fill their too-quiet afternoon.

Victtor strode down the road, oblivious to his surroundings. His fury had dissipated, which surprised him. For some mysterious reason, he believed Romane when he said that Rosa would be wedlocked. He didn't dwell on the missing promise of the obeying and following of husbands, but that would proceed of its own accord. It was the natural order of things.

He could victoriously return to reassure Mandra's fretting worries, hold her wringing hands. His stride softened, his jutting jaw lost its clench. Romane's magic continued to wend its diplomatic way into his heart. His brow unfurrowed, his teeth ceased their grinding. His breath slowed and drew deep as he opened the gate to Mandra's garden.

He found her huddled at the back of her tent. He looked over her round form, with its curled spine and tucked knees, hand fisted against mouth, eyes squeezed tight. A long-forgotten sensation of pity rose in his chest, and he sat next to her, hoisted her into his arms. "There, there, Mandra. Ease your fear. All is well."

He patted her cheek and lifted her chin. Her eyes sought his. He smiled kindly, his lips twisting into the unfamiliar expression. "All is agreed. Rosa will wedlock." He smoothed her damp cheeks. "She will obey her husband and follow his wishes," he glossed lightly. "All is well."

Mandra's eyes filled with gratitude, and she leaned her temple against his chest. He patted her arm, let her fall into sleep, then gently lowered her roundness onto its back. He smoothed her forehead until a gentle snore rumbled forth, and he wended his way between baskets and boxes, taking care not to jostle or dislodge, to raise no clatter nor crash, which might awaken his dear sister from her much-needed rest.

Chapter 31

Arrival, Redux

Willam Ulrich felt a dizzy lightness in his head, though he continued to hold it high. He must convey confidence and might, regardless of the uncertainty that clutched his heart.

Did he really want to marry into this contentious family? He quailed at the prospect. But all was arranged; nothing could be done. A different outcome had never been possible, not when this wedlocking had been backed by the power that Victtor wielded in their village, his stranglehold on every aspect of business and day-to-day life, inherited from his father, and his father before that. Since the dawn of time, for all Willam could know. Never had it been other than it was.

So, now, here he was, riding a stallion much too large, wearing a collar much too tight, his feet swimming and squelching in boots much too tall. He would wedlock the mysterious Rosa, lead her home to a house too large, with a garden too small, and continue his servitude to the fearsome Victtor, and in all likelihood to the terrifyingly daily proximity of the probably fearsome Rosa.

The house and the stallion were gifts from the world's most powerful man, too grand to be refused. In all truth, the collar and boots, too, and all that went with them, were themselves gifts, and though seemingly insignificant, could never have been refused. There was no refusal, when it came to the mighty Victtor. His haughty niece would have only the best, and Willam, himself, had been swept into that overall assessment of 'best.'

So, here he rode, head high, lip trembling, Rosa's village marching into view. "Take command!" Victtor had commanded. "Women respect only command, and you will show it! From the first moment, you will show it, if ever you hope to succeed. For succeed you must! You will! You are to wedlock my Rosa, and your sons will follow in my footsteps."

For Victtor had no sons of his own, nor daughters, if it comes to that, a deficit never whispered. He surely had tried, with a succession of wives, each following the former, but never a son nor daughter did he get. So his scheming grew ever more de-manding, as year followed year followed year. His eye roamed relentlessly and settled on Willam, who, though not born into greatness, was deemed the best of the best at hand.

Willam's forehead shone with sweat, not only from the sun blazing overhead, but also from the trepidation that sweated his palms. The stallion pranced its knees high, its bridle held by a groom, Zedar. For in all truth, Willam showed no gift to com-mand it on his own. Zedar had taken pity on the lad, whom he had known since toddlerhood, and was glad to help in any way he could.

An entourage followed Willam, his stallion, and their groom, as befitted a young man of high standing. Two wagons swayed, over-burdened with silks and feathers and all manner of apparel and glittering bobbles, finery for bestowing on a bride of high standing, for high-standing was proven by show.

The wagons and horses and grooms and helpers, every bit and bob that accompanied Willam, in all truth, 'twas all gifted. Willam felt the weight of it, had felt it every step of his journey. That weight had bowed his head and lowered his eyes, silenced his voice and doused his laughter. Every groom, every helper trudged every step of the journey alongside him, for they, too, had known Willam since toddlerhood. They each understood his burden, understood his plight, and silently thanked the stars to have been overlooked during Victtor's quest for the best of the best to receive his grandiose gift of heirship.

Victtor's nephew, one would think, would fit the bill entirely. But nay. He was his mother's favorite, and she could not bear to send him to Victtor, lose him to a far village, even though Victtor was her beloved brother. So Victtor had acquiesced to her pleas and cast his searching eyes elsewhere, and they had landed on Willam, not perfect, but, as has been said, the best of the best to be had.

They passed the first house with its burgeoning garden, several more, explosions of colorful blossoms lining the fine road. The road broadened and straightened, trees branched overhead, with a flock of turquoise birdlings chattering their arrival. Clouds sailed above them, mimicking the lambs who frolicked in the fields along the road's edge. As the stallion pranced 'round the final bend, the crowd came into full view, and Willam's jaw fell and his blood froze, his shy nature raising its terrified head.

The crowd waved flags, pink ones and white, and showered his path with petals. They cheered and they chortled, dressed in their finest, rejoicing his wedlocking on this glorious day, his wedlocking to the fearsome Rosa, niece to the fearsome Victtor.

Willam silently thanked Zedar for holding the stallion's head with such authority, seemingly adding to Willam's standing. For Willam's knees shook, and his neck dripped, as the stallion's high knees pranced them forward. Their path led under tassels of ribbons, past flowering trees, whose scent made Willam's head swirl in delirium. He blinked and he breathed, bewildered and forlorn, his heart pounding in his ears, drowning out the crowd.

Some unknown grace helped his legs swing him from his saddle, and he stood for a moment and had the sense to raise his hand in greeting. The crowd cheered anew, and he remembered to hold his head high, for first impressions were his only hope. He followed Zedar, who set a decorous pace, and the crowd parted, showing them the way.

Willam sloshed in his tall boots and choked within his collar, but he paraded forth bravely, for command her, he would, this terrifying Rosa. He must quell her with his manliness.

After an eternity, Zedar stepped aside and turned, gesturing him forward with a grand bow.

And there she stood, dressed in the palest pink, white ribbons fluttering, orchard blossoms gracing; there she stood, his fearsome bride.

Chapter 32

Wedlocking

"What will you say to him?" Draymon asked Rosa, his face worried.

"I could never know that, not until I'm standing before him. I'm not a fortune teller, divining what will be."

"But you could think on it now, when you're calm, gather ideas that you can tuck away and draw out when needed," Greggor suggested.

Rosa wished for Romane's presence, his reassuring smile, his ready support. But he had left that morning to return to his mother's house. "To make sure she is there for your wedlocking," he had whispered as he kissed the top of her head.

Rosa searched for words on her own, stepped forward bravely, on her own. "But they wouldn't be true, if I thought of them now and used them later. Every moment is new, and the past is unimportant. I will know when the time comes; my heart will surely guide me." A wave of surety filled Rosa's heart. The words did come when she needed them. She lacked only the practice of speaking them.

Bolin drummed his fingertips on one of the tables strewn with the final preparations for the afternoon's feast. Delicacies had emerged under Gosikk's murmured instructions, and they were truly a sight to behold. Tables squatted on the mown pasture next to the inn, and all manner of treats awaited the guests.

The sun approached its zenith, when the wedlocking would take place across the road in the sprawling orchard with its high canopy rich with blossoms.

"Rosa," Stevven explained, "everyone is expecting you to enter your wedlocking and ride off into the west with your husband, never to be heard from again. That doesn't appear to be your plan. It would help us to know what your plan *is*, so we know what to do, what to expect. Do you see?"

Rosa searched for an explanation. "Stevven, when you are working with wood, building whatever you are building, do you know ahead of time, which board you will choose? How you will hold it? What murmurs will empower your gift?"

"Well, yes. Pretty much. I have to make sure to have enough planks, to know what the customer wants, how high, how wide, how long. I might not know exactly which plank I will pick up first, but the wood tells me what *it* needs, and the murmurs come of their own volition. That being said, a lot of preparation goes into the project before I get to the point where I actually murmur the wood into place. I have a strategy fully prepared before ever I begin."

Rosa's heart lightened at the success of her comparison. "This is the same. I have enough words, and I have all of you. I will pick the words that are right, in whatever moment I happen to be standing. I can't pre-murmur my way through the day."

"But what do *we* do?" asked Jullia. "How will we know what you need from us?"

Rosa felt a moment of clarity. "Because you are my champions and you will know in the moment. For surely, that's what champions do."

"You sound like an auntie," complained Katernn.

"Do aunties know only lies?" asked Rosa, bemused.

Cam banked from his circles overhead and called out to the pondering heads sequestered within the inn. "They are coming," Bolin said simply.

"Come. Put on your dress, and I'll comb your hair," urged Jullia. "Unless you want to meet him here..."

Dread swept through Rosa, tingling her fingertips. She obediently turned and dashed up the stairs. She swept up a cloud of palest pink, and Katernn slipped it over her head. Rosa did not care for frills and fluffs, but this dress was the stuff of dreams. They pulled the soft folds into place, secured buttons and tied ribbons. Jullia coaxed Rosa's curls into a swirling pile atop her head and fastened an emerald clasp in its usual place.

They stood back to admire her, looked for any overlook, and nodded. She wiped her palms down her sides and turned on her heel. She heard them follow her out of the room, down the passageway, the stairs. She paused in the center of the common room and looked about her. Would she ever step foot in this room again? Or would she ride away at the side of a stranger newly husbanded, never to see her village again?

Mackey handed her a bouquet of orchard blossoms, extracted one and tucked it behind her ear. She buried her nose in the petals, drew in their intoxicating fragrance. She raised her face and stood before them, her twelve, and looked from one to the next. She saw smiles and grins, nods and eyes aglow, a wagging tail and clacking beak. She lifted her chin and gave a slow turn. They applauded and laughed, and stepped forward to hug.

Rosa drew in a deep breath. She was ready, this bridal Spring Maiden.

As the inn's double doors opened, the crowd hushed and turned toward her. The waving flags stilled, the gossip held its breath. The sun caught her as she moved down the wide steps, her twelve arranging themselves behind her. Her very presence stilled all hearts, and a calm descended. Awe swept through the crowd, a wave that crested and sprang into the air, to scatter under the sun and sprinkle over guest and villager alike.

Rosa glimpsed Romane as he raised his arms where he stood next to his parents, and a cheer escaped his throat. He waved his flag and scattered petals, his joyful heart showing clearly on his face. His cheer spread and caught, taking the crowd by storm. They waved flags, pink ones and white, and showered Rosa's path with petals. They cheered and they beamed, dressed in their finest, rejoicing her wedlocking on this glorious day, her wedlocking to the mysterious bridegroom, hand-chosen by the bellowing Victtor.

They opened a path before her, widened it for the twelve. The procession continued, deep into the orchard, until Rosa paused next to Romane, turned, and waited. Her twelve gathered behind her as she watched an opening of the crowd form before and close behind two figures making their way toward her. She knew that the bridegroom approached, setting a proud, unhurried pace. She saw the jaunty slant of a feather protruding from his hat, and his hand waving to the crowd on either side, and knew that the wedlocking, blessed be the stars above, the wedlocking was upon her. She prepared herself for who knew what.

A liveried groom stepped into the space before Rosa, moved to one side, and with a deep bow, ushered the bridegroom forward, to take his place beside her.

Rosa's first glimpse of her bridegroom revealed a haughty face and thrust chin. One hand grasped his belt at his side, sending his arm akimbo at a rakish angle. His other hand reached for his hat with its jaunty feather and swept it before him and to one side as he bowed deeply to her and her twelve. When he straightened, he would not look at her, which seemed odd to Rosa. Had she already disappointed him? She drew in a breath. Did he already sit in judgement of her? Had she no hope?

She calmed as she felt her twelve behind her. Together, they could conquer the world.

She scowled as he stepped forward, but he neither saw nor seemed to care. They stood side by side and faced her uncle, whose slitted eyes appraised them both. He took each of their right hands in one of his own and pressed those hands together, Willam's atop Rosa's. Victor wound a golden length around their pressed hands, again, and again, and again.

He held their bound hands, tightly between his two and raised all four overhead. He glared first at Willam, second, at Rosa, and released their stiffly raised arms. Sweeping his arms to each side, he declared in a voice resounding, "They are wedlocked!"

The crowd lifted their flags and cheered their cheers, waving their arms back and forth. It was done! They were wedlocked! All the gossip and rumoring had been for naught, 'twould seem.

As they lowered their bound hands, the couple found courage, and searched each other's eyes. What was his name? Rosa wondered. She saw pride and command, felt the stiffness of his arm, the grasping of his fingers, the jutting of his jaw. And yet, in his eyes, she saw softness, and hope, and kindness, and she smiled a wide smile, a smile that leapt to the heavens and splashed over her bridegroom to melt his heart.

The couple stood, breathless, and the twelve caught theirs, too. The world went still, no sound seeped in to distract the two, no sound from cheering crowd or whirling noisemakers or clapping hands. Rosa drew in her breath, and Willam's breath soon followed, and their smiles grew as wide as the sky as the scent of roses flooded the world.

Victtor paused in his acceptance of the crowd's admiration and noticed the quiet smiling of the wedlocked. This did not adhere to his view of decorum, so he stepped forward to take command once again.

He bellowed above the crowd's cheers and had to bellow a second time, a third. When finally the crowd settled, he bellowed to the couple before him, taking care that all would hear.

"You will vow your obedience and loyalty! Before all who have gathered here!"

A heartbeat, a second, and Rosa spoke, her voice clear; it carried far. She spoke the words always spoken after wedlocking, the words of obeyance and loyalty. The surprise that shocked them, that sent her uncle stepping backward, was that she spoke the words always, always! spoken by the bridegroom!

"Do you promise to live with me always, in full obedience and loving loyalty?"

And Victtor could not believe it, had no way to fathom its meaning: Willam responded, spoke the words always, always! spoken by the bride!

"I faithfully promise to live with you always, in full obedience and loving loyalty."

Then Willam lifted their bound hands and kissed her knuckles, never taking his eyes from hers.

They turned as one and left the way she had arrived, the silent crowd parting before them, the twelve following after, through the orchard, across the beautifully groomed road, and the inn's doubled doors swallowed them, whole.

Chapter 33

Celebration

The crowd, villagers and guests alike, awoke from their shock, as Romane broke into a loud cheer. They cheered their cheers and waved their flags, looked one to the other, and shrugged their shrugs. Darling Rosa was wedlocked! Despite gossip, despite furrowed brows, despite the wondering and the whispers, Rosa had stepped forward and entered her wedlock, just as was expected of her.

Well, except for the vow part...

The crowd cheered their cheers and waved their flags and strolled across the fine road to the inn's shorn pasture with its bountiful bounty. All morning, they had peeked at that bounty carried from inn to pasture, spread on tables, atop cheerful cloths. Aromas had wafted, bundled flowers had fluttered, tankards had beckoned, and everywhere, bright colors had welcomed. The time of celebration was now upon them.

The champions circled amongst the guests, encouraging another draught, another morsel. Laughter flowed amidst stories told, and overflowing platters emptied, barrels drained their last, and still the wedlocked couple remained awaited.

Rosa and Willam stood in her bedchamber, right hands bound, left hands held, and stared, one's eyes into the other's.

"My name is Rosa." The whisper broke their silence.

Willam nodded. "My name is Willam."

"I thought it might be."

"It is."

They pulled together two chairs, and sat knee to knee, and told of their lives, his life and hers, hearing the facts, intuiting deeper truths, through eyes, and expressions, and the fluttering of hands, somewhat hampered by the binding that bound them still.

Willam startled at the sight of a raven soaring through the window, circling over their heads, and disappearing once again into the sky.

"We must go down. My champions are calling." Rosa spoke as the raven exited.

"Champions?" Willam ventured.

"*That* story is for another time. Come. We must go."

Out they went, greeted by cheers renewed and much waving of tankards and spoons. They made the circuit, greeted guests, and hugged villagers, "So happy!" "So wonderful!" "So blessed."

When all had been drunk, and all had been eaten, when all the goodbyes had been waved, the last laughter laughed, the champions clustered around the wedlocked couple. They sighed their sighs, and nodded their smiles, smoothed Rosa's hair and patted her cheek, and hugged a welcome for Willam. They shooed the couple upstairs and returned to their straightening and tidying, pleased that all had gone wonderfully well.

At long last, Rosa and Willam unwound their wedlocking bindings. Willam kissed Rosa's hands, and Rosa kissed his. He whispered into her ear. "We could easily fall asleep, wait until we know each other better."

And Rosa whispered back, "Let's see how it goes." She placed her freed hands either side of his face and reached up to give him her kiss. He wrapped his arms around her and kissed her back, and little by little, they saw how it went.

Chapter 34

Spring Maiden

'T was Gosikk who told Willam the story of the night of double moons. The champions introduced themselves, shared a brief story each. Bolin offered Cam onto Willam's arm, while Willam scratched Pharlan's ears with his free hand. They took him to see Bolin's seedlings turned saplings. They settled there, around a strapping sapling, and told more stories, to help him understand, to believe. For the aunties' stories held sway, obscure though they were, warped over the ages. Willam couldn't resolve the sweetness of the girl sitting by his side with the grip of the aunties' stories terrifying his heart.

"So what does it mean, in all seriousness, to be a Spring Maiden?" he asked Rosa.

"I'm trying to understand that myself. These saplings happened, but otherwise, I have only the same tales and stories that *you* grew up hearing. Those stories are horribly frightening, and that doesn't align with how it feels to me. I feel only kindness and want only to help. If it weren't for these saplings, I'd doubt the belief my champions hold, that I am Spring Maiden."

Willam turned to the champions. "How do you know she's Spring Maiden?"

Mackey was the first to answer. "Because we were there. We witnessed it. We were part of it. Becoming a champion changed me irrevocably. From my earliest memories, I wanted only a full tankard. Nothing else mattered. Now, it's Rosa. Nothing else matters."

The other champions nodded agreement. Pharlan gave a soft yelp and Cam spread his wings, resettled himself.

"What does it mean to be champions? I should be a champion, too, don't you think, as Rosa's husband?"

Miichal cleared his throat, unaccustomed as he was to using his voice. "Champions are chosen by who is with the Maiden when the moonbeams find her. They revive her. Their number is always twelve. The fact that twelve were with Rosa cemented the certainty that Rosa was Spring Maiden. It was the final sign we needed. If there had been ten or fourteen or any other number, Rosa would not have been Spring Maiden."

"What would she have been?"

"Well. Dead, of course. Just as Romane would have died had not Rosa revived him."

"What? Romane?"

And so they told the story of Romane, how Mandra had found him and Rosa had revived him.

"Before the sun touched him," concluded Bolin.

"Why is that important?" Willam asked.

No one spoke for a moment.

Miichal said, "I don't know. Tronder had answers to every question I had, but, I don't have Tronder anymore."

"Who is Tronder? What happened to him?"

And so they told the story of Tronder. Miichal held his head and wept anew. Pharlan whimpered and thumped her tail. Mackey went down on one knee and drew Pharlan close, comforting her. Pharlan nosed his chin, then resumed her adoration of Miichal.

Everyone saw the flash of pain that crossed Mackey's face as he released Pharlan and regained his seat in the circle they held around Bolin's sapling. Miichal stood, and Pharlan padded after him as he walked a short distance away. Mackey bent his head and stared at his hands.

"What about the headman?" Willam spoke into the silence. "Surely he will have an opinion on who should bond with whom." Blank stares surrounded Willam, giving him pause. Was there trouble here with the headman? "Who is your headman? I don't remember meeting him."

"We have no headman," Gosikk answered Willam's perplexity. "We've never had need of one."

"Then who makes the decisions? Like this one?"

"Whoever is involved in the question. We decide for ourselves."

"But, who has final say?"

"Whoever is in the right."

Katernn wrinkled her forehead at Willam. "Is Victtor your headman? In your village?"

"Of course."

"And he makes decisions for others?"

"He makes all decisions. He holds all the reins and keeps things moving in the right direction."

"And he decides which direction is right?"

Willam was unaccustomed to discussions about the finer nuances of deciding right from wrong. That was the headman's job. A job that would one day be his, he avoided reminding himself. Sweat beaded his forehead, and his heart pounded, thumping against his ribs.

"Of course. He understands the intricacies."

Stevven asked, "Does everyone agree with his decisions? Do they think themselves better off having a headman?"

"Of course. Firstly, they have no other option. None of us do. Secondly, everyone has their own opinion, so the solutions are overflowing. Victtor chooses one, and everyone goes along with it."

Willam desperately wanted the questions to stop. His defense of his village's ways felt patchy, and he couldn't think how to fill the empty spots. He grasped a thought that would take the discussion back to the real question at hand, would free him from the spotlight.

"Rosa. Can you fix Miichal? He seems broken after his loss of Tronder. If you helped Romane, perhaps you could help Miichal."

"What would I do?"

"Give Tronder back. Restore their bond."

"I don't know how."

Thoughts bounced around Willam's head. He fought to bring them into focus.

"Did you know how to revive Romane?" He gestured toward the sapling. "To bring this tree to maturity?"

"No, but..."

Bolin said, "Let's try. I know I would rather die, than lose my bond with Cam."

All eyes turned to Rosa, waiting for her reply.

"Let's try," she echoed.

They scrambled to their feet, and Gosikk called to Miichal. "Let's visit Tronder, Miichal. Rosa hopes to restore your bond."

Miichal touched Pharlan's head as they turned to follow.

"Only one bond can exist," said Miichal and Bolin together, echoing what Pharlan and Cam declared.

"Let's try," replied Gosikk.

They trooped through forest, across fields, along the beautifully groomed road, talking excitedly, not only at the prospect of Miichal and Tronder's re-bonding, but also at the prospect of exploring Rosa's powers, what *their* role might be. Willam was unused to the pace they set and fell behind, quickly out of breath.

He caught them as they entered the stable and waited for Miichal to guide Tronder from his stall where he slept the days away, the nights as well. A tired horse, old with bowed back and lowered head, dull coat and uncertain gait.

Willam gasped, shocked at the sight of Tronder. He was no horseman, had not that gift; but never had he seen a more dispirited, listless steed, in all his years of being in the constant company of horses, the powerhouses of every village.

Rosa approached Tronder, ran her fingertips down his nose, looked into his eyes. She brought both hands up to palm each side of his head, closed her eyes, and rested her forehead on his. They stood motionless.

"Bond with Miichal," she whispered.

Everyone held their breaths.

"Only one bond can exist," said Miichal and Bolin together.

Silence fell. Nothing changed.

"Perhaps there are some things even a Spring Maiden cannot do," said Gosikk, his shoulders drooped.

A peaceful certainty drifted in waves from Rosa. She knelt beside Pharlan, who went into a crouch, whining, tail between legs. Rosa bent over the trembling dog and repeated her actions, holding Pharlan's head between her hands, closing her eyes, and touching foreheads.

"Bond with Mackey," Rosa breathed. "He loves you beyond measure."

Pharlan yelped and struggled to free herself from Rosa's grasp, which held firm. Jullia held her hand over her mouth, brow furrowed.

"Rosa, don't," said Willam, his face draining of its blood, aghast at what he had set in motion.

It was done.

Pharlan stopped her struggle, sat up, Rosa's hands still grasping her head. Pharlan licked Rosa's face once and then twisted away. She padded to Mackey and sat under his hand.

Mackey dropped to his knees and pulled Pharlan into his arms. Pharlan rose to place her paws on his shoulders, licking away his tears as they rocked together, back and forth.

"Ah, Pharlan. Lass. I've missed ye," Mackey gasped. He fell over sideways, taking Pharlan with him, and the two wrestled in the dust with much laughter, yips, and licking and petting of faces. Pharlan could not contain herself, wriggling and prancing. Mackey smoothed her fur and held her, wherever he could find a wiggling hold.

The champions slapped each other's backs, relieved over the outcome, yet casting glances to Rosa, who knelt where Pharlan had left her.

Her face showed calm detachment as she watched the bonded pair rejoice. Willam bent over her, placed his hand on her shoulder.

"Rosa, are you yourself again?" he asked, perplexed at her calm silence.

"Yes. Of course. All is well," Rosa replied, her face oddly wooden, without expression.

Mackey and Pharlan scrambled to their feet, ran from the stable to romp across fields, onward to the forest. Old friends, reunited, with a depth never imagined.

Rosa straightened and turned to Miichal. His face showed a collapsed emptiness, a crushing of soul. Miichal had curled into himself at this second loss of companion. Pharlan's struggle and subsequent joy upon reunion with Mackey had torn his heart, and when she left without a backward glance, bond broken, he looked as though he might die, that nothing, nothing, was left to live for. He sank to his knees, sobbing, broken anew.

Rosa helped him stand, braced his shoulders with her strong hands. She held him upright until he found his balance, then led him to stand next to Tronder.

"Miichal," Rosa breathed. "Come back to us. We have you. We love you."

Miichal's breath caught, his eyes cleared, his shoulders straightened. Rosa's grip slid from shoulders to arms as he turned to Tronder. She let him go.

Tronder stood, head high, coat gleaming. He tossed his head and pawed the dirt with a polished hoof. Miichal reached and encircled the horse's neck, face buried in Tronder's muscled shoulder. Tronder whinnied and tossed his head again. Miichal hoisted himself onto Tronder's back, now strong and straight, and threw a leg over Tronder's rump. Grasping thick mane, Miichal tightened his legs, and Tronder trotted to the stable door, gathered himself, and broke into a gallop.

The champions hurried into the courtyard, shaded their eyes against the midday sun, and watched as this second pair of companions disappeared into the forest. Cam launched into the sky, flapping after the foursome, and Bolin trotted behind, waving his hat, whooping.

Willam swooped Rosa off her feet and twirled her in circles. "You did it! You did it!" The horror of helplessly witnessing this challenge lifted from his heart, and he felt the rightness of his urging that she try.

As he set her onto her feet, her arms remained locked around his neck. "I knew what to do!" she whispered. "I just knew." A look of awe overtook the calm certainty that had radiated power during the bonding. The girl they had come to know once again stood in the midst of her champions. Willam found he could again breathe as they wandered into the inn, leaving the bonded companions to rejoice and reacquaint.

Chapter 35

Slip Away

"I want to tell Romane about Miichal and Tronder," Rosa announced as they walked into the common room. "He will rejoice over the happy outcome."

The others moved enthusiastically toward the double doors, but Rosa held up her hand. "I should go alone. I can go there and back without rousing my uncle's ire. If we all go, he is sure to take offense."

"Someone should go with you," Gosikk said. "What if you need help?"

"I don't need help to talk to my brother. We'll be brief."

The dismay at being left behind shone on every face, but Rosa held firm. She would be brief.

Rosa walked the road between the inn and her childhood home, keeping to the shade of overhanging trees, borne from concern of being watched by who knew whom. She glanced over her shoulder, surprised at how bereft she felt without her champions. Their constant presence had filled her with belief in herself, and now that confidence dribbled away with every step.

She glanced over the garden gate, gathered her resolve, and stepped inside. The tent remained, drooping next to the house, and spared a swift regard of the familiar façade of her childhood home, her mother's house. Her glance fell away. Truly, she would not return to her mother's house. Instead, she sidled to the tent and lifted the flap.

Romane looked over his shoulder at the sudden light spilling through the flap, and his face lit at the sight of her. "Rosa!" he breathed and strode the few steps to sweep her up and twirl her around the improvised kitchen. Rosa clung to his neck, smiling broadly. She regained her feet and the two siblings looked each other over.

"You are radiant!" said Romane approvingly.

"Well, I am newly wedlocked. Of course I'm radiant." She touched his cheek. "I've missed you so. Won't you come back to the inn? It would be lovely if you were with us again."

Romane shook his head, regretful. "It *would* be lovely. I've missed you, too. But Ma needs me here."

"Surely there's not much for you to do. There are only the two of you, with Papa gone all day and Uncle Victtor having his own cook and such. Mama can look after herself."

"That's the thing, Rosa. She can't. She's crippled with fear. She can't do anything for herself. I thought that Victtor could help her where I could not, but he is attentive only now and again. Ma needs closer assistance than he thinks to provide. I am the only one." Rosa's face fell in disappointment. "But never mind that now," Romane hurried to continue. "Tell me about you. How are you faring? And your champions? Tell me everything."

"Romane, it's wonderful. Everyone is wonderful. In fact, I came to tell you; Miichal is re-bonded with Tronder." She told him the story, with only a smattering of embellishments, all of them inconsequential but entertaining. Romane held her hands, face glowing.

"This is the best news, Rosa. Miichal's plight broke my heart. Thank you for telling me, for fixing him. *Both* of them!" His eyes narrowed with a sudden thought. "Could you fix Ma, do you think? Might you be able to relieve her of her fear?"

Rosa's thoughts clouded. She had not expected to see her mother. She realized she wasn't sure she wanted to help her. She had suffered long under Mandra's wrath, and now being free of it, any reminder darkened her heart.

"Please, Rosa." Romane tightened his hold on her hand.

At last, Rosa whispered, a child again. "Will you come with me?"

Romane nodded.

Still Rosa hesitated, heart thudding. She looked past Romane's shoulder, to the shrouded doorway leading deeper into the tent.

"Is she in there?" Rosa jutted her chin toward the doorway.

Romane nodded, squeezed her hand again.

Rosa dropped Romane's hand, stepped around him, and lifted the shroud to peer inside. Romane followed, let the shroud fall behind them.

Rosa could barely see the mounds of furniture piled floor to ceiling and knew not where to walk. Romane crowded past her and led her to a back corner. He lifted the flap from an opening in the tent wall and light trickled in.

Mandra lay curled on a mattress on the floor, a thin sleeping cloth draped over her. Rosa looked to Romane, who nodded encouragement. Rosa knelt at the edge of the bedding and leaned to touch her mother's arm.

"Mama?" she whispered. "Mama? It's me. Can you wake up?"

Mandra startled awake and gasped, "Get away!" She scooted as far as the tent wall allowed, holding her arm above her head protectively.

"Mama, it's fine. It's me, Rosa."

"Get away!" she cried, her voice taught and high. "Leave me alone!"

"Do you see?" Romane said. "Fear lives in her heart and gives her no peace. Please help her, Rosa."

Rosa sat back on her heals. She felt no calming clarity wrap itself around her. She felt only resentment, saw only the bane of her childhood. But still she couldn't leave Mandra like this. Her terror was obvious, and having lived in the shadow of fear much of her life, she wished that fate on no one, knowing its power to debilitate and crush.

"Don't be afraid, Mama. You have nothing to fear. No one will hurt you. Not even me."

Mandra lowered her arm and stared at Rosa, but said nothing, breaths slowing and deepening.

Rosa waited a moment more, could no longer feel waves of fear emanating from the woman who crouched before her. She rose, cast a wondering glance over her mother's prone body, and turned to leave. She stopped at her mother's soft voice.

"It has never mattered over the years, what I might say to you, has it?"

Rosa felt a flood of relief and blossoming hope. Her mother understood her at long last, that none of the meanness she had thrown at her daughter over the years had really mattered, that all along Rosa *had* known her mother loved her. At last, they could breach the wall that separated them.

"No, Mama," Rosa breathed in relief, with love. She turned to her mother, let her hands fall to her sides, open and welcoming her mother's love.

Rosa's breath froze at the look of disdain and loathing on her mother's face. Her mind whirled and re-heard the words, "It has never mattered over the years, what I might say to you, has it?" The words dripped loathing. They meant that Rosa was clueless, unheeding, rebellious. That despite Mandra's persistent efforts, nothing ever penetrated Rosa's thick skull.

"Oh," breathed Rosa, head lowered, thick with disappointment and embarrassment. She stumbled past Romane, through the shrouded doorway, smack into the unyielding chest of her uncle.

He grabbed her arms and shook her. "What are *you* doing here?" he bellowed. "Leave my sister alone!" He shook her again. The emerald clasp fell to the ground, and her hair tumbled around her shoulders.

Rosa trembled in her uncle's grasp, all thought of good deeds and champions fleeing her mind. She was a child again, cringing before the rage of someone who was meant to protect her. She turned her face away and shielded herself as best she could with shaking hands.

She felt Romane's arms grasp her from behind, twisting her away from Victtor's hold, so that he stood between her and her uncle, clutching her into the curve of his body. "Uncle, please!" he said over his shoulder.

"And you! I thought you were here to look after your mother!" He circled around them, and Romane turned with him, keeping Rosa protected. "You're just as worthless as she is!" Victtor jabbed at Rosa, reaching his jab past Romane.

Faced with Victtor's jabbing finger, Rosa felt power surge into her. She turned in Romane's arms and thrust her arm over his shoulder, straight into Victtor's face. "Stop your bellowing, Uncle!" she cried.

His mouth continued to work, his eyes bulging, but no sound emerged. Romane looked from Rosa to Victtor, wondering at his sudden silence. Victtor's face turned purple, veins pulsing at temple and neck, his rage mounting ever higher. He flailed his arms, struggling to reach Rosa, but Romane's shoulder kept him at bay.

All motion slowed, as though mired in molasses. Victtor choked on his own spittle, grasped his hands to either side of his head, slithered down Romane's back, and sprawled on the floor, eyes staring emptily at the cloth ceiling.

"No!" screamed Mandra, as she stumbled through the shrouded doorway. She threw herself across her brother's body. "No! No! No!"

Romane stood, holding Rosa, unbelieving. Then Romane thrust Rosa toward the door. "Go!" he hissed.

Mandra heaved herself to her feet and lurched toward Rosa. "You! You did this, you evil, evil girl!" The words were free from anger, but loathing coated each syllable.

Romane caught Mandra, holding her back. "Go!" he implored Rosa. "I will find you later."

Rosa turned and ran, straight into the arms of Gosikk, who scooped her up and carried her to the inn, her champions engulfing them.

The champions had arranged themselves along the steps of the inn, watching Rosa disappear into her mother's garden. They hated being separated from her and stood restlessly, awaiting her return.

At the first bellow, they burst onto the road and stampeded into the garden. Gosikk caught Rosa, and they brought her back to the safe haven of the inn.

When the bonded companions returned from their roaming celebration, they found their brethren clustered around Rosa, folded into Gosikk's lap, Willam at her feet, grasping both her hands. Jullia petted her arm, and Stevven offered her cool water. Greggor and Draymon leaned over Gosikk's shoulder, while Yonce and Katernn knelt at either side.

"What has happened?" asked Miichal, authority ringing in his voice.

They told the story, as best they knew. To learn the aftermath, Cam flew to the garden, watched and listened. Bolin relayed the newest news. A healer summoned. The shaking of heads. Mandra's wails. Romane's stunned silence. As full under-standing of Victtor's collapse dawned in the room, silence fell. He would not rise from this bellowing bullying. It had been his last. Soft glances and reassuring pats turned to sideways looks and covered mouths.

Miichal spoke the words that Tronder sent into his heart. "This is why the aunties speak fearsome tales. This is the bane of the Spring Maiden's existence. Innocent intentions easily lead to fearsome consequences."

Greggor spoke the hopeful. "She can revive him, same as Romane."

Miichal shook his head. "Romane was entranced. Victtor is dead. A Spring Maiden cannot revive the dead."

Miichal looked around the chastened gathering. "We must leave this village. She will be hunted."

Chapter 36

Denial

"Are we sure?" Jullia asked the others. "Do we know the truth of what's happened? Perhaps flight is premature." Her heart quailed at the thought of fleeing the village, which had sheltered her entire life.

Cam confirmed and Bolin relayed that no one had moved from Mandra's garden, giving the fellowship a moment to ponder. Cam held vigil on a high branch that gave an unfettered view of the garden.

"Perhaps he's not dead," Yonce ventured.

"The healer came, pulled a cloth over his head," Bolin recounted. "We heard Mandra's wails. Her grief was real. Is real." He glanced to Rosa.

"But must we flee?" Jullia asked. "Romane was there. Surely he will speak in Rosa's defense." She grasped for a different solution.

"And say what? That Victtor tripped and fell? That he choked on a piece of fruit perchance?" Mackey shook his head. "Mandra was there as well, and she will demand Rosa's head." His face took on the look of remembrance. "She's a mean one, is Mandra. She'll not rest until Rosa pays."

"Then Romane must come with us!" Jullia cried to the rest, her hand reaching toward Mandra's stunned garden, her eyes imploring. "It will be madness there, to face Mandra alone." Her eyes darted from one to the next. "I will fetch him. It will take but a moment."

Gosikk heaved a deep sigh. "Nay. Romane will be well, Jullia. He doesn't draw Mandra's wrath."

Bolin nodded. "And Mandra will need him, now with Victtor's death. Romane wouldn't agree to leave her. Not alone like that."

Jullia stood and paced, frantic for solutions, her heart refusing to accept conclusions that left her bereft. "Mandra has her husband. What need has she of Romane as well?"

Katernn caught Jullia's fist as her pacing brought her near. "Jullia." Katernn took a deep breath. "Leave him be. In this, his place is with his mother."

Jullia gulped back a sob, sank onto a bench. Her hand covered her crumpling face. She did not want them to see the desperation that swept over her at their words.

For the first time since Gosikk had scooped her from her mother's garden, Rosa stirred of her own accord. She stood. Her unsteady feet took her to where Jullia sat, hiding tears. Jullia refused to respond to Rosa's touch, Rosa's hand on her arm. Rosa stood silently, her quiet hand smoothing Jullia's sleeve. Jullia could barely stop herself from shaking off the quiet hand.

Rosa spoke so all could hear. "I swore to Miichal, and I remind you all now. If you seek release from me, I will grant it. I will grant..."

"Silence!" roared Miichal, springing toward Rosa at the sight of her rising arm. "Speak not another word!"

The assemblage stared at him with shock. Jullia's heart skipped painfully. Her mind went blank.

Miichal's power stirred Rosa's curls, her clothing, swirled a leaf at her feet.

Rosa turned at his roar, forced away a cower that was her lifelong response. Her eyes narrowed. "How dare you..." A familial rage flushing her face.

"Silence!" Miichal loomed over Rosa, grasped her hands and held them to his heart. His voice dropped to a whisper, a whisper that carried to the corners of the room and dropped into every heart. "Have you not learned the terrible power of your words?"

Jullia could bear no more. She knew that they would leave. She would lose Romane and all that was familiar. The need to flee, not only the wrath that was surely even now blossoming over the death of Victtor, headman, but more immediately, she needed to flee the terrible power that swirled around Miichal and Rosa.

She turned to Stevven, counting on his sweetness for her. Her face glistened with tears as she begged him, "Will you help me?"

Chapter 37

Pantry

Jullia slipped out the nearest door, Stevven following close behind. As they gained a backroad, Stevven caught her arm, pausing her flight.

"Where are we going, lass? What help do you need?"

Jullia choked back a sob. "We're fleeing." She pointed toward the inn. "We're going to take Rosa and flee."

Stevven followed her pointing arm. "It's not decided. Shouldn't we listen, to know?"

Jullia pressed the heels of her hands against her trembling cheeks. "It is decided. It only waits to be spoken." A sob tightened her throat. "Will you help me?" Certainty of the rightness of her plan grew, and with it, a calmness spread across her heart. "My pantry. If I can take my pantry, I could bear to leave…" She gestured feebly around her, the village, the only life she had known. Another sob threatened, and she pressed her hands to her cheeks again.

"Will you help me? If we hurry, we can gather it all. If I had my pantry…" her voice quavered. "…I could bear it."

"Show me," Stevven said, palming her arms, planting a swift kiss on the top of her head. "We'll do what we can. Together."

Jullia nodded and turned to hurry down a path, onto a second, and led the way to her tiny house, now empty of wedlocking guests, and pushed open the heavy door. Together, they dumped cloths from a sturdy basket, added jugs and jars, padding them with the dumped cloths.

"Best to take light things. We'll be able to carry more that way," Stevven said.

Into bags went herbs and sprigs, boxes of ground spices, bundles of roots. They secured bunches of dried flowers on top of the sturdy basket, which Stevven hoisted to gauge its weight.

"What else?" he asked.

"This is the best of it," she answered. Her heart felt calmer at the sight of the gathered abundance. She straightened and looked at Stevven, saw him fully for the first time. "Thank you, Stevven. I cannot thank you enough."

"We best go." He interrupted her thanks with an embarrassed shrug. "We best return to the others."

With a final scrubbing of cheeks, Jullia turned for a final scrutiny of her emptied pantry, and nodded. She shrugged two bulging sacks onto her shoulders, and together they slipped through the heavy door, into the bright sunlight.

Chapter 38

Lesson

Rosa stared at Miichal, mouth agape. She shook her head. "No. No. This has not been my doing. I brought you back to yourself, yes. And I bonded Pharlan to Mackey. But that is all. Nothing else has been my fault."

Miichal felt Tronder stir in his stall, gusting his breath forcefully.

Tell her.

Miichal put his hands to either side of the maiden's head, his eyes bore into hers, his thumbs brushed her temples. "I tell you it is, darling Rosa. All of it. You are Spring Maiden. The world revolves around you; you are its center. Everything, everything that has happened since the double moons and before, it all has been because of you." His voice dropped to a whisper; still all could hear. "And so it will be, for many years to come."

Miichal smoothed his hands down her neck, grasped her shoulders. "You must take care with your words, Rosa, until you understand your power."

Tell her.

Miichal's eyes held Rosa's eyes. "You took away Mandra's fury, Rosa, and left behind her fear. You took her fear and left her hatred. There is always another driving force hiding under the surface. You do not know what damage you do, when you demand a change in another."

Rosa stepped back from him, shaking her head. "No."

"Watch your words, Rosa, until you understand your power."

Make her see.

Miichal took a deep breath. "I tell you this, Rosa, not to punish you, but to force you to see your power. You stole your uncle's bellowing, and his fury had no escape. It flooded his mind and broke his heart. He could not live, denied of his bellows."

Rosa sank to her knees, spread a hand on the wide planks of the floor, clutched her heart. Miichal sank with her, gathered her clutched hand between his, kissed her knuckles.

Willam spoke from the double doors. "Stop. You have to stop, Miichal. She didn't know."

She must understand.

Miichal held Rosa's fist, her eyes. "It's true. She didn't know. But she *has* to know, Willam." He gently gathered Rosa into his arms and held her, petting her hair. "And it's our job to teach her." He kissed the top of her head. "We are your champions, Rosa."

He stood, bringing Rosa with him. "By the majesty of Ero, the sacredness of Era, through the mysteries of their crossed paths, and the wisdom of the ages, we twelve entered into covenant, one with the others, together to protect and defend, to serve and guide, through all of our days."

Rosa buried her face in Miichal's chest, wrapped her arms around him, and sobbed.

"There, there, darling Rosa. You're safe. We're here." He kissed the top of her head. "We must away," he whispered.

Chapter 39

Fractured

Muffled scrapes and clunks punctuated the flurry of hurried footsteps. Willam stood at the window, his frozen mind catching blinks and flashes of rushing motion. He turned his head to look out the window, eyes squinted against the glare. His bride had disappeared down that road, skirts billowing behind Miichal as Tronder flew from the inn, the village. From him.

As Rosa disappeared, his wedlocking vow cracked into a thousand shards and clattered around his feet, piercing the floor with their razored edges. Along with the clattering of his vow, his mind fell away. Sounds and sights jangled aimlessly against his bewilderment.

Willam turned, one hand clutching the window's sill, to peer, perplexed, at the chaotic bustle of the common room.

"Are you watching?" Katernn asked him as she swam into view, grasped his arm, squinted into his face. Did she expect something from him? "Willam?" He gaped, and his words scattered to hide from her. She shook his arm. "Willam!" He blinked to focus on her face, inches from his. He quailed and pulled back. He would have fallen, but for her grasp. He looked at the floor as he hunched and raised a protective arm.

Katernn softened. "You're fine, hon. No one's going to hurt you." Her grasp became a pat, and she was gone, a sleeping cloth trailed, fluttering, behind her.

His head swiveled toward a loud clatter and exclamation from the kitchen. Mackey bent to retrieve a fallen pot and hurried from view.

Greggor and Draymon descended the stairs, lugging a crate between them. Draymon's foot caught the edge of a step, and the crate tipped, spilling a cascade of unfurling bandages. Greggor braced his thigh against the crate until Draymon regained his footing. They shuffled down the last stairs and through the door into the courtyard.

Beyond them, Yonce led two mules, readying their harnesses for a wagon. Boxes and crates lay strewn across the cobblestones. Stevven loaded a stack of bowls and murmured them into place. Greggor's crate went in, and shadowed figures stooped to lift other crates, scraping them across the wagon's bed. The cobblestones quickly cleared of its chaos.

The double doors brushed Willam's arm as they opened to reveal Zedar. Willam blinked. Zedar?

"Where's Rosa?" Zedar rasped. Willam's words scrambled in confusion. Zedar grabbed his shoulder. "You've got to hide her!" Zedar's eyes swept the room, skipped past the courtyard, came back to Willam. "They're coming," he hissed and disappeared beyond the swish of the double doors.

Zedar left two words that Willam could use. "They're coming," he whispered, reminding his mouth how to form words. "They're coming," reminding his throat how to speak. "They're coming!" reminding himself how to shout.

A final crate tumbled into the wagon. Yonce murmured to the mules, and the wagon pulled out of view. Willam heard it rumble past the inn, heading down the road that had swallowed Tronder, had stolen his bride.

Jullia raced across the room, clutching a large bundle. She panted over her shoulder, "Are you coming?" She disappeared into the courtyard.

Willam's wooden legs lurched him into the empty courtyard where he stood, wits scattered. Stevven brushed past him. "Come on, lad. They're coming."

"They're coming," Willam whispered, offering his entire vocabulary.

Greggor turned to him. "Come along, now." His voice coaxed gently, but Willam's legs would not move. Greggor studied Willam's face, lowered his bundle onto the cobblestones, and put his arm around Willam's shoulders. Greggor guided Willam's faltering steps back into the common room. "You best stay here for now, lad. We'll get you once you're better ready for travel." Greggor's head turned to the double doors, head cocked toward the silent road beyond. "Stall them as best you can. There's a good lad."

Willam stood alone in the silent inn, breath shallow, mouth agape. The air held the memory of roses. He heard the caw of a raven and the distant bark of a dog.

Chapter 40

Conceal

Yonce murmured to the mules, and they picked up their pace. The well-groomed road passed under the wagon, the wheels leaving no trace of their flight. The first bend of the road lay at too great a distance still. Yonce looked over his shoulder at the receding village. No sign of pursuit yet.

The orchards masked much of the village, a roof showing here and there. The midday sun blanched the heavily blossomed trees, and Yonce's heart panged with regret. He had wandered through their rich scent daily, dreaming of the fruit soon to appear.

Bolin rode beside him, clutching the seat so as not to lose it. He pointed and hollered into Yonce's ear. "There! Where the forest crowds the road. We'll leave the road there."

Yonce nodded and murmured to the mules, preparing them for the unexpected route. They would resist the turn, preferring the open road to the uncertainty of the trees. They twitched their ears and slowed their trot. Yonce murmured to keep them in step, balancing each other and the wagon that jostled at their heels.

As they slowed to a walk, Bolin lowered himself, stepped onto the verge, and released his grip on the wagon. Yonce split his attention between the reluctant mules and the woodsman waiting for the wagon to pass. He turned in his seat, curious.

The mules tossed their heads and laid back their ears as the laden wagon bogged, leaving deep ruts in the forest floor. Yonce gave the mules his full attention, murmuring them into renewed effort, and the wagon slogged into the shade of the canopy. Yonce secured the reins, jumped from his seat, and smoothed the near mule's flank as he moved forward to grasp its harness, murmuring his fluid gift.

His eyes swept the ground, looking for firm footing, and guided the team toward a sunny glade. There he paused the straining mules, hushed their snorts, smoothed their necks. He stepped away, constant with his murmurs, to lean and look for Bolin.

Bolin crept, knees bent, hands outstretched to either side. Without hearing it, Yonce knew the woodsman was murmuring the wild ground. The wagon's ruts filled and smoothed, and leaves and unbroken twigs re-wilded their path, leaving no trace of tramping hooves and mired wheels.

As Bolin drew near, Yonce moved to regain his place at the mules' heads. "Wait!" called Bolin. Yonce ran his palms over the mules' necks, murmuring calmness, trust, safety. Bolin left off his murmuring at the wagon's rear, walked to the front of the wagon, and eyed Yonce.

"Are they well?" Bolin asked. "Is the wagon up to the task?"

Yonce eyed the hastily piled crates. "The mules will be fine. We'll repack when we reach the others. We can make it work until then."

"I'll strengthen our path." He looked toward the road, just visible through the trees and underbrush. "I don't think they'll see that we've left the road."

"They might suspect, when they don't see us riding toward High Pass."

"Yes. They might. We'll take care for long enough to make them second-guess."

Bolin walked in front of the wagon, murmuring the forest floor into a compact path. Yonce murmured the mules forward. His heart jumped at a rustling behind them, and he whirled, expecting an enraged posse rushing headlong. The forest remained empty, serene. The rustling came from the ground they had just covered, as it fluffed itself and resettled, Bolin murmuring the re-wilding that hid any sign of their passage. Yonce patted the near mule's neck, calming himself.

Bolin's gift of wild led them true, and the mules relaxed into a smooth rhythm. Yonce walked next to the team, adding an occasional murmur to remind them of their focus, his protection, their strength and accomplishment.

A raven's call broke the silence of the forest, and Cam swooped into view, banked, and landed on Bolin's raised arm. Bolin halted his murmuring to smooth a welcoming hand along Cam's back. He turned to Yonce and explained. "They're waiting for us, about an hour ahead."

Relief flooded Yonce. They had left without knowing if the others got away safely, and their passage, heavily laden as they were, was slow. Knowing the fellowship would regroup within the hour lightened his steps. His murmuring gained an enthusiasm that caused the mules to prick their ears and quicken their pace. Bolin trotted ahead, his murmurs fluid and sure.

Cam launched and flew to an overhanging branch where he waited. Bolin shifted their direction to follow Cam's lead. Yonce's heart lightened further at their increased speed, the certainty of their path. They would reach Rosa, darling Rosa, well before sunset.

Chapter 41

Gifts

"Hosting has been my gift for all my remembrance." Gosikk's eyes glittered from the glorb nestled in his lap. "I built my inn during my youth. Had it built," he amended with a nod to Stevven, "at the insistence of my gift. I knew just how the inn should be, how many rooms, the size of the common room, what to put in the kitchen. The artisans listened to my imaginations and brought them into being. I have led a happy life in that inn, with visitors coming and going, neighbors spending their evenings together." He mused. "The inn became the hearthstone of the village, the place where everyone came together."

Yonce nodded. "I pretty much grew up in the common room. I was there every chance I found."

Gosikk guffawed. "Always underfoot. I put you to work, just to give myself a moment's peace."

"You taught me to murmur."

"Nay, lad. You taught yourself. Tending things, especially animals, is your true gift."

Silence.

Rosa held her own glorb on the boulder next to her, keeping her face in soft shadow. Others held their glorbs so that their faces could be seen, a gesture deemed as friendly in their village. Rosa shadowed her face from a sense of shame.

Gosikk's glorb emphasized his shrug. "Now, hosting holds no charm for me." Dread iced Rosa's heart. Had she caused this, too? Had she broken Gosikk? "The inn seems of another world," Gosikk continued. "There is nothing in me that wants to go back."

"Nor I," said Yonce, tossing his glorb between his hands.

Gosikk motioned his glorb in her direction. "I want only to be with you, Rosa, to be wherever you are." Rosa frowned, embarrassed by his claim. Her eyes darted from face to face as the entire fellowship nodded in agreement.

Greggor spoke. "I don't know how to be a champion, or even how I became one. But it is all I want, Rosa." Draymon turned in his seat to wrinkle his forehead at Greggor, but said nothing.

Heads nodded. Rosa shallowed her breaths, yearned for invisibility. She found no comfort in their words. Heat spread across her face and ice crawled up her spine.

Stevven said, "I didn't have an auntie to frighten me into behaving. I know next to nothing about Spring Maidens or champions. But, I, too, want nothing of my former life. I am here for you, Rosa. I am enthralled."

Katernn said, "Perhaps not enthralled. At least not for me." Rosa grasped Katernn's words, expecting them to confirm her unworthiness. "But I don't want to be anywhere else." Rosa's heart shrank, closed itself from a kindness she didn't deserve.

Jullia said, "I keep thinking about my pantry. I am grateful we had time to retrieve it." Her eyes turned to Stevven. "Thank you." Her eyes glistened.

Katernn yawned and stretched arms overhead. "Oh my stars. Yes. Your pantry." In all remembrance, Jullia had carefully built her pantry. Everyone depended on Jullia's pantry. Now, the village would have to do without. Rosa closed her eyes. Another loss for the village because of her.

"I think it will be useful. Out here on our own, I mean," Jullia ventured. Rosa would have reassured her, had she the wits to gather words. The forest crowding around them held too much mystery. She could not imagine tomorrow, nor any of the days to come. What had she wrought?

Yonce spoke. "Nobody beats Gosikk's cooking."

Gosikk spread his hands. "Cooking is tied to hosting. I've the gift of hosting, to be sure. But cooking makes sense only in the company of guests. When I cook on me own, I'd rather eat a carrot than cook something." Rosa could not believe him. Delicious food always surrounded Gosikk. His familiar smile sank into a frown. "I fear I'll be of no use out here, with just us, and no guests to host. I haven't the heart. Or the gift."

Rosa couldn't understand his meaning, although she could absorb his despair. Her thoughts jostled uselessly, hidden in fog. She could not calm her tumbling emotions. Everything had changed. Everyone had lost everything dear to them. Because of her.

Mackey said, "I cook." He grinned at the wave of disbelief that turned to him. "Aye. It's my gift. I knew it well, before my gift of the drink swallowed it up. Back at the inn just now, I made sure we brought what we'll need."

Bolin broke the ensuing silence. "The forest holds everything we might want, in the way of eating. There's wealth beyond measure here." He swept his glorb in a slow arc, illuminating the nearest trees. "The wild forest is my gift. We have everything we need."

"That's good to know, lad. That will serve us very well," Macky said.

"And my medicinal herbs," said Greggor. "We managed to crate a good supply. We'll be able to keep each other healthy."

Gosikk stood up, his glorb palmed at his side. "We need to travel light, all the same."

"We brought only one wagon and both the mules to pull it," said Greggor.

Gosikk shook his head. "Even that might be too much. We won't be able to use roads much."

Stevven said, "I'll murmur the wagon into something smaller, better suited for the goods we carry."

Yonce said, "We couldn't leave the mules behind, Gosikk. Who'd care for them?"

Gosikk looked to Rosa. "What say you, lass?"

Rosa shook her head and hunched herself onto her boulder.

Miichal spoke for Tronder. "Let the Maiden be. She needs time." Relief and gratitude welled into Rosa's eyes. She blinked, desperate to keep tears from betraying her roiling emotions.

Katernn stood, rested a hand on her hip, playfully tossed her glorb up and down with the other. Rosa let her eyes follow the path of the tossed glorb, let it hypnotize her into a trance. "Setting out on this adventure feels right to me, and I'm betting it feels right to everyone else as well." Katernn's voice barely penetrated Rosa's stupor.

Katernn paused her glorb tossing, breaking Rosa's trance. She counted on her fingers. "We got Rosa away. We gathered what we need. We got us away." She looked at the forest surrounding them. "We have this beautiful spot for the night. What more could we want for?"

Rosa wrapped her arms around her drawn knees, buried her forehead in her elbow. Tears dampened her sleeve.

Chapter 42

Lesson, Redux

As the morning sun warmed the campsite, Miichal lowered himself to Rosa's boulder and stretched his long legs before him. Tronder moved to stand behind him.

Everyone must hear.

Miichal's voice carried around the glade, but his attention lay with Rosa. "We'll wait until everyone can settle, and then it's time to talk with the Maiden." Her wide eyes flew to his; her face blanched.

As the champions gathered, he spoke, his voice kind. "There are many things you need to learn; not all at once, but over the next season; maybe two seasons." Rosa's lips thinned into a frown. Her chin quivered. "These lessons are for Rosa," Miichal scanned the others, "but everyone must hear." His pause allowed time for the gravity of the moment to capture their attention. "If we all understand to the same degree, in the same way, we can work in concert, and better serve Rosa."

Greggor wiped his hands and took a seat. Jullia covered the herbs arranged on a drying tray, setting the remaining stems back in Bolin's foraging basket and turned her attention to Miichal. Pharlan settled next to Mackey, who rubbed her ears and rested his hand on her back.

What do they know?

"What have you seen and heard the last two days? Since leaving the inn? Anything unusual?"

Stevven replied without hesitation. "Rosa hasn't spoken."

"Yes," Miichal said.

Yes.

"Are you afraid to speak?" Miichal leaned toward Rosa, studying her face. She drew back, refusing to answer. "I'm not surprised." Miichal's gentle voice carried to all ears. "The events, since *I've* known you at least, have happened quickly and forcefully. They would silence even an elder, rich in wisdom. I expect they've shattered your soul." Rosa blinked back tears.

Miichal smiled and picked up her clenched hand, nested it between his own. After the joy of reuniting with Tronder and the drama of the fellowship's unplanned flight, it had been Tronder's sensibility that propelled him through the steps that followed, with barely a thought of his own. The fellowship out of breath, bereft of familiarity, stumbling bravely through their days.

They needed a more sustainable footing, *and only the Maiden can bring that.*

Miichal nodded his understanding and agreement with Tronder's conclusion.

"Only the Maiden can bring back our balance." He squeezed her hand. "We need you, Rosa. Let us help bring you into your natural strength. Your gift of inner strength."

Rosa's eyes widened, and she tried to pull her fist away. Miichal tightened his grasp, waited for her to settle. "Not all at once, Rosa. Let us help you take the steps that lead to your inner strength."

Her brow wrinkled. She shook her head ever so slightly, but they all saw it. The fellowship sighed at her denial. They sank back, crossed arms, drew knees to chins, closed down. Jullia lifted her hand to cover her frown. Mackey fidgeted.

"Let me begin your first lesson, which will probably be the easiest path to understanding my meaning. I actually yelled the lesson to you at the inn, at a time of great need. Let me tell the lesson more fully, now that we find ourselves in a peaceful setting.

"Maiden. You cannot demand that someone change what they're doing, who they are. As Spring Maiden, others have no choice but to follow your command. People are too complex, and you know only a small part of their story. Even those you've known your entire life." His eyes grazed the circled gathering. "Maiden, here is the core: You may only command yourself."

Think back...

"Think back to each unfortunate consequence over the last days, the days since the double moons. Every interaction proceeded as it should have, until you demanded someone be different." Miichal saw the truth clearly, and chose words carefully to describe the truth to the others, to Rosa especially. "You will be safe, others will be safe, once you learn to refrain from demanding something from others. Control *yourself*, not others."

He saw Rosa's eyes clear. The wrinkled brow smoothed itself. Her lips parted, softening her frown. "Do you feel clarity wash over you?" She nodded. "That clarity tells you that you're seeing *truth*. That feeling is your signal that you are aligning yourself with all that is." He opened her fist, smoothed her hand. "Always look for that feeling of clarity. Then you will *know* it's safe to proceed."

Her eyebrow lifted.

"Yes. It is safe for you to speak. If you take care, you will harm no one." Still she hesitated. "You can ask questions. You can make suggestions. Observations. Insights. Right now...your lesson right now, is to simply avoid making *demands* of others. Can you do that?" She nodded briskly and drew in her first deep breath in days.

"Where is Willam?" she asked.

Chapter 43

Confusion

They told the story of Willam, his confusion, his frozen mind, his dysfunction.

Rosa wrinkled her forehead. "What did I say to make him that way?"

Not hers.

Miichal elaborated. "Nothing that I heard you say would have caused his confusion."

Not completely.

"It may be that your own confusion seeped into Willam somehow, what with him being closely bonded to you."

Katernn said, "Willam had his own habit of cowering, I would wager. Given the bellowing that mayhap dominated his village, his upbringing."

Yonce nodded at Rosa. "You both have that in common, seems to me. You and Willam."

His vow.

Miichal sucked in his breath, understanding washing over him. He took Rosa's hand. "Willam made a vow to you, a wed-locking vow. He vowed to live with you always, in full obedience and loving loyalty. He would not come with us. His vow is broken. No one can break a vow to a Spring Maiden without consequence."

Jullia's eyes were huge, her mouth slack. "He wouldn't come, Rosa. We had to leave him behind." Her tone pleaded understanding.

Greggor nodded. "I told him we would come back for him when he was able to travel. He only needs time."

Mackey shook his head. "Nay. Willam stood broken the moment Rosa rode away. His wits scattered. It's not that he *would* not follow. He *could* not follow."

Rosa straightened, raised her chin. "I want...We have to..."

"Silence!" roared Miichal.

Rosa raised her arms to shield her head.

"Silence, Maiden." Miichal repeated gently, reigning himself in. She had to learn, but kindness was the tool to smooth her way. "Your mildest request becomes our command." How to point her in a better direction? "For now, for a long while perhaps, speak with questions. Your questions will draw solutions from us."

Rosa quenched her cower and sat quietly for several moments. "Can we go for him? Can we return to the village and bring him with us?"

Danger.

Miichal shook his head, a slight motion. "I believe we'll never return to the village. That village, at any rate."

Rosa's eyes went wide, her mouth forming a silent, "Oh." She drooped.

"All is always well, Maiden," Miichal assured her. "If Willam were meant to come with us, he would be here. We have to trust in the hidden path of the Spring Maiden."

"What is to become of their wedlocking?" Stevven asked.

Steadfast.

"It remains secure, despite the broken vow. Wedlocking is separate from vows." Miichal said. He closed his eyes, searched for a more complete truth, for Tronder's prompt. Tronder remained silent. Miichal shook his head. "I don't know the exact unfolding, but Willam is steadfast." He tasted Tronder's disappointment. Was there more he could say? He could feel nothing that held certainty. He shook his head again. "He has a role to fulfill that kept him from following us. I can say no more." Tronder's ears drooped. "The time has not come to know more." Tronder pawed the ground.

Miichal patted Rosa's hand, turned away, and made his way apart from the others. Tronder followed.

You knew more. Miichal's accusation came swiftly.

You could have known more if you would trust yourself.

You knew more and yet said nothing.

You must know for yourself. Speak your truth. I will not always be with you.

A familiar dread spread through Miichal. *I am nothing without you. That has been proven.*

You are more than you believe yourself to be. You must build on that.

I am nothing.

As long as you believe that, it will be true. Tronder's words paused. *The Maiden has much to learn, as do you. As do all of you. Grow not complacent. You must learn! You must learn to bring yourself out of your own confusion.*

Teach me!

I have taught you well. You must put the teachings into practice. Look within.

Miichal shook his head. *There is too much to risk.*

Practice when it's easier. Throughout your day. Practice when it's easier. Your certainty will grow.

Chapter 44

Alone

Rosa stared at the stars. Sleep often eluded her, since the night of the double moons, regardless of how far they journeyed, how trying the events of the day. The forest nights were filled with voices and melodies, calls and trills, breezes and moving water. Rosa, surprisingly, her sleepless nights.

Except for her dismay over Willam's absence. Could it have happened another way? Miichal's sweeping of her onto Tronder's back, their thunderous leaving of the inn, the village, had overwhelmed her sensibilities. She had complied; had not thought of resistance. Now, there lived a Willam-shaped hole in her heart. If only she had known. If only she had thought, resisted, implored. Would Willam be with them now? Would she have his arms to lull her into sleep on this glorious night?

Or would some other harm have befallen anyone within hearing of her unthinking voice?

The forest sought to fill the Willam-shaped hole in Rosa's heart. She heard its song, and knew it sang for her. She smiled and watched a falling star blaze across the moonless sky. She loved the nights filled with moonlight. She loved the moonless nights filled with starlight, a night such as tonight. Their delicate brilliance drifted across their stage, a stage bordered by treetops and high ridges; treetops that swayed their nocturnal dance; ridges brined in white that shown beneath stars and moons alike.

Rosa heard the call of an owl and its answering echo from some distant glade. She breathed the scents of flowering bulbs and watery herbs and the busy soil over which her sleeping cloth spread. She stretched her arm outside the cloth, to press her palm onto the forest's floor. The soil and its wealth responded to her touch and pressed itself against her skin in cheerful greeting.

Her awareness spread to follow the interlaced networks that spread themselves across the valley, splashing up the foothills to kiss the feet of mountains. Crawling things and their burrowing partners brightened at the passing of Spring Maiden's touch. The realm of Below glowed and quickened, awakening after generations of slumber. Rosa relished the realm of Below and marveled at the gift her palm bestowed.

After a moment that held eternity, Rosa threw back her sleeping cloth, and ignoring her slippers, gathered herself to stand beneath the sparkling heavens. With measured steps she strolled away from sleeping cloths that draped themselves over the fellowship, as they breathed their night away, steps that took her from the wagon and its sleeping mules, away from her twelve that championed her with every glance and motion. For she had her night to fill.

She followed the song of moving water, which led her to the bank of a wandering brook, slow and wide as it whittled its path across the forest floor. She sat on a boulder and lowered her feet into the busy stream and felt its song rise along her spine to burst in its fullness into the air around her. The brook sang of its journey from distant peaks, of its gathering of myriad trickles, to splash around boulders and beneath melting banks of crusted snow. Her awareness flowed downstream, where the brook joined fellow brooks, tumbling, united, toward their distant home in the sea.

Rosa held no knowledge of the sea, and yet she recognized it through the song of the brook and all its kin. She smelled the salt air, heard the pounding of waves, and glimpsed the expanse that stretched beyond sight, glistened under the same stars that sparkled their light onto this trickling brook. The brook danced and splashed its delight at the touch of Spring Maiden, and Rosa marveled anew at the breadth of awareness that her submerged feet lent to her imaginings, soothing her emptied heart.

The Maiden rose and trailed along a different path to wind her way back to the wagon and her sleeping champions who breathed below the faint hint of dawn. Rosa wrapped herself in her sleeping cloth and allowed the awareness of enthralled realms and broad seas to melt away as she at last slipped into sleep, even as the forest's song grew with the light of dawn. Birds and leaves and all manner of flying and roaming creatures stretched and yawned and joined the morning's chorus to jostle the day awake.

Chapter 45

Bradi

She rarely flew past dawn. The night was her domain, with her silent wings and enormous eyes. But the wandering people drew her, and they wandered during daylight, so Bradi followed them on her silent wings, despite the approach of eastern light in the shaded forest under its thick canopy.

She swept through her ancient forest that was at last awakening. After generations of dreaming through sluggish days and indifferent nights, the double moons had sparked an awakening. On her daily rounds, Bradi's heart rose in expectation of what was to come, a blind expectation, filled with curiosity of what blossomed toward her. She heard the forest stretch and flex, heard it whisper to its devas and sprites, coaxing them back from the realms to which they had retreated.

The awakening forest spurred her on, and she followed the rag-tag wanderers as they bumbled across the forest floor. The forest knew their names, so Bradi knew their names as well. She had followed them for days. Although they showed respect for the forest, they could not yet hear it, or even know that it could be heard. One man, Bolin, was familiar to the forest. He was an awakening friend. He guided the wanderers, taking care to not trample, not gouge.

One of the wanderers, Rosa, glowed. The forest had heard of her coming long before makta grew on High Pass, long before the double moons. Spring Maiden. The forest, the entire valley, had readied themselves for her arrival. Snow cleared. Air warmed. Birds appeared early from their winter seclusions. Insects hatched and grew and molted. Flowers opened and seedlings straightened and stretched furled leaves.

The early spring stepped hand-in-hand with the forest's awakening, which reached deeper still. An ancient wisdom raised its head and yawned after its deep slumber. The forest peeked from behind time-worn barriers and reached toward the sun. The soil grew busy, its biome awakening in all directions, enlivening ancient networks that sang its song forgotten. Roots lengthened and spread. Branches stretched and splayed. Ferns unfurled and wafted their subtle scents onto the breeze.

Bradi flew through her forest and blended into its songs. She heard the melodies and remembered the harmonies. She knew where to fly, where to follow, how to watch. She watched the wanderers, the kind one, the glowing one, all of them.

She swooped above the awakening encampment, some figures motionless beneath their cloths, some moving sleepily, rubbing eyes, yawning. Steam rose from an early kettle. She landed on a branch reaching high above the encampment and peered between leaves, watching.

Especially, she watched the one, the one whose name the forest whispered to her with a power that opened her heart, filled her with reverence. She knew the forest's whispers, its song. And she knew that this was the morning that she would speak his name.

Yonce.

She saw him pause his murmuring of the drowsy mules, look around.

Yonce.

He looked but could not find her. She sent a piercing arrow to his heart, and he swiveled, looked up, found her eyes, held her in his gaze. She felt his own arrow pierce her heart, and she opened her wings, fell forward, and glided silently to land on his uplifted arm. He bent his head; she lifted her crown; their foreheads met; their eyes closed. Their beloved companionship birthed, drenched in morning sunlight.

Chapter 46

Revolt

Rosa wanted to scream. She knew Bolin meant well, but oh the stars! She could not face yet another ailing tree.

"Could we find some bushes, Bolin? Or perhaps an orchard? Flowers! Can we work with flowers?" Rosa's voice slipped into a whine. Forgotten were her nighttime wanderings, her roaming of brooks and realms below. Her spirit strained against the restrictions of repetitive sameness, of anguishing monotony.

"The trees need your help the most, Rosa." He scratched his chin, thoughtful. "Cam suggests that you need only be near, for flowers and such to find their balance. The trees need more."

"But, why do I have to spend so much time with them? Why don't they get better, if I were to simply pass by but not stop, like the flowers and bushes?" Rosa stubbornly ignored his explanation. She only wanted her duty with the trees to be finished. She could not imagine beyond her boredom and restlessness.

"Do you not care for trees, Rosa?"

"I asked a different question." Why would he not answer her? Rosa wordlessly accused Bolin of her own stubbornness, searching for an angle that might free her. Despite her roiling rebellion, she took great care to not demand anything of Bolin. Of anyone. Great care. She took her lessons seriously.

"Trees are ancient, compared to bushes and flowers, Rosa. Their maladies lay entrenched." Bolin paused. "Should we go back to camp?"

Rosa's heart softened. She heaved a great sigh and hung her head. "How many more are there?" She could not quite remember the nurturing of Bolin's seedlings into saplings. The magic of that day remained elusive, and she could not recall it, hampered by the Willam-shaped hole in her heart as she was. It did not always flow easily, this Spring Maiden mystery.

"Cam can find as many as you have the patience for." He gazed at the trees surrounding them. "This is an ancient forest. No one has cared for it in many years. Generations, most likely." He turned his gaze to Rosa. "But we'll stop, whenever you want. Maybe you've practiced enough patience for one day."

Rosa drooped. Bolin knew her well, and she could not shrink from his honesty. 'Twas true. She had not the gift of patience. She closed her eyes and took a deep breath, rubbed her thumb across her itching nose. "Perhaps we could do a few more."

Bolin's face lightened. "The forest is ever grateful for your care, Rosa. Whatever you can do for it benefits it greatly."

He stood five paces from her. All the champions kept their distance, Bolin especially. Their words conveyed respect and concern, but Rosa often suspected the twelve were afraid; afraid of *her*. Could that be right? Were they afraid? Loneliness engulfed her.

"Do you ever miss the days when we used to wander the forest together, Bolin? You, me, and Romane?"

"I hardly remember."

Rosa swallowed her disappointment. He didn't want to remember back to the time when they had been friends. Or perhaps he didn't want to remember Romane. Or maybe he missed his own forest, abandoned days ago. "Where does Cam want us to go next?"

"This way, m'lady." He gestured and led the way.

M'lady. Rosa sighed. She tromped her way through what was left of the afternoon. They visited dozens of trees of every shape and size. They became a blur. She knelt at the foot of each, wrapped her arms around the trunk as far as she could reach, pressed her forehead against the tree, and poured love into it.

A spark of happiness lit her heart with each embrace, as she felt life quicken within the tree. But the sparked happiness was short-lived, given her Willam-shaped hole in her heart, and shone not as brightly as the day lengthened, given her subdued but not quenched rebelliousness. She had enough wits to suspect that the sparks came from the trees, some semblance of gratitude for her help. But she could detect no love from neither giants nor saplings, nor any size between. They could not touch her holed heart. Or perhaps her rebellion alone kept her from feeling any magic. What she could feel was that her feet ached. Her arms hung heavy at her sides.

As daylight waned, Bolin led them back to camp. Or perhaps it was Cam who led them. She didn't care or even wonder. She didn't feel more patient than she had that morning, despite another day of practice. She wouldn't sleep any better than she had the night before or the night before that, despite another day of purposeful activity. Tomorrow would be much the same as today, healing the forest while the fellowship moved their camp ever farther west.

Things would be better if only Willam were with them. She wasn't certain of how or why, only the certainty that it must be true, that his presence would put everything to right. She shuffled her slippers in the forest duff and hung her head.

The addition of Bradi to their fellowship delighted everyone, wild thing that she was, including Rosa. She coaxed the owl onto her arm whenever the opportunity presented itself. But Bradi would stay but a moment before flapping back to Yonce, bumping her forehead against his chin. That gentle bump swamped Rosa in a fresh ache of loneliness.

Spring followed them loyally. They didn't find the deep winter that Bolin predicted in the forest where he had harvested seedlings. It should have been encased in snow and ice still. Bolin said, again and again, "This can't be. This is impossible." And yet meadow flowers fluttered their heads in the breeze and birds trilled from above and all around.

Miichal merely said, "She's Spring Maiden, Bolin. Spring will always precede her and trail after."

Katernn, ever seeking the reason for things, asked, "Why do the aunties tell only stories of tragedy and doom? Bringing spring is surely the greatest gift. Why don't the aunties sing those praises?"

Miichal answered. "Early spring can be attributed to many things, brushed aside as rare but not necessarily magical. Stories of early springs are thought exaggerated and easily discounted. But the story of Victtor? That story will persist and grow darker with each telling."

Rosa's spirits sank further. She sighed a great sigh. Even her magic could not change things, it seemed. The Spring Maiden tales would remain stubbornly terrifying.

Mackey handed Rosa a bowl heaped with favorite morsels, a broad smile on his face. "Jullia found some lovely greens for us today, Rosa. Her spices and herbs might lift your spirits."

They all tried to lift her spirits. In return, she tried to show them lifted spirits. But she knew they weren't fooled. They watched her from the corners of their eyes, their stories stiff and predictable, their laughter forced. They were trapped in her misery, perhaps even more than she. Self-doubt and self-blame tormented her, and she could not find her way out.

One evening, Rosa slipped away from the circled glorbs earlier than usual and wrapped herself in her sleeping cloths, determined to find sleep to escape her dreary thoughts. She squeezed her eyes closed, her holed heart shutting out the forest's song.

"Rosa." The whisper breathed into her ear. A hand shook her shoulder. "Rosa."

Rosa rolled onto her back, peered at the shadow leaning over her. "What?"

"Come."

The night pressed around them, black and silent. Mackey helped Rosa stand and guided her hand to grasp Pharlan's fur. The trio crept away from the champions who slept unaware, using Pharlan's keen eyes as their guide. Rosa felt calm and trusting as they wound past trees, until she sensed someone ahead, waiting invisibly.

"Rosa." Rosa recognized Jullia's voice and the stealth that sheathed it. "Rosa, what would you think about returning to our village? We promised we would go back for Willam. Perhaps now is the time."

Rosa's heart brightened at the thought of Willam. "What about the others? Why go alone, instead of together?"

Jullia took a deep breath. "Not everyone agrees. Some feel it's too soon. But I think *you* should decide, Rosa. Do you want to find Willam? So he can be with us?"

Relief swept through Rosa. "Yes," she whispered. "Oh, yes. Yes." She strained her eyes, trying to see Jullia's face. Neither stars nor moons shone this night. "Should we bring glorbs?"

"No, no," Mackey answered. "They will do more to reveal our presence than to guide our path. Pharlan's eyes are true."

A long journey lay before them. Pharlan led the trio through the long night until dawn kissed the forest's canopy, grew strong enough to splash down to where they trod. They released their grasp on Pharlan's fur, more easily able to follow her by sight, to move at a faster pace.

Into the morning and throughout the day, the quartet made their way through glades and across meadows raucous with spring. Rosa's enthusiasm fed them all, and they had no need of rest. Rosa was certain of the rightness of their mission. Her fingertips tingled, and her heart pounded. She felt driven, sweeping the others along with her, trotting over the forest floor, through meadows, splashing across streams.

As twilight dimmed the sky, they reached the familiar fields, village rooftops poking above the orchard, its branches now peeping with emerging fruit.

"Let's find Romane." Jullia's voice was low, hushed, even though the village's ears remained distant. "He'll know where to find Willam." Rosa nodded.

"We'll wait for you here," Mackey said, nodding to Pharlan, who sat at Mackey's side, panting. "The fewer we are, the less likelihood of discovery."

Rosa chose her careful words. "If Pharlan were to come with us, she could lead us. She would know if others came near, and warn us."

"We should wait for full dark, then."

Was Mackey agreeing with her because he had no choice? "Or perhaps we should go on now," she ventured. He didn't answer. "Or I could go by myself. Even less chance of discovery."

"No!" Their combined gasps rang into the twilight.

"No. We'll all go together, m'lady."

Rosa couldn't tell if his agreement was forced or true. She didn't know what to decide, how to move forward.

"If something happened to you, we wouldn't know about it, or how to help," Jullia said. "I would feel better if we kept together."

Rosa nodded. Misgivings filled her, yet it was most likely wiser to follow Jullia's wishes. They would wait for nightfall and go together.

As night swallowed twilight, stars once again filled the cloudless sky. Such was their brilliance, lighting the world below, that Pharlan's guidance of their steps was unnecessary, leaving her free to focus on seeing and smelling what lay at a distance. The quartet slunk along the edges of fields until they gained the shelter of the inn, once the center of their lives. Rosa felt the eeriness of its desolate courtyard and shuttered windows, a desolation that seeped beyond the walls of the inn, seemingly enveloping the entire village.

No lights glowed in windows. No voices bandied back and forth. No laughter drifted along the empty road. A shiver crawled up Rosa's spine as they crept from inn to Mandra's garden gate. The tent had been removed, leaving behind a garden trampled by uncaring steps.

Mackey's hand cupped her ear and whispered. "Pharlan and I'll wait here, keeping watch. You two lasses go and rouse our Romane."

Rosa nodded and traded glances with Jullia. Keeping to the shadows, they slunk through the garden, raised the latch of the back door, which soundlessly swung into the familiar kitchen. Rosa took Jullia's hand and led her to the curtain that hung in the doorway separating the sleeping room. She turned, and lifting a shushing finger to her lips, she dropped Jullia's hand and slipped through the doorway alone.

Familiar scents and shapes filled Rosa with a nostalgic aching. Her childhood rose to swallow her, engulf her with memories and swirling emotions. She paused to calm her heart.

Marlow's snores rumbled in her parent's corner. Rosa gathered her resolve and moved along the near wall, taking the few steps that led to Romane's bed. She bent over the mounded sleeping cloths to shake his shoulder awake.

A scrape behind her gave a too-brief warning before a rough hand covered her mouth with a stinking cloth. Powerful arms held her silent struggle until darkness overcame her.

Chapter 47

Pursuit

"How do we find them?" Miichal paced, wiping his forearm across his eyes.

"Cam will search," Bolin offered.

"And Bradi. They're our best bet." Yonce paused a moment. "They headed east. Bradi saw them, but paid little heed."

Miichal could feel Bolin watching him. Everyone was watching him. He always had the answers, didn't he? Or he was supposed to. But not today. No. Not today.

At first light, Rosa's absence had raised no alarm. She often wandered with one or another champion, learning some small thing, some large thing, or simply escaping the pressure of learning too much too quickly. When Rosa and Jullia didn't return for the midday meal, the usual assumption would have been that they had taken lunch with them. Usually, even a missed lunch would raise no sense of alarm.

The thing was, Mackey was missing, too. That was odd. Mackey always cooked the midday meal. After, they would pack up, move camp, and wait for Rosa to return. Mackey's absence was what set Miichal to wondering. It was then he admitted that he couldn't sense Rosa at all.

We should look for them.

Tronder didn't respond. He was doing that more and more lately, leaving Miichal to understand things for himself. Miichal felt anxiety and irritation grip his gut, just as it always did when Tronder went silent. Now, with no midday meal, no Mackey, no Jullia, no Rosa, Miichal's nerves bristled. Now, he wanted Tronder's help.

He strode to where Tronder stood, chewing on leaves from a low bush. He smoothed his hands along Tronder's neck, willing the horse to acknowledge him. Tronder raised his head, looked into Miichal's eyes, and continued chewing. They stared at one another.

How do we find them?

Silence.

Miichal drew a deep breath, closed his eyes, and bent to press his forehead against Tronder's cheek. Tronder chewed.

Miichal fought down rising panic. He wiped his sweaty palms along Tronder's neck. He settled his mind, let his thoughts drift, waited for one to bring him insight.

Pacing helped. He turned from Tronder with a final pat, and paced.

Miichal pushed away his panic and faced the others. They expected him to lead, so lead he must.

"Right." He watched the others. They watched him. "We've lost most of the day. Maybe most of last night, too." He looked to Greggor and Stevven. "Did anyone see them go?"

Greggor narrowed his eyes. "We would have said, had we seen anything."

"Bradi saw them, as I've said. Headed east." Yonce stood, hands on hips, staring at him.

"Right." Miichal looked at the ground, shook his head. "Of course. Just thinking out loud." He took another deep breath. "Let's secure camp." They needed something to do while they waited. "Once Cam and Bradi find them, we'll be ready to leave."

"Camp is already secure," said Gosikk. "We're ready to leave now."

"If they're headed east, they're probably headed back to the village," Katernn said.

"We don't know that yet," Miichal huffed.

They were all watching him, questioning him with their silence. Why was it always up to him?

"I've got to clear my head." Miichal turned and strode into the forest.

He heard the crunch of footsteps following him. He glanced back. Katernn. He waited for her to catch up.

"Talk to me," Katernn said.

"Rosa's gone!"

"We know."

"I don't know where she's gone."

"None of us do."

"I always know where she is."

"So do we."

"No. I don't mean knowing she's with Bolin or sleeping behind the wagon. I mean that..." His voice trailed off. He couldn't find the words. He jabbed his forehead with clustered fingertips. "I always *know*. I can sense it. I can close my eyes, and just *know* where she is."

"So can we."

"What?"

"We all know, instinctually, where she is. How far away she is. Whether she's hungry, or asleep." She wrinkled her brow at him. "We don't know how we know, but we always know."

"You do?"

"Yes."

"How about now?"

"No. None of us can feel her just now."

Miichal stared in disbelief and floundered through his thoughts. "How can you know?"

"You mean knowing where she is?" Miichal nodded. "We're champions." She shrugged. "I guess it's part of being a champion."

Miichal's knees began shaking, and he clumped onto a boulder. "I thought it was just me."

"You seem to think that a lot." She sat next to him, watched his face.

Miichal bent forward and held his head in his hands. "I do?"

"Yes, Miichal. The rest of us will agree on something, and then you walk in and declare the obvious as some kind of a command, or insight, or something. It's pretty arrogant, truth be told."

"How is it that I don't know this?"

"You keep to yourself. You get lost in your thoughts and don't pay attention to what's going on with the rest of us." She watched him. "You're a loner."

"Why has nobody said anything?"

Katernn shrugged. "It wouldn't be kind. Or helpful, more's the like."

Miichal leaned back, slid lower on his boulder, leaned back his head. He stared at overhanging branches. "Tronder won't talk to me."

"Maybe that's a good thing."

"Why would that be a good thing?"

"Because Tronder's doing it."

"What's that supposed to mean?"

"He's pretty smart, our Tronder. If he stops doing something, it's probably a good idea that he stops." She waited. "Why do you think he's stopped?"

"He says I need to understand things for myself."

"Well, do you? Do you need to understand things for yourself?"

"He knows so much. He always knows the best thing to do. He always knows what's going on. From the very start. Things always went better when I listened to him."

"That was probably the only way to get things started. Now that you know more, maybe it's time for you to accept responsibility and make decisions for yourself."

Silence.

"When I lost him? When our bond got...crossed, and I was with Pharlan? I was pathetic. I had no idea what to do, what to say."

"That was a pretty traumatic time. A lot happened that night, for all of us. Of course you were thrown. Anyone would have been."

"But afterward. When everything calmed down? I still couldn't think straight. I still didn't know what to do."

"This is different."

"Why?"

"Because you have Tronder again. Because he's telling you to start figuring things out for yourself. He's very wise. You should trust him."

"I do!"

"Do you?"

"Yes!"

"Then follow his advice. Start figuring things out for yourself." She got up and brushed dust from her overalls. "Start trusting yourself." She stood there, waiting.

Miichal took in a jagged breath. "I don't know what to do."

"None of us do." She waited. "But we'll figure it out." Waited longer. "Come on. Let's go back and talk with the others." He didn't move. She toed his shoe. "Come on, Miichal. Maybe you could try trusting us, along with all the other trust exercises Tronder wants you to do." He looked at her. "We're champions. We have a lot going for us."

Miichal clambered to his feet, brushed himself off, and glinted up through overhanging branches. "It's as good a start as any, I guess."

"There you go!" she mocked. "That's showing us you trust us!"

He crossed his arms and stared at his feet, embarrassed at her reaction.

"Come on." She jerked her head toward camp. "Baby steps. Trust is built on baby steps. You'll get there."

She's right.

Oh, now you speak up!

Chapter 48

Disjointed

Rosa swam up, out of the black and groaned. She blinked at the light seeping in around the edges of a boarded window. The stinking rag was pushed onto her face. After a weak struggle, she sank back into the black.

***

This time, no light peeked. She squinted into utter darkness, coughed. She turned away from the stink of the rag, but it found her anyway. Dizziness took her down.

***

The cold woke her. Her hand searched for a sleeping cloth to pull over her shoulders. Her hand forgot its search as the stinking rag pressed over her face.

Chapter 49

Contact

Bolin sat up, almost spilling his bowl of beans. "Cam found Pharlan." He stared at the others. "They're at the village."

"I knew it!" swore Katernn. "Jullia couldn't leave Romane alone. She had to go back for him. I *knew* she would." She scrunched her eyebrows. "But why did she take Rosa with her?"

"Bradi's coming back," Yonce reported. "We'll need her eyes in the night forest."

Bolin continued relaying Cam's messages. "Cam doesn't know where Rosa is. Only Pharlan. Pharlan is frantic. She doesn't know where Mackey is. She can't find any of them."

"What *does* she know?" Miichal asked.

"They went to the village to find Willam." The group went still, thoughtful. "They were in Mandra's garden," Bolin related.

"I knew it! I knew she went for Romane!"

"Hush, Katernn. Let Cam tell us." Greggor patted the air in front of him, quieting her outburst.

"They were in Mandra's garden. Jullia believed that Romane would know where to find Willam."

"I knew it," hissed Katernn.

"Jullia and Rosa went into the house to find Romane. They didn't come out. Mackey went in to find them, shutting out Pharlan. Mackey didn't come out. There were lots of voices; shouting. Then nothing. Pharlan was trapped in the garden all night. She clawed through a rotten board in the fence and escaped. She could find no scent of anyone. She doesn't know where they are."

"Will Cam bring her here? Back here?"

Bolin closed his eyes, listening.

"Pharlan won't leave without Mackey."

"Mackey is probably locked up somewhere," Greggor suggested.

"Pharlan won't leave without Mackey."

"They may have taken Mackey somewhere else," Draymon added.

"Pharlan won't leave without Mackey."

"I should go." Miichal stood.

"Why? What can you do?" Gosikk asked.

"I can help Pharlan find them."

"As could we all," pointed out Katernn with a meaningful glare to Miichal.

"Yes. Yes, we all could. But I can ride Tronder, get there quickly."

"I should go, too," Bolin said. "I know the village and the forest. Cam and I can help find them."

"We should all go," said Yonce. "All of us can help."

Michael shook his head. "It's true that the more of us help, the better our chances of finding them. It's also easier for *them* to find *us*. Plus, if all of us go, our travel will be too slow. Tronder and I can be there more quickly, if we go alone."

"I'll ride Tronder with you," Bolin argued. "Cam has the best chance of seeing something, now we know where to look. I should go."

"Tronder can't carry both of us," Miichal said.

Don't be stupid. Of course I can.

Miichal backtracked. "Tronder says he can." He looked at the others. "What will the rest of you do, while we're gone?"

"We'll figure it out, lad," said Gosikk.

"Of course." Miichal nodded. Trust was a hard thing to build, especially at a time like this.

This is the best time to learn trust.

Miichal nodded again. "The three of us can go, and Cam...and Bradi?...can help us find each other once we've found Rosa." He saw Katernn's renewed glare. "How does that sound?" he added hesitantly.

Stevven said, "And Jullia and Mackey."

Miichal looked at the ground and nodded curtly. "Yes, of course. And Jullia and Mackey." He kept saying the wrong thing. When would he get it right?

Bolin moved toward Tronder. "Time to go."

Both men mounted the horse, and Tronder turned east. As he picked up speed, they leaned forward over his neck, hands knotted in his mane.

Tronder covered ground at breakneck speed. Miichal knew to not distract him with questions, questions that cluttered his mind. How would they find her? Would they find her? Why hadn't he been able to know where she was? For an entire two days now.

She didn't want you to know.

She can block me at will?

Tronder thundered on. Miichal worried that he might tire quickly at this speed. They might have to walk most of the way.

Tronder didn't tire. They rode into the night, and at long last, with starlight brightening their way, they skirted the forest near the village and slowed to a walk. They slid from Tronder's back; Cam fluttered down to land on Bolin's shoulder, who reached up to smooth black feathers as Cam butted his head against Bolin's ear. Pharlan crept from beneath a low bush and sat under Miichal's hand, which automatically scratched her ears. Pharlan panted and let out a soft whine.

"Now what?" Bolin asked.

"Let's see what we can find."

"What can we find that Cam and Pharlan couldn't find?"

"We can open doors."

Chapter 50

Search

The search didn't take long.

Bolin eased through Mandra's garden gate and propped it open with a stone, to prevent a repeat entrapment of Pharlan. Just in case they would be taken, just as Rosa and the others had been taken. Pharlan eagerly led them to the back door, which Bolin opened slowly. Pharlan pushed her way in.

"No one is here," reported Bolin.

"How can you know?" Miichal whispered.

"Pharlan told Cam."

"Pharlan and Cam can speak to each other?"

"Well, yeah."

"Do they speak to Tronder?"

"Tronder's not a champion." Bolin wished Miichal would save his questions until later. Keeping track of Cam and Pharlan was enough to think about right now. Apparently, Miichal figured that out, because he went silent.

Pharlan padded into the sleeping room and the remaining two rooms.

"Lots of scents here. It's confusing," Bolin whispered to Miichal.

Pharlan pushed past the two men and trotted out the door. They followed her across the garden and into the street. Cam landed on Bolin's shoulder as soon as they cleared the trees.

There's nothing to see from above. I'd rather stay with you.
It's pretty dark to see, I expect.
That's part of it.

Bolin smoothed Cam's back, pleased with his presence.

"Let's check the inn. Maybe we can learn something there," Miichal suggested.

Bolin nodded, and they made their way along the road, keeping to shadows.

"No one's here either," Bolin said. He pushed the double doors. They didn't budge. "Maybe in back."

They tried all the doors, but the inn was shut tight, barred from the inside. Bolin looked up at the roof and said, "I know a way in."

He climbed a maple whose limbs reached over the inn. Lowering himself onto the roof, he crouched and made his way to a dormer. This latch hadn't worked for years. As long as Stevven hadn't fixed it during the remodel...

He hadn't.

Bolin shouldered his way through the window after Cam. He trotted down the stairs to open the back door for Miichal and Pharlan. Tonder waited in the courtyard. They made a circuit of the entire inn, looking for clues. Miichal disappeared into his own room and returned carrying a wrapped packet.

"I should have brought this before. I was in such a rush to get the Maiden away, I didn't think of it. It's a miracle it's still here."

"What is it?" Bolin asked.

"Makta."

"Makta!?! Where did you find makta?"

"At High Pass. When we first came through. It'll help Tronder, after all the galloping."

"Lemme see."

Miichal passed the packet to Bolin, who carefully peeled open the fabric to expose the broad leaves. "I thought makta was just a myth. I've never seen it growing." He lifted it to his nose, inhaling the pungent aroma.

"It is rare," Miichal agreed. "It was one of the first signs we had for Spring Maiden."

Bolin looked at Miichal. "What do you mean?"

"I'll tell you later." Miichal accepted the rewrapped packet and tucked it beneath his shirt. "Has Pharlan found anything helpful?"

"The timing of the scents means that Rosa and the others were carried here after leaving Marlow's house. The same sleeping herbs were in both places. Pharlan didn't recognize the herbs, but I do." He grimaced. "They've been drugged, Miichal. That's why we can't find them. And, no signs of struggle." He gestured around the common room.

"Tronder said that Rosa could block us out. He said that's why we didn't know where she was."

"Well, yeah. At first. But once they got captured, she would have abandoned her block. We should have been able to find her, once that happened."

"Except they drugged her."

"Yeah. Except they drugged her."

"Mackey and Jullia, too." Miichal stood silent for a moment. "What about Willam?" Any sign of Willam?"

Bolin listened to Cam's reply. "Willam was never at Marlow's. He was only here. Not for a while, though."

"Any reason to check other houses? Like Jullia's? Or yours and Katernn's. Mackey's?"

"No reason not to, since we're here."

They searched the village as thoroughly as they dared. They found nothing obvious. Pharlan was more discerning.

"There's a common scent, everywhere we've searched." Bolin had to concentrate to catch the words. "Zedar. Willam's groom.

He's been all over the village, including the empty houses we just searched."

"Willam's groom?" Miichal asked.

"Yeah." Bolin shook his head. He had no idea why this was important. "Pharlan pointed it out specifically, so it must mean something."

"Is he still around?"

"No. He left the same time as Willam. Long before Rosa came back." He paused, listening. "Pharlan's ready to leave. She wants to take the road west."

"West?"

"That's the way they went."

"Who?"

Bolin shrugged. "Everyone."

Tronder met them at the western edge of the village. They paused while Miichal opened the packet of makta and offered it to Tronder. The horse accepted two leaves and chewed, eyes closed. It took a while, but no one wanted to rush the tired horse's obvious enjoyment of makta.

"Should we ride? Or walk?" Miichal asked.

"Pharlan wants to run." Bolin looked at Tronder. "What about Tronder? How's he doing?"

"Two leaves of makta, and he can conquer the world," Miichal relayed.

"What about the others back at camp? They're most likely fretting, waiting, knowing nothing."

"Can Cam fetch them? Lead them to wherever we end up?"

"Yes! Cam says 'yes.' He can stay with us until daylight, then fly to meet the others."

"They'll travel slowly, with the wagon and mules."

"We don't need the wagon. That was just to coddle Rosa. They can bring the mules, take turns riding, if need be. They'll move fast."

Miichal tucked the packet of makta inside his shirt and hoisted himself atop Tronder. He reached down for Bolin's elbow and heaved him aboard. Once Cam had a secure perch on Bolin's shoulder, the trio leaned into Tronder's gait.

Tronder matched Pharlan's pace, who paused from time to time to investigate scents lingering along the road. Bolin voiced her thoughts, through Cam, along to Miichal; a meandering monolog.

Bolin's mood lightened as they gained distance from the village. His lifelong home felt menacing, even more so now, with Rosa's disappearance. He hated knowing she remained endangered, kidnapped out of her mother's home, out of his reach. He hated feeling helpless.

Chapter 51

Connection

Pharlan's nose led her along the road. She was sure of their direction.

The complexity of scents in the rooms Bolin had opened for her earlier that night had sorted themselves into a logical grid. She discarded the enticing aromas of food and soft pillows, the omnipresence of dust, soil, greenery, and orchard petals that lingered under bushes. She focused on human scents, since Mackey was most likely linked to the humans.

The garden where she had waited, trapped, held a trove of human scents. She knew that Mackey had been inside this house, and once Bolin opened that door, she highlighted the human scents that overlapped his presence in the house. She couldn't find his exit from the house. Since he was no longer there, he had exited somehow. Where? How?

The inn gave more clues. She found his scent, an hour more recent than his scent at the house. The background aroma of his everyday scent waved at her from every corner, reminding her that Mackey had lived here, immersed in tankards. She concentrated on his fresh scent, which she knew coincided with her entrapment in the garden. She found the same fresh scent splashed onto the cobbles behind the inn. He had been there, briefly, laying on the cobblestones. His head had touched here.

His feet, there. Again, she could find no clear exit taking him from the inn or its courtyard.

His fresh scent lingered, though. She found it caught on the leaves of bushes along the road outside the inn. The detours into other houses frustrated her, with each expectation of discovering him within, fed by the optimism of the men who opened each door for her eager nose. Every door opened into a yawning emptiness of not-Mackey. She tagged along patiently, waiting for the men to finish their search. They knew not what they might find, but were insistent on opening doors, on searching.

In the end, the house-search was helpful. Her scent grid shifted and took on vibrancy. She knew where Mackey had been. She knew where others had been and who they were. One scent brightened on the grid. This particular scent was everywhere. It was an old scent, a man's scent, never overlapping Mackey's, so she ignored it at first. But its vibrancy on her grid plucked her attention.

Cam put a name to the scent. Zedar. Willam's groom. Cam passed the information to Bolin. Now they all knew. Exactly *what* they knew lay shrouded. They had a name and a connection to Willam. They filed the information away.

But Pharlan had the scent.

As she trotted westward along the road, her scent grid moved Zedar's scent to bump against Mackey's scent. Zedar's scent brightened.

Pharlan pondered the connection. She picked up her pace, trotting along the tidy road. If she concentrated on Zedar's scent, which, although old, was persistent, prevalent, she could move faster. Mackey's scent, though newer, was masked, intermittent, harder to find. But it was there, right alongside Zedar's scent.

Zedar's scent glowed brighter. Pharlan broke into a run.

Chapter 52

Quandary

"Should we leave?"

"I don't know. I have been thinking about it, though. What do you think?" Greggor frowned as he spoke. He wasn't sure what to think, himself. Over the last several days, what with Rosa healing the forest and all, these thoughts hadn't occurred to him. Now, with Rosa gone...

Draymon finished his sentence, as was his way. "With Rosa gone, what's the point in staying?"

"Well, yes. Quite." Greggor drew a deep breath.

Draymon pressed his point. "Everyone here has a connection to Rosa. To each other. You and me? We're outsiders. We don't belong anyway. Why stay?"

Greggor shook his head. He couldn't quite put his finger on it. He didn't want to leave. But why? Draymon had a good point. They were outsiders. What reason did they have to stay, really?

"What about the mules? The wagon? We have no way to carry our goods, without mule or wagon."

"We'll take them with us."

"But...Is that right?" Greggor motioned toward the campsite, just visible through the trees. "They need them. We can't just leave them here, stranded."

"They've been talking about leaving them anyway. We'd be doing them a favor, mayhap."

"They talked about it, but decided they still needed them."

"Well..."

They sat in silence for several breaths.

"It's just..." Greggor began.

"What?"

Greggor shook his head.

"Just say it."

Greggor looked down at his feet.

"We've always been able to talk to each other, Greggor. Don't stop talking now. 'It's just' what?"

"I don't want to leave Rosa. I can't think why, I just don't."

"Are you falling for her?" Draymon's voice was unnaturally neutral. Greggor hated the sound of it.

"No! No. Don't be daft." Greggor put his hand on Draymon's leg, edged closer to him. "Don't be daft."

Draymon let out a held breath. "What then?"

"It's sort of..." Greggor heaved a sigh, struggled for words. "I feel like Rosa needs us."

"How? We don't cook. We don't drive the wagon. We're useless in the forest."

"I know. I know. It doesn't make sense whichever way we look at it. Maybe it's something still to happen. Maybe we're needed in the future somehow."

Greggor flailed his way through the words. He was the logical one, the smart one with the answers. He didn't have the answers now, and the uncertainty nagged at him.

"Well," said Draymon, "I know what you mean, really."

"You do?" Relief brightened Greggor's mood.

"Well, yes. Yes, I do. I can't think of the words or how to make sense of it, but when Rosa is here, I have no thought of leaving. I want only to stay and make sure she's safe."

"Me, too!"

"But with her gone...I don't know what to do with myself."

"Yeah. Feeling at loose ends."

"Yes."

They sat in silence.

"But with her gone," Draymon continued, "I begin to wonder whether we should leave."

Greggor sighed. "I don't, truth be told." He looked sideways at Draymon. "I'm at loose ends, but at the same time, I just want to be here when she comes back. I don't want to leave."

Draymon echoed Greggor's sigh. "Well. Let's not then." He met Greggor's eyes. "Let's not leave until both of us want to."

"You'll wait for me?"

"Of course! Don't be daft."

A sudden busy-ness at the campsite caught their attention.

"We'd better get back," Greggor said with a final pat to Draymon's thigh. "Something's up."

"Hey." Draymon caught Greggor's arm. "We can't stop talking, right? We'll be okay, as long as we keep talking."

"Just keep prying it out of me, should I forget."

"Let's get back. Maybe they've found Rosa."

Chapter 53

Convergence

A tawny owl swooped across Pharlan's path, startling her out of her compulsive focus. She heard Cam's call and stood panting, looking over her shoulder to the figures trotting toward her along the rutted road. She sat to wait for them, gazing around for another glimpse of the owl. She found it, staring at her from a low branch. She sniffed the air.

Bradi. Bradi is here.

Pharlan heard Cam relay the information to Bolin.

The others?

Pharlan sniffed the air.

They're coming.

Pharlan trotted toward Bradi's tree and sat, looking up at the owl, head cocked. She couldn't hear the owl's voice, but she understood her intent. She looked to Tronder, judging the time until the others joined her. She would wait.

Bradi will take us to them. They're close by.

As Tronder drew near, Bradi launched and flapped silently into the forest. Pharlan looked longingly at the abandoned road with its scent trail. She forced herself to trot after Bradi and Tronder. She would know the return path.

The two groups of champions and their companions converged under a giant oak. Bolin and Miichal slid from Tronder's back, shaking out numb legs. Cam flew to join Bradi on an oak branch. Pharlan sat below them, Tronder circling to scrape the forest duff, to stand and rest his hoof on its tip once he found solid rock.

Pharlan could hear Cam's thoughts clearly, a gist of Tronder's, and something of Bradi's, now that she could see the owl. She felt a kindred spirit with the owl, a connection that grew when she sat herself nearby. She pointed her nose up to the owl to catch her scent, her thoughts. She panted her long tongue.

The fellowship exchanged news, pondered their next move.

Gosikk folded his arms across his chest, shuffled from one foot to the other, shook his head. "We don't know who has them." He pointed his chin at Pharlan. "We'll be able to track them, but we don't know what to expect once we get to wherever they're being held."

"Who would want to take them?" Greggor asked. "She's just a kid, and the whole village knows them all."

"Mandra is out for Rosa's head," Yonce reminded them.

Gosikk nodded. "But if Mandra is behind this, Rosa would still be in the village. Mandra wouldn't care about Mackey or Jullia. I don't think it's Mandra."

Katernn added, "Plus, Mandra doesn't know anything about herbs. Her garden is full of flowers; nothing useful. She wouldn't know how to knock out anyone."

Gosikk said, "And no one in the village would help her. They might be wary of Rosa, but their dislike of Mandra is greater still."

Yonce asked, "Do you think they...killed her?"

Pharlan gave a short bark at this mention. Rosa's scent had floated at the edges of the road, along with Mackey's. And Jullia.

Cam sent Pharlan's message to Bolin, who said, "We're on Rosa's trail as well. She's alive."

Miichal said, "The fellowship would have dissolved if the Maiden were dead. We would know."

Pharlan felt the silence that fell over the group. A somber silence, laced with relief and foreboding, in equal measures. She whined softly.

Bolin said, "We should get moving."

"We need to think about what we'll do when we find them," Gosikk insisted.

Bolin shook his head. "We won't know what to do until we see what's happening."

Pharlan stood. She gave a low growl, impatient to resume the chase. People spent too much time talking, and not enough time knowing.

Gosikk looked at her, nodded. "Let's find them and then figure out a plan."

"First..." Katernn opened the satchel at her side and drew out red leaves.

"Where did you find that?" Bolin asked, incredulous.

"This morning. Along the way. Back there." She waved a vague hand.

"That looks like linsel. Let me see it." Bolin took the leaves that she offered. He sniffed them, gingerly separated them to peer at a single leaf.

Pharlan sniffed as well. An eager longing drew her to Bolin's side. She sat, thumping her tail. She yipped. Bolin looked down at her, hesitated, and offered her a leaf. She took the leaf from his hands, delicately taking it into her mouth. She let it dissolve on her tongue. She closed her eyes.

"I think it is linsel." Bolin watched the dog closely. "What made you collect these leaves, Katernn?"

She shrugged. "They're beautiful. I couldn't leave them behind."

"Why did you offer them to us now? It's not time for a meal."

She shrugged again. "We've been running since dawn. I remembered about them when we decided to move again. They might be a pick-me-up."

"They're certainly a pick-me-up. From what you're telling me, this most certainly is linsel. No one has seen this for generations..."

Pharlan stopped listening to the chatter. The red leaves flooded her as it dissolved across her tongue, a tingling sensation that reached to her toes, the tip of her tail. A deep stillness stole over her and kept her motionless while the fellowship handed 'round the red leaves. She felt Cam replicate her experience and knew that Tronder and Bradi felt the same. Their companionship brightened. She could hear Tronder and Bradi's thoughts more clearly.

She came back to herself and opened her eyes. The others were standing silently, arms frozen where they had lifted the linsel to their mouths. She waited until one, two, all champions opened their eyes and exchanged glances.

Miichal's words fell softly. "The forest is awakening. Linsel is a powerful sign. A Spring Maiden sign."

Gosikk wiped his hands down his shirt. "Let's go find her."

Chapter 54

Found

Cam circled the large village, spiraling over the squat building that held Pharlan's focus. The sun rode high in the sky, flooding the world with too much light.

Cam glanced at the fellowship crouched behind enormous piles of debris next to the squat building, waiting for news of this foreign village, of the companions' assessment of the battlefield. The stench from the debris rose to assult Cam's nostrils as he circled above, spiraling down to the squat building.

This one?

Yes.

Pharlan's eyes held the single window in her intense gaze, a window that lay shadowed below an overarching eave. The window was unglazed, too small for a man to breach, especially with the metal bars spanning it, top to bottom. Cam saw what Pharlan saw; sniffed what she sniffed. Pharlan had the ability to filter out the filth behind which she crouched, focusing on the important clues. They smelled Mackey clearly, heard his rattling breath. He was not well.

Pharlan whined and sank onto her belly.

Mackey! Cam heard Pharlan's call. They heard no answer.

I will look.

Cam spiraled lower, banked, and landed on the sill, fit easily between the bars. The dim room was empty but for a curled form pressed into the corner. Cam fluttered down, perched on Mackey's shoulder.

Beware his breath! Bolin recognized the smell of the drugging herbs, knew their danger. *Leave! Quickly!*

Cam flapped to the high window, slipped between the bars, and flew to the mounds of debris that shielded the fellowship from view. He landed on Bolin's shoulder.

"Katernn," Bolin hissed. "Pass me some linsel." He took the red leaves and crumpled one, smashed it in his palm. Adding a drizzle of water, he offered the emulsion to Cam. *Put this in his ear.*

Cam scooped up the liquid, taking care not to swallow, and returned to the dank cell.

Beware his breath!

Yes.

Cam fluttered to the drugged man's side, tipped his beak into an ear, and let the liquid linsel trickle in. He startled back, wings flapping, as Mackey pawed at the tickling ear. He lay still again. Cam hopped forward and added the remaining trickle to Mackey's ear and jumped back. Mackey did not stir.

It's done.

Come away. Back to the window sill. Avoid breathing the air in the room while you wait.

Cam hopped onto the sill, cocked his head at the piled debris, listening for sounds from the room behind him.

Bradi says someone is coming.

Cam flapped to the roof and squatted, unmoving. Metal scraping metal clanged from the room. The outer door squealed on its hinges. Footsteps shuffled into the room, paused. Water sloshed into a container and metal rattled onto the stone floor. Silence. Footsteps receded, hinges squealed, the door slammed shut. Metal scraping metal.

Cam regained the window sill and peered inside. Mackey's bleary eye watched him. Cam called softly. Mackey coughed.

He's awake.

Cam heard Pharlan's excited whining. She would not be contained. She streaked across the open space adjoining the shed and jumped her front legs to stretch up to the window. She whined.

He's awake, Cam told her.

I know! I can hear him!

He's not moving. His eyes are open.

But he's awake! He's awake! I found him!

Make no sound. Cam cocked his head to listen outside the window. *The others might come if they hear us.* Cam found it hard to keep calm in the face of Pharlan's excitement.

Yes. I found him! I found him!

Stevven is coming to murmur him out. Bolin's thought reassured Cam. He looked into the cell. Mackey was sitting up, rubbing his face with one hand, digging a finger into his damp ear with the other. He gathered his legs under him, using the wall to prop himself to his feet.

Stevven crept carefully around piles of shattered pottery and broken glass, abandoned bricks and dented glorbs. He paused below the window and set himself to murmuring a wide board of the wall. It was an old board and took some time to yield under Stevven's murmurs. At last he lifted it aside and started on the next.

I found you! I found you! Pharlan wiggled her nose through the opening, tail thumping. Stevven murmured around her.

Cam looked to the piles of rubble that shielded the fellowship. Greggor and Draymon were scuttling toward the shed, crouched. Cam felt the need to leave.

Yes. Come. Greggor and Draymon will help bring Mackey here.

Cam flew to the rubble that hid Bolin.

I found you! I found you! whined Pharlan.

Cam pressed his head to beloved Bolin's neck, understanding Pharlan's overwhelming joy at finding her companion.

Chapter 55

Retreat

The fellowship retreated an hour's walk from the foreign village. Strong hands helped Mackey slide from Tronder's back. He stumbled, tried to gain his feet. Strong arms hoisted him upright, stumbled him along the forest floor, helped him sit against a sturdy tree. Pharlan nosed her way between the strong arms, licking Mackey's face, her entire body wiggling in overwhelming joy.

"Ah, lass," he whispered. "I knew you'd find me." His head nodded against the tree, and he slumped sideways into sleep.

***

Black night greeted him when next he opened his eyes. He drew in a deep breath of the sweet forest air. Immediately, Pharlan washed his cheeks and neck.

I found you. I found you.

Yes, lass. You did. I knew you would.

His fingers dug into the fur at her neck, scratched her ears. His arm melted onto the ground.

***

Bright light bit through his eyelids, and he squinted, turned his face away from the midday sun filtering through the canopy of the ancient tree that held him in its energetic embrace. He blinked his eyes open, raised his hand to shade out the day's brilliance. He took in a deep breath. Stars, it felt good to be out of that putrid room.

His hand found Pharlan, stretched beside him. She was calm now, her delirium faded into complacency. He blinked his eyes open, patted Pharlan, and struggled to sit up. They were alone.

I told Cam you're awake. They're coming back.

Where are they?

Watching the village.

We should get as far away from that village as we can.

Spring Maiden is there.

Rosa's in the village? Is she in danger?

Cam doesn't know. They haven't found her. They need my nose.

Well, go! Go!

They want you well first. We'll have to travel fast, once we steal Spring Maiden.

Dismay washed over Mackey. He was aghast that Rosa was captive in the same village where he had been held. They had blacked him out before he knew her plight. He hated the thought of her being there, perhaps in the same hands that had treated him roughly. He hated thinking what they might have done to her, where they might have thrown her.

Who are they? Why did they take Rosa? And me?

They have Jullia, too. We think Jullia is in another shed, like the one where I found you.

Can they get her out? Why would anyone take Jullia? Everyone loved Jullia. Everyone loved Rosa, too. Mackey's thoughts swirled, and he caught himself from tipping over, dizzy with confusion. He wasn't surprised that he had been imprisoned. He was a self-determined derelict, worthy of stewing in his own mess. But why Rosa and Jullia?

Mackey could barely remember that the world had changed; how it had changed. His years of drunkenness overlay his days of fellowship, and he couldn't quite sort it out. His thoughts reeled, and he caught himself from tipping again.

Bolin wants you to eat some linsel.

What?

Bolin wants you to eat some linsel.

What's linsel?

The red leaves. It makes you strong. Pharlan turned her head to point her nose at the pile of red leaves laying within reach.

Mackey followed her gaze and blinked at the red leaves.

Linsel? I thought that was only a tale.

It's come back.

What?

The forest is awakening. Linsel is growing again.

What?

Eat some linsel. It will clear your head.

Mackey sat, befuddled. He steadied himself with one arm and reached for the red leaves with the other.

Eat it?

Yes.

Mackey brought the leaves to his nose. Sniffed its tantalizing aroma. His head cleared. He sniffed again. His memory fell into place. Rosa. Spring Maiden. Fellowship. Companionship. He remembered everything. He pushed leaves into his mouth and chewed. Energy seeped into his groggy limbs. He splayed his knees to sit cross-legged. He swiveled to look around him. The wagon sat nearby, and the mules grazed on a meadow just beyond, chewing contentedly, ears twitching at butterflies jockeying around their heads.

We have Bradi now. She's an owl. She's Yonce's companion.

Bradi?

Yes. She came some days ago...Wait! She came before you left with Spring Maiden. You already know Bradi.

Yeah.

Why did you pretend not to know her?

I like hearing you talk.

Pharlan licked his hand. He rubbed her face. He looked around for water.

There's a jug next to the tree. Just behind you.

Right. Mackey reached for the jug, drank long and deep.

How did you find me

So Pharlan told the story of being locked in the garden, digging her way through the rotten fence, finding Tronder and Cam, Miichal and Bolin. She embellished as she told, the drama of every door opened for her inspection, her dismay at finding him not here, not there, her impatience with the search, of her discovery of Zedar's scent intermingled with Mackey's own, their race west, through two valleys, a third, meeting the others, the talk that went on and on and on...

Mackey grinned at her telling, laughing outright over the frustration of talk, talk, talk. He rubbed her ears, picked up a paw, held it, watched her eyes, relished her thoughts flashing across his heart, telling her story of search and rescue.

And now, here we are. Waiting again. Probably more talk, talk, talk to come.

Pharlan panted happily, rolled on her back to invite a belly rub. Mackey happily complied. Belly rubs turned into wrestling, the dust puffing around them in their happy scuffle.

Pharlan jolted to her feet.

Wait...

What?

Wait...They're back.

Cam flew into view and landed on Mackey's dusty knee.

Cam helped find you. He put linsel in your ear.

In my ear? Mackey wiggled his finger in his ear.

You were asleep. Bolin told him to do it.

That's how I woke up?

Yes.

And then Stevven murmured the wall away and you *came in.*

Yes!

Mackey rubbed her ears. *I remember.* He looked up to see the fellowship winding their way past trees and bushes, headed their way.

"Did you find her?" Mackey called to them. Cam flew to Bolin's shoulder.

"Not yet," Gosikk answered. "There's been quite the flurry once they discovered you were gone. Stevven sealed the wall again, so they're baffled how you escaped."

Greggor said, "They've spent the entire day yelling at each other."

Draymon nodded. "There's a lot of fury in that village."

Yonce added, "A lot of fear, too."

Katernn said, "We retreated quite a distance to stay out of their way. Let things settle down a bit while we plan our next stage."

Talk, talk, talk.

Mackey grinned.

"You know." Gosikk brought his hands up to plant them on his hips. "All that fury and fear seems familiar."

"Familiar how?" asked Miichal.

"I think this might be Victtor's village.

Younce slapped his thigh. "Of course it is. We should have guessed that. They took her to Victtor's village, where they'd have free reign to punish her."

Chapter 56

Discovered

Yonce fumbled from a deep sleep when his arm was roughly grabbed.

They're coming.

Aahh! Yonce swung his captured arm away from his assailant, swiping against the iron grip. His hand met feathers covering a solid shape. He felt a sharp pinch on his ear.

Ow! Don't hit me!

Bradi hopped to the ground, ruffled her disheveled feathers and glared at Yonce as he sat up, rubbing his eyes awake.

You hit me!

What?

Wake up!

I'm awake! I'm awake! Yonce scrubbed his hand over his face and looked around. *What's wrong.*

You hit me.

I didn't mean to, Bradi. You startled me.

So you hit me?

I didn't know it was you. I'm awake now. What's wrong?

They're coming. She swiveled her head to look over her shoulder. *I went to the village to watch and saw nothing the entire night. On the way home, I heard movement. They're searching just beyond those trees. They'll find us soon.*

The forest was barely visible in dawn's early light. Yonce rolled into a crouch and scrambled to shake the closest shape, curled under a sleeping cloth.

"Wake up!" He rasped, hastily shaking another shoulder. His heart pounded. "We've got company." He didn't explain further, simply moved to the next shape, shook its shoulder. He heard others stirring, quick whispers, a hushed choreograph that brought them together behind the wagon.

Yonce pointed the direction that Bradi had shown him. Pharlan stood, ears alert, staring, lip lifting in a silent growl.

"There's a half dozen of them. Bradi can't see any weapons." Yonce wiped sweaty palms down his shirt. He was grateful for the growing light. Or, maybe not. The intruders might have missed them in the dark of night, passed them by completely. They would certainly be discovered in the brightening light of dawn. He heard Greggor next to him take in a deep breath.

"Whaddoo we do?" Draymon whispered. "I've never been in a fight."

Gosikk breathed, "We'll rush them and tackle them. We outnumber them."

The fellowship crouched, keeping their alarmed breaths silent.

Yonce heard a twig snap. A heavy footfall. A voice called softly, "I smell wet ashes."

"Mayhap we've found them after all," muttered another.

"Sshhh!" hissed another.

More twigs snapped. The branch of a bush swished and snapped back to hit a leather boot. Yonce scowled. They weren't being very careful. He risked a peek beneath the wagon. Heavy boots appeared.

"There's a wagon," came the whisper. "No one's here though."

"They won't be far."

"Keep looking."

"Do you hear anything?"

As one, the fellowship roared to their feet and poured from behind the wagon. Yonce heard Bradi's screech and Pharlan's barking attack. He yelled his loudest, tromped into the open, waved his arms, and ran straight at the nearest man. His tackle was clean, and the man went down with a heavy grunt. Yonce forced the man onto his stomach and sat on his back, pinning both arms.

Yonce looked around wildly, adrenaline pumping, to see how the others had fared. He kept yelling, adding to the cacophony. He glanced down at his captive, who seemed to be having trouble breathing. He relaxed his pressure and the man took a ragged breath.

"Help," the man choked out. He panted, and Yonce relaxed his pressure further still. "Wait," the man coughed. "We need your help."

Chapter 57

Conspirators

Draymon prided himself on being a good judge of character. He could sense a schemer within a sentence or two after first acquaintance. He kept his distance from schemers, just on principle. You never knew.

He also knew honesty when he heard it. Honesty could take longer to detect, because, oh my, honest people could go on and on being completely neutral before opening up and revealing their honesty.

This gang was honest. Draymon was sure of it. He knew it even as they rushed from behind the wagon. The unfamiliar faces had been completely taken by surprise. They showed no resistance to the tackles that took them down. Not one of them had struggled. Draymon saw it immediately.

Draymon had held back, waiting to see if his help was needed, but no; the others were completely adequate. Even Greggor joined in a tackle, and Greggor did not throw himself in the dirt for any reason whatsoever. It was one of the things that Draymon admired about him, his fastidiousness. Maybe over-fastidious, truth be told.

Yet there he was, screaming like a banshee and throwing himself on top of one of the intruders, moments after Katernn took the man down. It was a sight to see. Draymon couldn't quite believe it!

Luckily, no one was hurt, other than the wind being knocked out of a couple of them. No hard feelings, though. After all, they had been slinking through the bushes, uninvited, unannounced. With all said and done, they couldn't resent getting trounced.

But all of that was in the past. Miichal had even shared some of his makta, to help them recover, you see. Bolin looked a little sheepish, Draymon thought, and Katernn had settled down right away. Mackey, on the other hand, still had a bit of a squinty-eyed glare about him. To be fair, he had been treated pretty rough at the villagers' hands. Draymon didn't blame Mackey one bit for being suspicious. Not one bit.

But Draymon knew the gang was the real deal. He believed their every word. They had started out as a posse, truth be told, but they had promptly disposed of their two leaders, ruffians in their own right, truth be told, tied them to a tree and left them to stew in their own juices. Apparently, it was hard to leave the village. No one allowed out, you see. So this gang, finding themselves out and about, had jumped at their first opportunity to take out the two ruffian leaders and set out on their own.

They'd been looking for the fellowship. They wanted help. Help in their village. Things were bad.

Apparently, the widow, everyone called her the widow, the widow came back from the wedlocking all important and full of herself, started ordering everyone around. The villagers didn't buy it, though. She had no authority! She was a woman, after all, even if she had been married to the mayor, or whatever he called himself. The lord. Maybe that was it. The lord. Yes.

Anyway, no one would do what she said, so then she started saying that she spoke for Willam. Willam was the lord's heir, apparently, so *now* they had to do what she said, since Willam was in charge.

Thing was, no one had seen Willam. Not since they first got back from the wedlocking, bride and groom in tow. But no one had seen hide nor hair of either of them. Well, you can imagine. The grumbling! So the widow hired the ruffians to bring some of the villagers in line. You know, the trouble-makers. That's how the lord had run things, so that's how she would run things. Excuse me. That's how Willam would run things, so the widow said. Now everyone was too frightened to stand up for themselves, which, apparently, was how things had been for years and years.

But the trouble-makers were tired of it, you see. Things had been so pleasant when the lord and lady were off at the wedlocking, taking the ruffians with them. People came out of the shadows and got a feel for what it could be like if no one was lording it over them, dictating what could happen and who could do it. That made it even worse when the widow returned and tried to put everything back to how it had been.

Draymon believed the gang when they said they wanted help. He knew they were being honest. The real deal. He was ready to help, and he could tell that Greggor and Katernn were ready, too. Miichal was hard to read. So was Stevven. But Gosikk and Bolin seemed ready to give it a go. Yonce, for sure.

First, though, they had to figure out where Rosa was.

Chapter 58

Conspiracy

The sketchiness of their plan bothered Katernn. The posse and their deputized fellowship planned to move camp to the far side of the village, an hour into the forest. Katernn was skeptical. She chewed her lip.

"Why take the time?"

Zedar answered. "We searched that part of the forest for the whole of yesterday. It won't occur to the widow to send anyone in that direction again."

Katernn nodded. She liked things to make sense. If she could see the pattern, then she knew how to fit into it.

"How did you end up in the posse, Zedar?" she asked.

"I'm a good tracker."

Katernn narrowed her eyes. "And yet it took you two days to find us, an hour's walk from the village." How did that fit? Skepticism nudged her cynicism forward.

Zedar looked to the rest of the posse. "Well. Not everyone agreed that we should...subdue Duke and Lloyd." He sat, nervously bouncing on his toes while they talked. "It was risky."

"But it was your best plan?" Katernn's cynicism pushed her to more questions, even though it could be a waste of time.

"It was our only plan." Not the brightest rocks in the river, then.

"What's the plan now? Do you have one? Or are you fresh out of plans?" Katernn kept her voice friendly, but Gosikk wasn't fooled.

He interrupted her interrogation with his own hesitation. "It'll take some time to circle around the village and set up a new camp. A good part of the day, most like."

Yonce stood. Katernn figured he carried his own store of nervous energy, same as the rest of them, and needed to move around. "I can take the wagon around with the mules and have it ready for you after you find Rosa."

Zedar cleared his throat. "In all truth, we don't know where Rosa is." His feet shuffled, betrayers of his feigned calm. "But we do know where Willam is."

Katernn frowned. "We're looking for Rosa. We can worry about Willam later." The man was starting to irritate her. Maybe this was a mistake after all. Maybe they should figure it out themselves, just the fellowship. Why complicate things with these strangers, posse or no?

"Once we have Willam, we control the village."

Aha. The picture cleared. If the widow was claiming that Willam was in charge, they would make him available to *be* in charge. Katernn was confident of the newly wedlocked. The two youngsters doted on each other. If Rosa was being held against her will, most likely drugged, then in all likelihood, Willam was being held, too. Katernn doubted that he would go along with any plan that included Rosa as prisoner. If they could set Willam up to take command, the widow would be hard pressed to sway the rest of the villagers to follow her demands. Maybe the fools weren't fools after all.

Gosikk asked the sensible question. "How do we get Willam?"

"Three or four of you can walk in and make a ruckus. I'll sneak your carpenter," he nodded at Stevven, "to the room where Willam is, and we'll break him out."

"Why move the camp, then?" Katernn needed to fill in the holes.

"After you make the ruckus, you'll head in this direction, and we'll take Willam to the new camp until he recovers. Then Willam will set things to rights."

Miichal asked, "What if they lock us up for making a ruckus?"

"They won't. Duke and Lloyd are in charge of keeping order, and they're...indisposed. The widow doesn't have anyone else to carry out orders of lockings-up."

"What about the widow herself?" Katernn couldn't decide if she liked this plan or if it was hare-brained.

"She'll holler and scream, and everyone will hide."

Katernn shook her head. "I don't know."

Stevven said, "It's more of a plan than any we've had so far. If I don't have to put the wall back together after we bring out Willam, I can work real fast. The ruckus distraction just might work."

Katernn clambered to her feet. "Well, if we're going to do this, we should get started. The morning's half-gone already." She bent to scoop up sleeping cloths that lay strewn around the small clearing. She tucked several under one arm, using her chin and her free hand to fold the first cloth into some semblance of order. Chin down, she walked to the far side of the wagon, patted the cloth away, shook out a second one to start folding.

That's when she saw the fox.

It was the most beautiful creature she had ever seen. It sat demurely in a shaft of sunlight, tail wrapped around its feet, fur glowing a deep golden red, brilliant in the morning sun. Katernn froze. She forgot to breathe. The sleeping cloth slid from her grasp and puddled at her feet. She didn't notice. She took a step forward, and the remaining cloths dribbled to the ground.

Aarvil.

Katernn's head reeled. She heard the word clearly and finally understood the silent communication that flowed effortlessly between people and their companions. And she knew without a shadow of a doubt. Aarvil had come for her. Aarvil was her companion.

Katernn walked toward the magnificent animal and went down on her knees in front of her.

You are so beautiful!

Aarvil cocked her head, her green eyes lustrous. Katernn reached out her hand, paused.

May I touch you?

Yes.

Katernn touched the fox's cheek, stroked an eyebrow. Aarvil's nose sniffed the air, sniffed Katernn's arm, never breaking her gaze.

"Katernn! What are you doing?" Gosikk's voice floated to her.

Will you come with us?

I will always go with you.

A tiny sob clutched Katernn's throat. *How did I get so lucky?*

"Katernn! We're going!"

Katernn rose and returned to the wagon, Aarvil trotting regally at her side.

Chapter 59

Discontent

Mandra didn't like it at all. She had long dreamt of returning to her childhood village, of being close to her dear brother, but this homecoming resembled not at all her dreams. Where had the beauty gone? Why was everything in wretched disrepair? Gardens had vanished. Gathering places had been torn out. Rocks jumbled the edges of walking paths, and debris filled every corner.

This village was not the village she remembered, filled with people who, even when she didn't know them, always tipped their hats in her direction, showing respect. This village, this village where she now found herself, was filled with slanty eyes and turned-away faces, people who hurried in another direction whenever they spotted her round figure.

And throwing a bitter shadow over everything, Victtor was gone. Her throat closed at the thought of her brother. He had always championed her, and now she had no one. He had been her anchor, and now she had nowhere to belong.

She was more miserable here than she had been in Marlow's village. Her eyes filled with self-pity.

Victtor's widow had been so gracious and lovely when she invited Mandra to return with her, to reclaim her childhood home. Mandra hadn't thought twice. She didn't ask Romane or even Marlow whether they wanted to leave, what they thought of the widow's proposal. She had simply and immediately agreed to leave her wedlock home, incapable of clear thought, heavy with grief and a yawning sense of loss, transformed into hope at the promise of returning to her childhood dream.

Romane stayed by her side, and Marlow trailed along somewhere. She gave no thought to her daughter. Her wedlocked daughter was no longer her concern, thank the stars. Mandra simply walked out of her wedlocked home, clambered onto the wagon that awaited her, made room for Romane on the high seat as he climbed to sit next to her. She was driven away. She cast no backward glance. She sat, buried in a grief so black that the sun could not dazzle her, the flowers and birds could not delight her, ponderings of her future could not rouse her.

But this was worse than anyone could have imagined, relegated as she was to this single-room hovel. Ramone stayed by her side, murmuring comfort, sharing her tiny house without complaint. Marlow was somewhere; she knew not where, nor cared. And her Victtor was gone. Her eyes brimmed anew.

And now, now that the widow's ruffians had disappeared, she, Mandra, was suddenly expected to care for her comatose daughter. That had been a rude shock, learning that Rosa was here. On top of everything else, she was expected to endure the presence of the simpering fool of a daughter that she thought she had left behind. When the widow led her into the low, dark cell, pointed at the still figure curled on the floor, and said, "Make sure she doesn't awaken," Mandra couldn't even see who it was that she was expected to hold as prisoner.

Ramone found them there, reluctant mother and estranged daughter. He took over Rosa's care, thank the stars. Mandra didn't dare return to her own hovel, wary of arousing the widow's retribution for disobeying her. Mandra and Romane squeezed themselves into Rosa's tiny cell as best they could, turning their noses from the stench.

As the day went on, Mandra sank into a dark cloud of despair. Romane placed a bowl of gruel into her inattentive hands, poured clear water into the clay mug that passed for a drinking cup, combed her hair and twisted it into a simple bun at the nape of her neck.

Mandra felt her tension drain away at Romane's touch. The comb tingled along her scalp and sent waves of comfort flowing down her neck, along her spine, out through her fingertips. The cool cloth on her face and neck soothed and refreshed, rinsed in water scented with spring petals and the tiniest of herbs. Romane bathed her hands, her feet. His ministrations revived her enough for her to look around the tiny cell, to watch the quiet form curled beneath the barred window, and she remembered that it was her daughter who lay there, so still, so vulnerable.

A brightness fluttered in Mandra's chest. She reached out and pulled Rosa's skirt straight, tucked a blanket around her feet. Those feet were so cold. Mandra scooted closer and rubbed the cold feet, bent to breathe warm air onto them, rubbed them dry with the rough blanket. A faint glow shimmered under her ministrations. A tune hummed in her throat. A lullaby. Her lips formed the words, and she sang breathlessly to the poor, poor girl who lay with pale face and dusty curls.

It wasn't right. No one should be treated this way. Always, Mandra had been pampered, by her father, her brother, her husband for a time, then Romane. Never had she experienced the disdain and disinterest that was her daily treatment ever since Victtor collapsed and breathed his last.

Victtor.

How could she continue without Victtor?

And why did Victtor's widow take no interest in her? She was Victtor's sister! She was important in this shabby village, by association. Bafflement shrouded her thoughts as she curled herself around Rosa's still form, pulled Rosa into the curve of her round body, shared her warmth with the chilled girl. The glimmering glow spread from Rosa's warmed feet and ankles to seep through her still form wherever Mandra's embrace sheltered her. Tears seeped across Mandra's nose, tickled her temple, and splashed into the dust. She buried her face in Rosa's curls, breathed her sweet scent of roses and forest floor. Mint.

She slept.

Mandra swam out of a dream of her garden thick with blossoms and the buzzing of bees. She swam into the awareness of a hand rocking her shoulder, a whisper in her ear. She blinked and turned her head to gaze into Romane's smiling eyes.

"It's time to give Rosa another dose, to help her sleep."

Mandra rubbed her eye and peered at the window, a dense sprawl of stars glistened, a warm breeze rustled the leaves of the bush that waved at the window's edge. She gathered her wits, turned her head to breathe in the faint scent of roses that hovered over the still form glowing peacefully in the corner of the cell.

"No. It's not right. No one should be treated like this. We should let her awaken."

She felt Romane's surprise. "But the widow..."

"The widow is wrong. Rosa does not need sleep. Rosa needs to awaken."

"But..."

"It's time for Rosa to awaken."

Mandra knew that Romane's silence meant obedience. Always it had been so, in all her remembrance. He would question in order to gain understanding, but never in defiance. If he had no more questions, she had won his complete cooperation.

Mandra raised herself, rolled away from Rosa and struggled into a sitting position. "Bring me a comb."

Mandra drew the comb through Rosa's tangles. Curls fell gracefully, released their chaos willingly, sprang into glowing life. Romane brought the cool cloth, redolent of herbs and petals, and leaned to wipe the dust from Rosa's face. Mandra took the cloth from Romane's surprised hand, exchanged cloth for comb. She bathed her daughter, Romane always there with a freshly wrung cloth. Mandra sat with legs spread wide, held her brightening daughter reclined against her sturdy chest, and bathed arms, legs, hands, and finally feet, murmured her mothering murmurs, wrapped in the glory of Spring Maiden's magic.

The Spring Maiden's glow spread into Mandra's round embrace. Mandra's grief for Victtor's death softened and melted into a reverie of pleasant memories and loving gratitude. Mandra's indifference for husband and home melted into a wondering of his whereabouts, their upended fortunes. Mandra's clinging and dependence on son and the support he readily offered melted into respect and pride for the fine man he had become. Mandra's disdain and indifference for daughter acknowledged the beauty and power of Spring Maiden.

Mandra felt Rosa's stirring, craned her neck to see Rosa's eyes flutter and squint at the flame of Romane's glorb. Mandra helped Rosa to sit on her own, then clambered to her feet and shook out her long skirts. She waited for Rosa's wits to gather.

A raven fluttered at the window, perched on the sill, cawed into the silent room. Romane recovered himself from his startle and stood, shushing the excited bird. "Hush, Cam. You'll draw others."

Somehow, Mandra was not surprised that Romane knew the raven's name, that it fell silent at his remonstrance. The raven fluttered to the ground and hopped onto Rosa's thigh, rubbed his head on her arm. Rosa lifted a weak arm to pet the bird's head, and he leaned into every stroke.

An owl alit soundlessly on the window's sill and squeezed itself through the bars. It held a twist of leaves in its beak. It fluttered to Rosa's other thigh and lifted the leaves toward her.

"Thank you, Bradi," Rosa whispered, took the leaves and gave them into her mouth, chewed with eyes closed.

Mandra stood in unsurprised amazement at this invasion of the forest into the rancid meanness of their cell. Rosa chewed and swallowed, rested two hands on two birds, and looked at Romane, at Mandra.

Mandra smiled at Rosa, nodded. Rosa stared, breathed, ventured a smile in return. Rosa clambered to her feet, upsetting both birds who fluttered away as she moved into Mandra's arms.

"Mama!" Rosa cried, burying her tears in her mother's neck.

Mandra rocked her, murmured her mothering murmurs, smoothed her curls down her back. Unfamiliar tenderness and joy blossomed in Mandra's heart, tears wet her cheeks, sobs shook her round belly.

Mother and daughter startled apart as Miichal burst into the room, his crouch readied to vanquish all threats. Tronder stood just behind, thrusting his head and shoulders into the low doorway. Rosa straightened from her mother's embrace and threw herself into Miichal's arms. Miichal, who bent to fold himself around her, even as his eyes swept the room, assessing possible danger.

"We must away, Maiden," his voice low and urgent. "Our entry into the village carried no stealth."

Rosa gathered her mother into her arms and whispered in her ear. "Thank you, Mama. We will be back to make certain you are safe." Rosa hugged her brother, spoke the same assurance to him, and turned to follow Miichal and Tronder into the night.

Chapter 60

Ruckus

Being unplanned, the ruckus unfolded better than Rosa had imagined.

They burst into the village, Rosa and her ten, while Zedar and his conspirators crept with Stevven along its opposite edge.

"Where is my husband?" Rosa shouted as she strode onto the main square. Villagers turned in disbelief, stared out windows, peeped around doorframes. An unfamiliar vibrancy brightened the green of the square, blossoming outward from Rosa's footsteps. The scent of roses drifted amongst the awakening grasses. By the time Rosa shouted her second shout, "Where is my husband?" villagers were trotting into the freshening square, curiosity overcoming their cowers.

Upon Rosa's third shout, the widow swept through the wide doorway of her fine house, stomped down her veranda's steps, and sailed onto the square that spread, innocent and square and deepening into a lovely shade of spring green. The widow's fury stopped the villagers in their tracks, yet their curiosity held them, ensnared by a reluctance to retreat.

"How dare you command your husband! How dare you command him before all to see and hear! You are once again proving yourself to be an unworthy bride for the leader of us all."

Rosa fervently renewed her vow to only ask questions, to avoid demanding others to be different than they were. "What have you done with Willam?"

The widow's eyes darted around the square, blinked at the unexpected colors, noting that her ruffians remained disturbingly absent. Rosa noted that the widow appeared suddenly unsure, pausing in her tirade, hesitating, if only for a moment. Then the widow drew herself tall, a leading lady readying herself for performance.

"Willam has denounced you, Rosa." The widow's words carried clear and far. "You abandoned him in his time of need, and he has denounced you and your betrayal."

Rosa blinked, took a step back. Willam? Had he, contrary to her assumption, not come to her because she had been absent all these days? Had he, in fact, turned from her, perhaps disgusted with her for riding away from him, for laying sick and feeble for hours and days? She stared at the widow, stole a glance around the square that steadily regained its glory. Was their plan for naught, dependent as it was on Zedar's assurance that Willam himself lay captive, the widow's captive? Uncertainty swept through her. Would Willam refuse their help, sneer at her, before one and all?

She felt the ten at her back. She drew in a deep breath. She narrowed her eyes at the widow, wondering. She felt the ten, remembered her mother's love, Miichal's rescue of her from the wretched cell, his strong arms holding her secure on Tronder's back, her return to fellowship. She felt the ten, the burgeoning green, a rejoicing expectation beneath her feet, and wondered no more.

"Are you being truthful, Widow? Why is it that Willam does not speak for himself?"

The widow paused a breath too long, and Rosa knew her connivence. The widow's eyes flashed as she sang out her newest refrain. "He remains secluded, secluded in the aftermath of your betrayal and his lord's sudden death. He prepares himself to take on the mantle of leadership in his lord's stead. I am his messenger and confidant. He will appear when the time is come and take his rightful place before his vassals."

"I doubt your words, Widow. My Willam is strong and knows truth. He would not need to hide behind your skirts."

"How dare you! How dare you mock your husband and question me."

"I do not mock my Willam. But I do question you. Have you forgotten that you have no right, no authority, to lead your fellow villagers? You call them vassals, but I look around me, and I see men and women of value, men and women worthy of respect. A leader should inspire, rather than demean. Could it be that you wrap yourself in fear and bellow, only so others will cower? Is your sway so shallow?"

"How dare you! How d..."

"Yes! I dare!" Rosa stood tall in the rightness of her demand, in the exaltation of the awakening green. "Where is my husband?"

"You deserted your husband. You rode away and left him behind. You do not deserve him, and you will not have him. Because he will not have you." The widow's sneer drove itself into Rosa's heart. She knew that sneer well, had cowered before it all her life.

She felt the ten behind her, smelled the billowing scent of roses, and leveled a commanding stare at the widow.

"I did not desert my husband. He dwells always in my heart. My every thought lays with him. And he has not deserted me! This I know in my every fiber. I have vowed myself to him, and him to me."

"Your vow!" The widow's disdain dripped from her stony stare, her raised nose, her hissed words. "Your mockery of a vow.

His empty-headed echo back to you. You spoke no vow. You spoke heresy." She spat the words. "Your wedlocking cannot be valid when vowed under such heresy."

Rosa ignored the widow's diversions and returned to the central issue. "Why do you keep him from me? Why do you keep him from his friends and neighbors? Why do you keep him from his loved ones, of whom he has many? Is that the only way you can control him? By keeping him away from the world? Does he also lay drugged at your hand, just as I have lain?"

The widow shook with fury, eyes darting from Rosa to the green, confusion boiling into the air around her. She choked out her words, her voice thin and high with fear. "You have waited these many days without a thought for him. You come now? Today? Demanding the world of him? You should have come sooner. But you waited, and your waiting showed him the truth of your betrayal."

Rosa saw through the widow's act, saw her confusion, tasted her fear. Rosa drove her purpose home. "I declare before all who stand as witness this day. I lay poisoned at your command! This day is the first I have drawn clear breath, held clear thought! And I come now, immediately upon gaining coherency, and demand of you, where is my husband?"

"Rosa?"

Rosa's glare shifted to the figures who staggered beyond the widow's shoulder. The blood drained from her face, and her knees went weak as she recognized Willam, his arm draped over supporting shoulders, stumbling forward eagerly.

"Willam!" His name escaped her lips, a whisper filled with alarm and relief. She ran across the green, arms spread, sobs catching in her throat. "Oh, Willam!"

As she passed the widow, her arm was wrenched, twirling her around to face the renewed fury of the widow, whose eyes poured rage and hate into Rosa's heart. She pulled her arm away, but the widow's grip was iron.

The ten were on them in an instant, pulling the widow away, prying her grip from Rosa's arm, engulfing Rosa in protective embraces. And then Willam was there, gathering Rosa in his arms, whispering her name again and again, smoothing her hair back from damp cheeks, kissing her forehead. She held him upright, supporting his weakened frame, while sobs shook her belly. "Willam! I've missed you so!"

The newly wedlocked stood, swaying in each other's arms, for all the world to see. The scent of roses flooded the square. Cheers and laughter, clapping hands and pumping fists erupted from all sides. Villagers swarmed them, pounded Willam's back, petted Rosa's hair. The ten stepped back, making room for the relief and hope that poured onto the newly wedlocked couple. The two who stood swaying, reclaimed, rejoined, rejoiced.

Beyond the jubilant throng, the widow turned, lifted her black skirts, and mounted her veranda steps to disappear behind her wide door.

Chapter 61

Shards

The widow had found Willam standing, vacant-eyed, in the common room at the deserted inn, on that disastrous day when Victtor had fallen and Rosa had fled. A flash showed Willam the silhouette of a tall woman dressed in black stepping through double doors. The next flash showed her peering into his eyes. He startled at her close proximity. He turned his head as a raven fell from a high rafter, spread its wings, and swooped through an open window.

***

Willam toppled from his high seat and tumbled to the road. He stared at the wagon wheel that turned to a halt and heard scuffling footsteps. Arms hoisted him onto a pallet.

***

Sunlight flickered through green branches to stab his staring eyes. The bounce and clatter of the wagon boards beneath him shook him awake.

***

A white curtain fluttered above him. A fresh breeze carried the scent of orange blossoms.

***

He spluttered at water poured down his throat.

***

A sharp slap set his ears to ringing. A demanding voice hissed in his face. He ciphered no words.

***

Strong arms lowered him into warm water.

***

A bright moon wandered into his staring eyes, forced him to turn his head away.

***

Shouting drifted into his awareness. Willam blinked. He moistened his dry lips, a grimace drawing his brows together. He lifted an arm to rub crusty eyes. Thirst panged his empty belly.

A wooden plank cracked. Light tumbled through the wall opposite Willam. The opening widened. Voices whispered. Firm hands sat him upright, brought him to his feet where he wobbled clumsily. Leaves were tamped into his mouth where they lay unnoticed, drool trailing from his lips. A hand grasped his wrist, lifted his arm over a shoulder. Another arm encircled his waist, propped him against a sturdy hip.

Willam turned his head, blinked, squinted, bringing someone's head into focus. His head swayed down, leaves fell unnoticed, and he concentrated on moving his feet, stumbling forward, finding balance, lurching above noodled ankles and knees. The arm around his waist tightened. The shoulder under his arm hitched him more securely. They moved forward. Willam wobbled his head toward the new head, blurred next to his own.

"We got ya," said a familiar voice, soothing, gentle.

Behind it all, the shouting. Who was shouting? Why would they shout? It was foolish to shout. Repercussions. Willam checked his own mouth, making sure it wasn't him who shouted.

Who was that? Familiarity whispered in his ear.

His legs wobbled him down stairs and onto a dirt lane. Willam brought fresh air into his lungs. His pantleg caught on a dead branch that sprawled beside their path. He peered at a building they passed, a broken window. They didn't go in. Dust trailed their steps.

Who was shouting?

Willam squinted at bright sunlight that grew closer and broadened across a wide square. He recognized the square, blinked at its vivid color. He turned his head to the man propping him upright. Zedar. He recognized Zedar. Willam coughed, his throat dry. He blinked.

Who was shouting? He gasped shallow breaths, remembering how to form words. "Zedar," he whispered. "Who's shouting?"

"Rosa!"

Rosa? Willam swung his head forward, squinting in the direction of the shouts.

"Rosa?"

She stood in full sun, arms crossed, a crowd behind her, glaring at a woman in black. The widow.

"Rosa?"

Her eyes found him. She took a step, broke into a run, arms outstretched.

"Oh, Willam!"

The widow grabbed her. The crowd swarmed around widow and maiden, pulled them apart. They swarmed around him, brought him into Rosa's arms, Rosa who enfolded him, whose waist he clung to, whose rose-drenched hair he breathed.

And the shards came together. Full remembrance flowed into his heart. His wedlocking vow swept over him and pieced itself together. "I faithfully promise to live with you always, in full obedience and loving loyalty," Willam whispered in Rosa's ear. He held her close, clenched her against him, and remembered everything.

Chapter 62

Remembrance

Miichal tensed and relaxed his muscles, starting at his feet and working his way to his neck and jaw. Rosa was holding her own. He knew to give her room, to use her own power to stand against the widow's wrath. But he was ready. All of them were ready, the Maiden's champions.

A calm knowing rose along his spine as he tensed and relaxed. His gaze swept the crowd surrounding the brightening village square, noted each person, their stance, their expression. Rosa was safe for the moment.

Rosa faltered, only briefly. The cower melted from her shoulders and she straightened her spine, stood in her full height. She leveled her chin and firmed her jaw. Miichal watched her childhood slip from her shoulders, the weight of doubt and shame and fear evaporate from her heart, to stand firm and shimmer in the bright sunlight.

Remembrance flooded Miichal. His own childhood of doubt and shame and fear swept a cold dread through him, a dread that evaporated from his own heart, leaving its own shimmer as it melted in the sun.

Remembrance. Finding Tronder. The months of training under Tronder's careful instruction. The teachings swirled through his remembrance and spiraled into a coherent whole.

He was not defined by his past. He was free to create his own future.

Miichal watched the Maiden transform and was himself transformed. He mirrored her posture, the casual relaxation of her hands, the tilt of her head. He heard the clarity of her shouted truths and knew his own. He fed courage to her, and she brightened and fed her courage back to him. They stood, champion and maiden, bolstering each other, blossoming and shimmering beneath the morning sun. Together, they stepped into their future.

Miichal felt Tronder's joy burst across his heart. He knew beyond doubt that this self-knowledge was the very threshold that Tronder had led him to, time and time again, urged him to cross at every opportunity. He alone could gain the self-knowledge, in his own way, in his own time, and Tronder rejoiced that the time had arrived.

Miichal stepped into his own power, and Tronder released him to stand with his own energy, his own knowing, his earned wisdom.

Motion swept across the tableau before him, and Miichal stood in razor awareness at its unfolding. He knew the widow's intent before she knew it herself. He bolted after Rosa, who careened toward Willam. He grasped the widow's arm even as her hand clenched the Maiden. His glare blazed into the widow, and with a sharp intake of breath, she released Rosa, swept back by the champions' momentum, whisked away from darling Rosa. Whisked to where she could do no harm.

As the crowd cheered and clapped, as the widow melted away, Miichal found Katernn's eyes. "Jullia," he mouthed. Katernn nodded. Followed by horse and fox, they moved across the square, away from the celebration of love and hope. They knew exactly where to find Jullia, could feel her, were drawn to her like arrows to their target. They found her, where she stood in Romane's embrace, blinking her own remembrance into a coherency that stretched across years of admiration, patience, and certainty.

Miichal and Katernn stepped through the open doorway, ensured the room's safety, then, with a quick glance at the enthralled couple, stepped into the sunlight once again, closing the door behind them.

Chapter 63

Elders

Of course the widow called a meeting of the elders. Yonce shook his head in disgust. It wasn't convincing enough that Rosa had exposed her in front of the whole village. The widow had to twist things around and claim *she* had been wronged. Poppycock.

He would much rather be out with the mules, or even better, wandering fields and glens with Bradi; anything other than sitting in this crowded hall listening to the widow's lies. But he'd be mashed if he would abandon Rosa, who sat accused. Accused of murder.

Murder?

Poppycock!

He had to say, though, Rosa did not look cowed in the midst of her circumstances. She sat alert, shoulders back, chin level, facing each speaker with calm eyes, quiet hands. She'd always been a great kid, but always a bit scared around the edges, fluttery-like. That was gone now. Rosa was every inch a Spring Maiden.

The elders sat at the front of the room. Hand-picked by Victtor, most likely. Had the most to lose, if things went against the widow, most likely. Yonce shook his head.

He was ready, though. They'd rescued Rosa before, and they would do it again. They were good at it. They'd outrun posses and made out just fine on their own, out in the forest. That life suited Yonce to a T. Perfectly happy out there. He did not need this village or any other.

Yonce shifted on his bench. He closed his eyes and concentrated on Bradi, dozing in a tree at the edge of the village. He smelled the duff at the base of her tree, the leaves that tremored above her head. He heard bees buzzing beneath her branch. Bradi may be sleeping, but her senses kept her aware of the world around her, and Yonce could share everything she heard and smelled.

He didn't want to wake her, though. Let her sleep her daytime sleep.

He opened his eyes and refocused his attention on the healer who now stood before the elders.

"I warned Victtor many times that his anger would be the death of him."

Yonce sat up, glanced at Gosikk beside him. Gosikk was nodding. Yonce returned his attention to the healer. His fingers tingled, and his breath quickened. The healer's declaration would surely help Rosa.

"Victtor took no heed of his health. He overate, overdrank, overslept. He refused activity of any kind. He had not the stamina for the journey to his niece's wedlocking..." The healer gestured toward Rosa, gave a slight nod. "...despite its importance. I told him forcefully that he should not go. But Victtor would not hear my entreaties."

Yonce heard the widow muttering. The healer continued, ignoring her, his focus on the elders and the tale he must tell. "I had to content myself with traveling with his entourage, make myself available for whatever he might need, to do whatever might be done."

The healer looked to the floor, shook his head. "Victtor kept himself in a frenzy the entire journey. He would not be content.

He railed at every turn." The healer looked at the elders. "As was his way." The elders nodded, raised an eyebrow, shuffled the papers before them. "I saw all the signs, his flushed complexion, his grip over his belly." The healer placed his hand over his own belly, showing where Victtor's pain had gripped.

He frowned, shook his head again. "I expected his collapse at any moment. Hearing the child's recounting of her defiance before her uncle, I am not surprised that his abused body finally gave out. But it was not she who brought him down. Victtor brought himself down."

"Lies!" the widow shouted, roaring to her feet. "You pronounced him in the best of health."

"Lady, I did not." The healer's voice was calm and clear, his conviction unwavering.

"I would never have allowed him to travel, had you given the slightest indication that the journey might tire him." The widow's rage purpled her face, hinting at the possibility of her own demise.

The healer turned to face the widow directly, stood unflinching in the face of her furious stubbornness. "Lady, I implored you many times. You held no more influence over Victtor than any of us."

The color drained from the widow's face. A vein beat a frantic staccato at her temple, along her neck. "How dare you! You speak nothing but lies!"

"Lady. For the first time in many years, all of us have the freedom to speak truth. Just as I speak it to you now. Just as I spoke it to Victtor many times. As I spoke it to *you* many times, imploring you in private, in the hope that you would influence him toward health. But you cared not to exert your influence, Lady. Not in the least."

The healer turned to the elders. "If anyone shares guilt in the death of Victtor, it is the widow, for refusing to fulfill her wifely duty of ensuring her husband's continued health."

The room was deathly quiet. Yonce remembered to breathe, despite the drama unfolding at the front of the crowded room.

Yonce started as the widow slammed her chair against the table from which she had erupted. She stormed toward the healer, who brought his arms up as a ward against her, even as he stood in unflinching honesty.

"You lie!" the widow hissed, coming within arm's reach of the healer. "You despicable, crawling, ungrateful idiot. You will never find profession in this village again!"

The crowd gasped, murmurs and exclamations flowing from side to side.

"Luckily, Lady," said the healer, his voice calm and clear, "that is no longer under your persuasion."

The widow stared at him, trembling with rage. She swept her glare across the neutral faces of the elders, at the staring crowd, turned on her heel, and stormed from the hall. The outer door slammed.

The center elder pushed himself upright and spoke above the mounting exclamations. "Thank you, Healer. We hear your words and hear the truth of them." His gaze swept the faces crowding the hall. "Are there any other voices that would be heard?"

Heads turned to the widow's ruffians, newly freed from their tree. The two looked at their feet, frowned, shook their heads. "No, Elder," came their doubled admission.

One of them stood. "If you please, Elder." His feet shuffled themselves beneath him. "The widow's hold on us was fearsome." The second ruffian stared at his hands. The first continued. "We have done much wrong to many of you. Though we may not deserve it, we ask your leniency. Should you ban us from our homes, we will go." He paused a moment to regain his composure. "But we ask, most hopefully, that you will allow us to stay and help repair the damage we have done, in any way you decree."

The ruffian thumped onto his bench, wiped a sleeve across his wet eyes.

The elders rose to stand together before the village, before their neighbors and friends. They spoke, one after the other, directly to the ruffians, but deliberately within hearing of the villagers, presenting their decree.

"Remain with your families; stay in your homes."

"Become useful in our village."

"Use kindness, rather than bullying."

"Use willingness, rather than disdain."

The elders turned their attention to Rosa, spoke, for all to hear.

"The child is blameless."

"All the village witnessed Victtor's wrath."

"The widow's wrath."

"We welcome you, child."

"And all who wander with you."

Finally, they turned to Willam.

"Willam, as Victtor's sworn heir, will take his house,"

"and all of his holdings."

"The widow will make her own way."

"May Willam lead us with wisdom,"

"with his bride at his side."

The elders fell silent.

Yonce glanced at Gosikk, somewhat astounded, much relieved. Gosikk met Yonce's glance, looked back to the elders in time to see Willam rise.

"We thank you, revered elders, for your wisdom and your truth." He looked to Rosa, who beamed at him. "We have pondered well, the truth of this village and our place within it." He looked at the floor, perched his hands on his hips. With resolve, he faced the elders. Rosa stood to be at his side. She slipped her hand around his waist as he relaxed his stance, glanced at her, and smiled.

"I have lived in this village for all my remembrance, content with my place within it. I have watched as neighbors and friends cowered beneath Victtor's thumb, his injustice and meanness."

He rested his hand on Rosa's shoulder, standing tall by his side. They faced the elders, a united front.

"Never have I desired to rule, to lead. Always I have wondered why the village did not lead itself, that all of you," his gesture took in the villagers crowding the hall, "being kind and wise, knew best what was best for yourselves." He paused. "Visiting Rosa's village, I saw neighbors and friends making their way from day to day, creating beauty and welcome and camaraderie at every opportunity, using their own truth, using their own knowing, to guide themselves, and be at peace with each other."

Willam swept his gaze across the row of elders. "I propose to you..." He turned to include everyone in the room. "...to all gathered, that the village lead itself, to come before the elders in times of disagreement and perplexity. I implore the artisans and craftsmen to come forth and re-establish the beauty and calm that we once knew.

"I ask that you release me from the burden of heirship. I propose that the widow remain in Victtor's house, that it become her own, that she be given the chance to choose kindness and truth, which, with time, she may discover as worthy guides, just as others are likewise guided by their very nature."

As a first speech, Yonce thought it well presented and well received. The elders went through the formality of asking the villagers' opinion of Willam's proposals, and cheers and whistles erupted in wild agreement. The elders joined hands, raised them above their heads. The villagers mirrored the gesture. The shout reverberated around the hall, as though from a single throat, "So say we all!"

Yonce pounded Gosikk's back, who pounded in return. They shouldered their way to the front of the hall, where Miichal swept Rosa into a twirl, her skirts billowing, curls flowing. The champions engulfed the pair, then shuffled aside, as hand after hand shook Willam's, as hug after hug welcomed Rosa.

At long last, the hall emptied, leaving Rosa with her husband, truly wedlocked, surrounded by her champions, every face a-grinning.

Chapter 64

Secret

Alone figure detached itself from the shadows in the far corner of the hall. Rosa and her champions turned at the sound of measured footsteps approaching. The man walked purposefully to Rosa, eyes troubled, despite the friendly smile he presented to the Maiden.

"Parker?" Willam stepped closer to his bride.

The man nodded to Willam. "M'lady." He bowed respectfully over Rosa's cautious hand, even as she glanced at Willam, her eyes questioning.

"Yes, m'lady. The name's Parker. I accompanied the lord and lady to your wedlocking."

"I remember, Parker. We didn't have room for your party at the inn." Rosa looked at Gosikk and his dawning remembrance. "I'm glad we're able to meet under...kinder circumstances."

"Yes, m'lady. Much kinder. Thank you." Parker cleared his throat. "Thank you for all you have done to help our village right itself. I have great confidence for our success."

"I have no doubt of your success. Everyone has been helpful and...so very kind."

"Yes, m'lady." His lips thinned and a film of sweat glowed on his forehead. "M'lady. I want desperately to assure you that I have made no mention of your...status to anyone here at the village. Nor did I hear talk of that...particular topic while attending your lovely wedlocking, from anyone in the lord's entourage."

"My...status?"

Parker leaned closer and dropped his voice. "Spring Maiden, m'lady. The kind gentleman here...Gosikk, if I remember correctly..." A nod to Gosikk, whose frown accompanied his short nod. "Yes. He mentioned that you...introduced you to me as...Spring Maiden."

"Yes. Newly birthed only days before the wedlocking."

"Yes. Yes. Newly...birthed..."

Willam placed a hand on Parker's elbow. "Parker. Is everything well with you? You seem...distraught."

"No. No. Not at all, Willam. Not distraught. Everything is fine. That's what I wanted to tell you. Everything appears to have gone well today, and I believe that is in part due to the fact that no one, except me and your fine...comrades..."

"Champions," Rosa said.

"Yes. Yes. Champions." He cleared his throat again. "I've not mentioned any of this to anyone, and with things going in your favor today, I wanted to assure you that everything will, in all likelihood, continue to go well for the remainder of your stay." He patted Rosa's hand, which he still held. "I believe you to be safe here, m'lady. No one need know."

"Why would we keep this a secret, Parker?" Gosikk asked.

"Your village knew Rosa before...before she was Spring Maiden. They have much to weigh in her favor." He turned to Rosa. "Here, these folk, though fine and honest and well-meaning, they do not know you, m'lady. Things could turn for the worse, were they to learn...your secret. We saw you step onto the green and bring back its life. We smelled the roses. People may wonder, but I will not confirm, in deference to your safety."

"The aunties have a strangle hold here, do they?" Gosikk asked.

"Some would claim that, good sir. Some would claim that quite strenuously."

Willam's face cleared with understanding. "Some would claim that the widow was Spring Maiden. That would explain her evil nature."

"Yes, Willam. That's exactly it. There is still that...belief to settle." Parker released Rosa's hand, stood tall, and clasped his hands behind his back. "As I say; no one knows your secret here. I wanted only to give you that assurance, to allow you to leave with grace and dignity."

Chapter 65

Conclave

*M*aiden.

The single word drifted into Rosa's heart and brought her immediately awake. She opened her eyes to the deepest dark of a moonless night. She heard Willam's slow breaths next to her and felt the dew of early night damp upon her cheeks. A calm peace enveloped her, and she smiled into the invisible world surrounding her and her champions.

Maiden.

Yes?

It is time for us to meet.

Curiosity chased the last remnants of sleep from Rosa's mind, and she sat, taking care not to disturb Willam's dreams. She slipped from her sleeping cloth and gathered her feet to stand and take a tentative step. Soft fur brushed under her hand, and she grasped Pharlan's shoulder, embedded her fingers in her ruff, and followed the dog unerringly past sleeping champions, wagon, and drowsing mules.

The pair moved soundlessly around bushes that brushed Rosa's arms, white petals that perfumed her hand, across moss that caressed her feet, night sounds whispering their soothing melodies from above, below, and all around. Pharlan moved with purpose, choosing their path surely, easily. Rosa heard the clump of hooves join them, the padding of a second set of paws, grunting huffs, a conclave of forest creatures moving in harmony to their destined meeting place.

At last, Pharlan stopped and stood still, tongue panting. Rosa waited a breath, two, wondering who had called her here. But she knew; some part of her had known at the first call across her heart. It came again.

Maiden.

Yes?

This may be the last time in many moons when we all can come together, to be in conclave with you. It is time for you to know.

Rosa heard not a *single* voice, but a *chorus* of voices, richly blended, perfectly synchronized, attuned, one to all.

Tell me.

We are your companions; the companions of your champions. We are the ambassadors of all that is.

Rosa furrowed her brow, reviewing the animals who had joined the fellowship. Cam and Pharlan from the beginning, Tronder, Bradi, Aarvil only recently...Rosa heard more voices in the blend than faces with whom to match them.

I have not met all of you, but I have met some.

Yes. Not all of your champions are ready to meet their companions. But that will come. We gather now, to bond with you, to complete the circle that will seal your power.

Rosa wondered fleetingly why she had not heard any voices before. Companions had been part of the fellowship from its birthing, and she knew the champions heard their own companions; that is, those who had already met their companions. She had heard no voices in her own heart; not even Miichal's voice. And this voice rang clearly, in her heart. It did not reach her ears; no whisper; no echo. Why now, in the dead of night, on the darkest of nights? Why was she alone summoned?

She keenly felt the absence of her champions.

The questions and wonderings bumped across her mind, but she paid them slight heed. All was always well.

They walked on.

Do I need more power? The power I have now holds unexpected danger, pitfalls I do not see until too late. Perhaps I shouldn't have more power. Perhaps I don't need more. The fellowship is strong and balanced in its own right.

Rosa slowed her breath as she waited for the voice to whisper into her heart.

With understanding and wisdom, power can be of benefit to all. We have waited through many generations to bring forth a Spring Maiden who can hold the understanding and the wisdom, who can hold her power within those boundaries.

Rosa's steps faltered, but Pharlan's steady pace pulled her forward. Hadn't Miichal awoken her? Miichal and the fellowship?

You brought me forth?

Yes. We heard the signs and made ready. Many Maidens have perished under the double moons, lacking the twelve who could awaken her. There have been awakened Maidens whose twelve lacked the courage and wisdom to guide and protect, thus unleashing aggression and cruelty that took time and hardship to vanquish.

We could prevail because we had Miichal. Miichal made the possibility of you...possible. When Tronder found Miichal, we knew that you were possible. When the twelve awoke you, we hoped that you could become a true Spring Maiden. When you were wedlocked, we feared you would disappear into obscurity, but you sustained your inner self. You have proven yourself adequate to the task before you.

And so, it is time for us to meet.

Rosa felt an ocean of peaceful calm. These statements, which normally would have caught at her breath, unsettled her peace, instead produced no alarm. Only the peaceful calm that floated around her, trailed behind her.

What is the task before me?
To heal the world.

Rosa drew her brows together in a frown. She clutched Pharlan's fur more securely. She raised her chin.

I don't know how to do that.

You are already healing everything you touch, everywhere you go. The forests are awakening. The streams and rivers are remembering. The animals are emerging from their long stupor. The devas and sprites are returning.

Your twelve and we, as their companions, will guide you and help you. Through you and your twelve, humankind will remember all that is. The breach with all that is will be closed, and the world will be healed.

Come. It is time.

Rosa came out of her walking stillness and opened eyes she did not remember closing. An eerie light had crept into the eastern sky.

It is time. Come.

Obscure shadows took shape around Rosa and moved with her from beneath trees into an open meadow. The eerie light blossomed quickly, and the shapes resolved into animals who converged, sniffing the air. Some she recognized; some she did not. A sweep of wings brushed the air beside her and an owl landed on a large boulder. Bradi bent to release the mouse she carried in her beak. Rosa smelled spring bulbs and heard the hum of bees, as if a dozen hives crowded nearby.

A dazzling moon burst above the eastern ridge. Era, on her erratic course, blazed across the sky and bathed the Maiden in magical brilliance. Rosa stared into Era's eye, and her companions swirled around her, a shared ecstasy.

By the sacredness of Era, through the mysteries of her solitary path, and the wisdom of the ages, we enter into covenant, one with the others, together to protect and defend, to serve and guide, through all our days.

The vow echoed across Rosa's heart, and she breathed the full power of Spring Maiden deep into her lungs.

Chapter 66

Aftermath

"Should we go back to the inn? Gosikk's inn?" Katernn sat on the elders' table, swinging her legs. The room gave no sign of yesterday's drama, and it was the easiest place for the champions to gather, now that it remained unbarred, open to all, to gather, to linger, to fraternize.

"Why would we go back?" Jullia asked.

"It's the perfect spot, the inn. We can all stay together as before. Cook together. Live our days together."

"And do what?" Yonce asked.

Katernn thought about that. She hated being bored. "Well; we had things to do before. We'll find things to do again."

Yonce stood at a window, watching villagers at their business of the day. "We had the wedlocking before. Even that didn't keep us busy for long." He turned to the room. "Think about it. What would we do?"

Jullia spoke into the silence. "I'd like to stay here." All eyes widened and turned to her.

"And do what?" Yonce asked. "I'm not trying to argue. I simply can't think what to do, myself. I've been pondering, all the while we wandered through the forest. What can I do?"

"Why do you want to stay here, Jullia?" Katernn felt restless, too, but wasn't drawn to this village. Nor to Gosikk's inn, truth be told; much as she'd loved it there. She didn't want to go back. Unless the others went back. Unless Rosa went back.

Jullia blushed. "Romane wants to stay. Mandra wants to stay, especially if the widow leaves. She feels an expansive enthusiasm for restoring beauty in her childhood home, to remind others of their forgotten gifts, to bring the village back to life. But even if the widow does stay, Mandra yearns to stay. She sees it now with new eyes, remembering old haunts, old friends. Marlow is willing to stay, to foster friendships and camaraderie. So, Romane is staying, too." She looked to Rosa. "Will you stay, Rosa? With your family?"

"I vowed never to return to my mother's house. I won't stay."

"But that was before. Besides, you have Willam's house." Hope shone from Jullia's face.

Willam shook his head. "My house is the widow's house. She and Victtor roped me in long ago. They demanded a big house to be built next door to them, for you and me to have." He smiled at Rosa. "But it's a monstrous thing; not at all to my liking. I truly have nothing that is my own."

He pursed his lips. "We could build a new house." He watched his bride. "What do you think, Rosa? Should we have Stevven build us our own house?"

"I could do that," Stevven agreed.

All eyes turned to Rosa. She stood and wandered to the window that opened toward the widow's house. "Tell me more about people thinking that the widow might be a Spring Maiden."

Willam looked at his feet. "She turned mean. Everyone knew she was mean, even before Victtor died. But Zedar talks about a new level of mean. From fear, probably. She would know that she didn't have power of her own. Without Victtor, her only chance to keep her position was to be a front for me. It was a pretty slim chance, but she was willing to take it."

"How does Spring Maiden work into it?"

Miichal ventured a guess. "Whenever people encounter evil, they remember the aunties' tales, and wonder."

Willam nodded. "She's not from here. Her village lies further west. She's an unknown. Arrived as an unknown, hid behind Victtor as an unknown. When her mean side flared, people...wondered...if she had power of a magical sort."

"Why does that threaten me?" Rosa asked.

Willam shrugged. "It's easy for people to harbor suspicions. Out of fear from generations of being under someone's thumb." Willam shrugged again. "The village had only a couple of weeks without Victtor and the widow, while they traveled to the wed-locking, to feel what freedom might mean. Even after so short a time, they would refuse to go back. They could easily rear de-fensively at the specter of an actual Spring Maiden who would rule them against their will."

Miichal said, "We'll meet this kind of ingrained blend of be-lief and superstition wherever we go. I'd like us to have more time together before we have to tackle the big lie that the aun-ties love to tell."

"A lot of it depends on whether we stay here or move on." Willam's comment brought them back to the current question. "What do you think, Rosa. Do we stay or do we go?"

"I don't know. What do others want? If I say what I want, then everyone has to agree. I'd rather hear what you think."

She turned her back to the window, leaned against its sill, crossed her arms, and waited.

Gosikk spoke with assurance. "I'd like to go back to my inn. Just to see. I can't say I want it opened again. 'Twould be dif-ferent. Not like before." He nodded at Yonce, Jullia. "I'd have to find a new crew." He raised an eyebrow at Katernn.

Confusion swept Katernn as she thought about the inn. She felt no pleasure at the thought of returning to her old life, simple as it had been. She liked simplicity. It would be easy to go back, pick up where she had left off. But was that what she wanted? She wrinkled her forehead, bit her lip.

Jullia said, "I want to stay here with Romane. And I don't want any of you to go. Not you, Rosa; not any of you. We'll find something."

Katernn understood Jullia's yearning, a yearning that pulled in two directions. But, she couldn't see a clear solution. She agreed with Yonce. What could they possibly do? What purpose would they have here? Or back in their own village, for that matter. Perhaps this is what happened with Spring Maidens. Perhaps the twelve just wandered away, back to their separate lives. That would be too boring an ending for the aunties, so that would never be told. What did Spring Maidens do, really?

"Miichal. What do Spring Maidens do?"

Miichal looked up in surprise. "What?"

"What do Spring Maidens do? We have one. We woke her. We saved her from the mob. Now what? What do Spring Maidens do?"

Katernn heard Aarvil's whisper across her heart, in cadence with Bolin and Yonce and Mackey speaking the words to the room.

"The Spring Maiden awakens the forest."

"She heals a world that has forgotten what's important."

"She brings nature back into our lives."

"She saves the world."

"She reminds us of all that is."

Greggor spoke into the silent room. "How does she save the world, then?"

Katernn chuckled. "Well. She has us, for a start."

Another silence.

"I don't think I need all of you, though."

All heads turned to Rosa.

Katernn felt a cold dread seep into her belly. "What do you mean?"

"Well. Look at the good that happened here. The village is free to grow into whatever it chooses. We couldn't have done that from Gosikk's inn. We had to come here to see for ourselves what was happening. Yes; we came for Willam and Jullia and Mackey. They drew us. But when we got here, we quickly learned what was happening; what had been happening for years.

"By opening the possibility that people could speak their truth, they spoke it. By defying the widow, breaking her hold over everyone, we gave them back their voice. It wasn't what we set out to do, but we made a difference here. We brought the difference that was needed, even though we didn't know it was needed or how to bring it."

Rosa pushed away from the window. "I'm not saying we should storm into village after village and tell them how to make their lives better. But by following the signs, by walking in the direction that opens before us, we'll find those places that need our help. And if we take the time to understand what we're meant to do, we'll know what it is and be able to find a way to do it."

Miichal entwined his hands behind his head, looked at the ceiling, imagined the sky beyond. A broad smile lit his face. "Well spoken, Maiden."

Rosa continued. "But, as I said, I don't think it has to be all of us. We may have to leave people behind here and there, mayhap to meet again, when the time is right."

"We have been sort of tripping over each other, out there in the forest," Yonce remarked.

The dread sitting in Katernn's belly lightened. A pattern began to take shape in her mind's eye.

Ambassadors, Aarvil remarked.

"Who would you leave behind?" Katernn asked.

Rosa turned to Willam. "First. Willam, how badly do you want to stay here?"

Willam's face turned pale. "You would leave me here?"

Rosa strode across the floor to where he stood, wrapped her arms around his waist. "No, no, Willam. We will always be together."

His arms encircled her shoulders, and he kissed the top of her head. Katernn's throat tightened with emotion, seeing his sweetness. "I faithfully promise to live with you always, in full obedience and loving loyalty," he said softly.

"Yes, yes," She shook him lovingly. "We all know that. This is a different question. Do you want to stay here, in the village of your birth?"

"I can't separate the two. If you leave, I leave. Without a backward glance or a pang of regret. I will live with you always."

She kissed his chin, turned to look at the others. "Jullia."

Jullia raised her eyebrows, looked at Rosa without flinching. "What would you think about staying here with Romane?" Rosa asked.

Jullia's eyes darted from face to face. "I would miss you terribly. I always want to be with you."

"You would be our ambassador," Rosa said. "We would always be connected, regardless of distance. And we would meet from time to time, when our roads lead us together once again."

"How would we be connected? I haven't a companion."

Bolin spoke for all of the companions. "That will come."

Jullia blushed, stared before her at nothing.

"Do you need to think about it? Talk it over with Romane?" Rosa asked.

"I don't need to think, Rosa. I will happily stay if you ask me to stay." She swiped her hair behind her ears. "It's not yet time to include Romane in my decisions. 'Twould be presumptuous, for one thing." She stood tall. "For another, this is my decision, Rosa, and I say, yes; I will stay here if that is your wish." Her eyes filled, at odds with her conviction.

Rosa turned her attention to Gosikk, standing beyond Jullia.

"And you, Gosikk. Will you return to your inn? Indulge your gift of hosting anew?"

"If you ask it, darling Rosa, I will gladly do it."

Rosa's eyes danced. "You also have no companion."

Gosikk crossed his arms. "Perhaps he awaits me at the inn." He laughed aloud. "Now wouldn't that be something? An ambassador and a companion, all at once! Brought together at my inn? That would be something indeed."

The glow in Katernn's belly chased away the last tendrils of dread. Jullia with Romane! What a glorious matchmaking for them both. And Gosikk with his inn. The rightness of it plastered a grin on Katernn's face that set her cheeks to aching.

"And what of us, Rosa," Katernn asked. "When shall we begin?"

Stevven cleared his throat. "I would like to build a house for Jullia." He looked at her. "I've long fancied you, Jullia, and building you a house would be a great pleasure. A sturdy house, with a pantry fit for a queen." He cleared his throat again and looked around the fellowship. "Who will help me?"

The fellowship chortled their enthusiasm and noisily traipsed forth from the meeting hall, leaving its doors wide to welcome whoever might wander by. They crossed the green to explore the village and its encircling forest, questing after the perfect site for Jullia's house and the perfect trees with which to give it shape.

Chapter 67

Homecoming

Dust motes floated in the slanted sunbeams that striped the common room. Gosikk shook his head, hands on hips. He gave a great sigh. Might as well start.

Gosikk had the gift of hosting. He liked nothing better than opening the double doors to any wanderer and every villager, serving delicious meals, immersing himself in the chatter and laughter of an evening friend-spent. But he had not the gift of householding, and in its current state, his inn was not ready for wanderers or villagers. He rolled up a sleeve and opened the householding cabinet and lifted out a basket of clean rags. Might as well start.

"I'll do that," said a familiar voice at the back door. Katernn strode into the common room followed by a glorious fox who sniffed the stale air. Gosikk lost his words and stood grinning as Katernn lifted the basket from his hands, set it on a nearby table, and selected a single cloth. She smirked over her shoulder. "Don't you have work in the kitchen?"

"Why are you here? And not with the Maiden?"

"Oh. Rosa's here. They're right behind us." Katernn disappeared behind the swinging door of the kitchen, from which the splash of water emanated, and returned with a wooden bucket brimming with soapy water. "Greggor and Draymon want to take some rugs and such for Jullia's house. Finishing touches, as it were. And we all want to help you with your new start."

She hoisted the bucket onto the table next to the basket of cloths, bringing the scent of soaking herbs and lemons to waft and mingle with hovering dust motes. "We might not stay long enough to welcome back all of your guests, but we will get your double doors open to all passersby." Katernn stood, hands on hips, watching her glorious companion explore the room that had been Katernn's realm for years.

The thought of Katernn moving through her well-worn duties, relieving him of the need of talents he did not possess, bemused Gosikk. A nostalgia niggled at his heart, opening a space for contentment to replace astonishment. He circuited the room, opening shutters, flooding the room with streams of sunlight, giving the dust motes an expanded stage on which to display their graceful ballet. Herbs and lemons overtook mustiness and weighted the motes to bring them coasting to the floor, ready for broom and mop.

Aarvil seemed right at home, despite a lifetime in the wild forest. She inspected corners with her busy nose, perked her ears at every window. She completed her consideration of the room, sat with tail curved across perfectly posed feet, cocked her head, and watched Katernn as she made her way, damp cloth in hand, from window sill to bench, from trestle table to wall glorb, humming as she went.

"Gosikk," Katernn called. "The kitchen?"

Gosikk roused himself from his reverie and made his way between tables and past benches to the kitchen that had been his domain for decades. As the door swung shut behind him, chaos halted his steps. The fellowship's hasty departure weeks ago had left shambles where once an efficient kitchen had glowed in readiness. Gosikk sighed. Bowls lay strewn amidst discarded spoons and spatulas. An overturned basket spilled its cache of wrinkled potatoes and sprouting onions across a work table and onto the floor. Mildew and old cheese assaulted Gosikk's nose, and he moved to open window and courtyard door.

Two mules and their wagon chose that moment to roll into the courtyard, clattering over cobblestones and squishing water from rotted straw. Yonce jumped from the wagon's high seat and set about releasing the mules from their harness and leading them into the stable. He stopped on its threshold. "The mice have certainly been busy in here," he called over his shoulder. "And squirrels and skunks and all manner of mischief-makers."

Gosikk grunted, knowing Yonce's gift of husbandry would soon set the stable to rights. He turned back to the kitchen and spotted the mouse sitting on its haunches in the middle of the work table as if it owned the place. Which it probably had during the inn's weeks of abandonment. Gosikk huffed and shuffled around the perimeter of the kitchen, intending to chase the intruder into the courtyard and away to the fields.

The mouse gave no sign of alarm, simply sat, its black eyes following Gosikk's waddling progress. It cocked its head.

Gosikk.

Gosikk froze as the word lit his heart.

Who are you?

And then he knew, not knowing or caring how he knew.

Strellahonerajanera?

Janera, to my friends.

Gosikk crossed to the work table, reached a hand to his newly-found companion, and delighted at her touch as she scampered onto his palm. He raised hand to chin, watched the twitching whiskers.

You need a pocket.

A pocket?

Yes.

Why a pocket?

My legs are too short to match yours. And, I'm easily trodden upon.

I'll get someone to make me a pocket.

Don't ask the Maiden. She has not the gift of householding.

Chapter 68

Anniee

Jullia stood in her garden and hugged her arms across her chest. The house was finished. Light poured through tall windows framed with golden wood trim, showing white-plastered walls beyond. Even the floor was murmured into perfection by Stevven, stretching from wall to wall, gleaming under soft rugs that Greggor and Draymon had scattered here and there, adding rich hues of the rainbow.

Stevven had murmured sturdy furniture, which Romane covered with soft batting and bright fabrics. Light streamed from every window to fall across inviting chairs and couches.

The pantry lay behind tall doors next to the kitchen, deep shelves along one wall, shallow along another, while bins lined a third. Drying rods marched across the ceiling, and a clever drying cabinet rose in one corner. Jullia had more than enough room to house her current food stuffs, with plenty of room left for storing the season's fresh harvest. This pantry would easily serve the village, which was much larger than Jullia's old village, with plentiful bounty.

Jullia strolled barefoot across the clover and chamomile that covered the garden paths at the back of the house. Roses climbed fences, encouraged by Rosa to spread and flourish. Fruit trees, heavy with blossom, edged the side gardens, and flowers of every shape and color danced across the front garden, available for admiration and thrilling delight for any and all passersby. The scent of roses flooded the newly murmured pathway.

Jullia's heart burst with happiness, her belly filled with contentment. Yet, running through it all was a shadow of sadness and regret. Today, the fellowship would leave, and she would stay behind.

'Twas only the beauty and promise of her house and garden, new neighbors and friends, the burgeoning forest filled with the season's forage that kept Jullia from turning her back on this house and garden to wander away with Rosa and her champions. Their adventures-to-be might hold little allure, but Jullia could not bear to think of the fellowship's absence. She would surely crumple and waste away, if she allowed those thoughts to dominate her heart.

She knew she was right to stay. Her efforts, along with Mandra and Marlow and her beloved Romane, would inspire the villagers to remembrance of the magic of their gifts. Her mere presence would help the village blossom into kindness and inspired purpose. Bullying had been a predominant part of village life for decades. Another way of being would take time, patience, and perseverance. Jullia knew in her bones that she was needed here.

She turned at the lifting of a gate latch, and Romane let himself through to the garden. His bare feet strolled across clover, the scent of chamomile fluffing into the air with every step, and he gazed through tall windows just as she had done. He saw her and came to stand by her side, to drape an arm across her shoulders.

Jullia fought back tears. "It's finished." She forced a smile. "Down to the last pillow and coverlet." She brushed a wet escapee trailing down her cheek. She blinked quickly, fighting the spilling of more tears, but spill they did.

"There, there, my sweet," Romane whispered as he wrapped his arms around her and kissed her head. "I'm here. You're safe."

She nodded against his chest, took his offered hankie.

After a time, she shook her hair away from damp cheeks, rubbed the heels of her hands across her eyes, and let her sadness melt into the sunshine. Taking Romane's hand, she said, "Come and see the trees. Rosa brought them into blossom yesterday."

They ambled, elbows locked, around the corner of the house. Romane's gaze swept the young trees, but his face froze in shock as he stopped at the orchard's edge.

"Aren't they amazing?" asked Jullia.

"Yes; yes, they are. They're beautiful," Romane assured her, but frowned. "Only, look!" He pointed at a low lilac bush, heavy with scent. "What in the world is that?"

She peered along his pointed arm. "The lilac? Oh!" Her hand covered her mouth. A gruesome mound of pulsating brown covered several branches of the lilac. The sight sent a quiver down Jullia's spine. The blob was certainly alive and looked to be from another world. It appeared to be devouring the beauty of the lilac.

Dread swept through Jullia. Dropping Romane's arm, she stepped toward the strickened bush, narrowing her eyes against the morning sun. "What in the world?" She heard the hum of ten thousand bees and suddenly knew they swarmed over their queen.

"Anniee?" Jullia whispered.

Jullia.

"Anniee?!?" asked Romane just behind her.

Jullia's hands came up to cover her mouth, tears flowing anew. "It's Anniee. Oh, Romane; it's Anniee!"

"Anniee?"

"Yes," breathed Jullia. "It's Anniee." She walked closer to the bush and reached out her hand.

"Jullia!" Alarm rang in Romane's voice.

"It's fine. It's Anniee." She palmed the pulsating swarm, and they flowed over her hand, spread up her arm. Jullia's laughter burst from her despite her tears, as she turned, delighted, to gape at Romane. "Look, Romane. She's my companion."

"Bees? Bees are your companion?"

"Yes! Oh, this is perfect. Aren't they beautiful?"

Romane skipped past the question. "And their name is Anniee?"

"The queen's name is Anniee, so all of them are named Anniee. Look, Romane! Ten thousand bees, and I can tell you the name of each and every one of them." She beamed at him. "Anniee and Anniee and Anniee. Anniee times ten thousand."

Romane could only stare.

Jullia turned to the bees boiling on their bush and offered her second hand. The swarm flowed up her arms, across her shoulders. Airborne bees buzzed around her head.

"Look, Romaine. Here she is, Here's Queen Anniee." She thrust her hand toward Romane, who took a step back, putting up a defensive hand. "It's all right, Romane. They won't hurt you. Look." She showed him her hand again. "Right there. In the middle of my palm. See the one bee who's bigger than the others? That's Anniee."

Romane edged forward and narrowed his eyes at Jullia's unsettling hand, swollen with swarming bees. He nodded, watched the busy-ness of the hive rolling and jostling over Jullia's hands and arms. He looked at her. "That's alarming. But, amazing just the same."

"Isn't she?" Jullia brought her hand closer to her face, gazing at the large bee who turned and looked at her. "Hi, Anniee. You are the most beautiful thing I've ever seen!" Anniee and Jullia gazed at each other, enthralled.

"Oh!" Jullia turned to Romane. "We have a house for them."

"They'll live in the house with you?"

"No. No. My house is much too big for them." She walked deeper into the orchard and knelt before wooden boxes stacked one upon the other. The rest of the swarm flowed off the lilac and followed her, a buzzing cloud jostling the air. "Stevven made hives for me. They're perfect for Anniee." She held her hands above the stacked boxes, and the queen released from Jullia's palm, landed on the top box, and wiggled inside.

The swarm dripped from Jullia's arms and hands, flowed around her head and onto the boxes. They followed their queen into their new home.

"You know what this means." Jullia stood and faced Romane, her eyes brimming, errant bees buzzing around her head, tickling her ear, exploring her hair. "Anniee is Rosa's farewell gift."

"How do you mean."

Jullia wiped an eye with the back of her hand. "Stevven built this hive yesterday, even though I don't have bees." She gestured toward the stacked boxes. "Rosa blossomed the trees yesterday, and it was she who told Stevven to build their home, here, where it wasn't needed until this very moment. To make everything ready for them. She sent Anniee to me this morning as a farewell gift."

Rosa looked down at the humming boxes, where a tear splashed, dark on the perfect wood. The entire swarm flowed onto the boxes, finding their way around their perfect home. Anniees rose to visit ten thousand blossoms. "Rosa sent Anniee to me, so I could bear their leave-taking."

Chapter 69

Journey

Rosa relaxed against Miichal's sturdy chest, their hips rolling in the rhythm of Tronder's steady gait. Silence was their friend this morning, this morning of leave-taking. Gosikk was settled with his new companion, awakening his inn to the welcoming delight of the entire village. Jullia was settled with *her* new companion, nestled into a home lovingly murmured by a loving artisan's graceful farewell. Both villages would find their way under the covert guidance of the two champions, aided and guided by their companions.

Rosa looked to Willam where he rode next to Yonce, the two fast becoming the best of friends. Bradi perched in her specially murmured cubby within the fellowship's wagon, head tucked under wing, dreaming her day away. The mules pulled the wagon with prancing hooves and flicking ears.

Bolin led the fellowship confidently through his wild forest, Cam darting from tree to tree. Greggor and Draymon walked contentedly at Bolin's side, listening, rapt, to his gift of wild, following his gesturing arm and pointing finger, enthralled by his story-telling.

Stevven followed in the rear, a lingering smile for Jullia and her newly murmured house.

A glade away, Katernn and Mackey chased Aarvil and Pharlan across a meadow, who, in their own turn, crouched in ambush behind a boulder, tails swishing the tender grasses behind them, ears perked.

The morning sun trickled through the canopy to splash on moss and grass. Ferns raised their fiddleheads, and a stream gurgled nearby. The scent of blossoms and herbs filled the air. Linsel grew with wild abandon, and fawn twins, triplets raised their heads, ears twitching in the morning breeze. Birds warbled and trilled their songs of spring and love and nest-making, and woodpeckers staccatoed their beaks into a tree's bark. Insects flew and crawled and dug, flirting with a myriad of blossoms. The soil busied its vast self awake, glowing in its secret depths.

Spring stretched before and lingered behind, as the Maiden and her champions passed through the wild, the scent of roses trailing in their wake.

You Can Make A Difference

In our digital age, product reviews have taken on an astounding importance. You can make a significant difference in visibility for this book for others who would not otherwise be aware of its existence.

A star rating helps. Writing two or three sentences about the book and your impression helps enormously.

Why share your thoughts? So you can be a beacon for others. Your perspective is invaluable, and in the vast world of algorithms, your review can be the guiding star for another reader.

Characters

The Fellowship

	Gift	Companion
Bolin	wild woods	Cam
Cam	bright things	Bolin
Draymon	selling	Craidon
Gosikk	hosting	Janera
Greggor	herbology	Embra
Jullia	preserving	Anniee
Katernn	understanding how things work	Aarvil
Mackey	cooking	Pharlan
Miichal	leadership	Tronder
Pharlan	scents	Mackey
Rosa	helping	Willam
Stevven	carpentry	Bishoor
Tronder	wisdom	Miichal
Yonce	husbandry	Bradi
Willam	husbanding	Rosa

Villagers

Duke	Ruffian in second village
Lloyd	Ruffian in second village
Mandra	Rosa's mother
Marlow	Rosa's father
Parker	Assistant to Victtor and his wife
Romane	Rosa's brother
Victtor	Rosa's guardian

Victtor's wife   Manipulator
Zedar   Groom and friend to Willam

Terminology

Glorb   Glowing magical orb used for lighting
Linsel   Ancient plant that grows in mature forests
Makta   Ancient plant that grows at high elevations
Murmur   Ancient art of magical craftsmanship

Other Books by This Author

Awareness, A Journey of Truth or...Treachery, **Book 1 of** *The Airon Chronicles*

Ava was brazen enough, driven enough, to convince 108 people to join her, to flee their trapped lives in a broken world.

Had she led them into a trap?

Awareness follows a group of 108 people who escape encroaching nanotechnology on Earth by embarking on a journey across the stars to colonize a recently detected planet, Airon. They travel aboard an intelligent spaceship who, after arriving on Airon, recycles itself into buildings, vehicles, and technologies that benefit the Earthens, as well as mysterious creations that eerily appear from the ship without explanation.

As The 108 establish Home Base, they venture forth to explore Airon's forests, rivers, and mountains. Some Earthens readily feel a profound bond with Airon's life, while others keep themselves hidden within the confines of Home Base. Despite growing connections with Airon and the life that surrounds them, suspicions mount, as mysterious technologies and events occur on Airon. Some Earthens feel threatened by the ship's abilities, which seem similar to the invasive nanotechnology that they so recently escaped.

The story explores themes of humanity's connection to nature, finding inner wisdom and cooperation amongst diversity, and exploring the mysteries of life. There are hints of a deeper calling behind The 108's journey to Airon, an inner wrestling with existential questions about their purpose and destiny.

Remembrance, A Journey of Awakening, **Book 2 of** *The Airon Chronicles*

The Narsis are dying out, and nobody understands why. The gentle custodians of Below have no choice but to face the inevitable collapse of their species.

And yet Vargad, Head-er, plagued with despair, prepares himself to launch the unimaginable: Rebellion.

Remembrance is an epic science fiction tale following the journey of an unlikely group of space travelers. When cultural collapse threatens life on Earth, The 108 are handpicked for a desperate mission to establish an Earthen colony on a distant planet called Airon. However, upon arrival, they find this luminous world is far more than it first appeared.

Airon's ethereal inhabitants and mystical wisdom compel the travelers on a profound inner journey, challenging their notions of consciousness and cooperation. As the truth of their purpose unfolds, The 108 must learn to blend their awareness with the living planet in order to transcend long-held fears, false beliefs, and their own limiting nature.

With vivid descriptions and fully-realized characters, Remembrance immerses the reader in an astonishing vision of awakening. Amidst tender moments of connection and startling twists, each traveler faces their inner darkness on the path toward embodying light. Ultimately, this is a story of humanity's potential and the courage required to remake ourselves.

Intrusion, A Journey of Friendship, **Book 3 of *The Airon Chronicles***

Ten years have passed since The 108 arrived on Airon. They've settled into a comfortable existence, immersing themselves in the awareness that is Airon, bonding with the friendly Aironians, and starting families of their own.

One quiet day, the ship detects an anomaly in the familiar night sky: a decelerating mass. The ship knows the mass is a ship, and it's traveling from Earth, heading straight to Airon. The ship is fully aware of the Earthen penchant for conquering, ruling, and overwhelming. The 108 must now decide how to protect themselves, and all of Airon, from the intrusion hurtling toward them.